THE GHOSTS OF RUE DUMAINE

By

ALEXANDREA WEIS

World Castle Publishing, LLC

This is a work of fiction. Names, characters, places, and incidents are products of the author's imagination or are used fictitiously and are not to be construed as real. Any resemblance to actual events, locations, organizations, or person, living or dead, is entirely coincidental.

WCP

World Castle Publishing, LLC
Pensacola, Florida

ISBN: 9781939865649
First Edition World Castle Publishing, LLC September 1, 2013
http://www.worldcastlepublishing.com

Cover: Karen Fuller
Photos: Shutterstock
Editor: Maxine Bringenberg

For Jerry, Irwin, Lee, Milton, David, and all the souls at 627.
Thank you, JW, for directing the adventure.

CHAPTER 1

The rays of the oppressive afternoon sun were beating down on the blacktop of Dumaine Street when a sleek, silver Mercedes E350 sedan cut across the cracked and uneven surface. The eye-catching car pulled in front of an unassuming Creole cottage and a woman's round face peered out the passenger side window. Her inquisitive blue eyes gazed up at the single-story, rectangular building, drinking in the pale yellow stucco on the walls and dark green shutters over the front window and double front doors. A sloping roof cast an afternoon shadow over the sidewalk in front, and to the right, a black iron gate rose over seven feet in height, securing the alleyway that led to the rear entrance of the home.

"It looks exactly the same as I remember," Danica Giles mumbled.

A loud snort came from the driver's seat next to her. "Hardly the same, darlin'," a platinum blonde scoffed. "It's been redone from top to bottom since you were last here, Danica. There's a new roof, new plumbing, renovated courtyard and carriage house, not to mention all the termite damage that had to be repaired. Damned Formosan bastards are eating up the Quarter."

Danica turned to the woman seated next to her. She was petite with striking features, which Danica deemed to be a bit too perfect. Her gleaming white porcelain teeth and voluminous breasts, bulging beneath her blue pantsuit jacket, only added to her factitious appearance.

"I hadn't realized it had been redone, Pat," Danica said to the woman. "I got the impression from the pictures on the Internet that it had just been updated."

Pat gave a deep throaty laugh that screamed of too many cigarettes and not enough exercise. "Honey, updated in the Quarter means overhauled." Her big brown eyes swept over the cottage. "There's been ten renters since you and your parents left here in ninety-two."

Danica was momentarily distracted by the extreme length of Pat's eyelashes and wondered if they were as real as the rest of her.

"Yeah, damn place has run more than a few people out of it, what with its history and all." Pat sneered, making her thin lips disappear. "After you and your father left, the owner, Mr. Caruso, rented the cottage to a costume designer. They found her strangled down by Jackson Barracks. Police said it was drug related." Pat rolled her eyes, accentuating the lines beneath them. "What isn't drug related these days in the Quarter? After that, there was some business guy from Texas...Hewitt, that was his name. He worked for an oil company and only stayed about a year, until he got called back to Houston. After him, there was a young couple from up north somewhere. I think they were street musicians. They stayed for about three years and left owing three month's back rent. Then there was a chef, an artist, and a stripper. Each stayed about a year or two." She sighed and sat back in her seat. "The longest tenants we ever had for the cottage was that gay couple. Their deaths ended up plastered all over the front page of TheTimes-Picayune."

"What exactly happened?" Danica asked. "My father mentioned something to me, but I was working in Seattle at the time and never got the full story."

Pat feigned a shiver and reached for her car door. "Still creeps me out, thinking about those two men." She opened the door and ventured into the sweltering late September air.

As soon as Danica climbed out of the car, the legendary New Orleans heat and humidity enveloped her. As she stepped onto the sidewalk, she heard Pat's high-heels clicking on the street as she came around the front of the car.

"Well," Pat went on as she flourished a diamond-clad hand in the air. "One of the men had a stroke while working out at the New Orleans Racquetball Club in the CBD. He was taken to Charity Hospital, and when his significant other arrived at the ICU, he damned near had a fit when he saw his lover was basically a vegetable. The next day he came to visit, and when no one was looking, he pulled out a gun and shot his lover in the head, and then turned the gun on himself." She removed a ring of keys from her blue jacket pocket. "I had just started with Wagner and Truax then. I had to get the spare set of keys from old man Caruso and open the place up for the police." She stepped toward the gate at the side of the cottage. "The inside was torn up real good. Papers and clothes strewn all about, and furniture was thrown everywhere. There was strange stuff scribbled all over the walls, too…weird looking symbols that I could not make any sense out of. The police discovered later that the guy that pulled the trigger had a history of mental illness. When his partner had that stroke, it must have set off something in his head."

"Those poor men. It's all so sad," Danica commented.

Pat shook her head. "That's the French Quarter, darlin'. Never a dull moment."

As Pat began to go through the selection of keys on her chain, searching for the one that opened the gate, Danica took in the surrounding street.

Directly across from the cottage was the famed Madame John's Legacy. Built in 1788, the older French Colonial style mansion was a reflection of the architectural traditions of those who had learned to adapt to the semitropical Louisiana climate. The exterior had been heavily stuccoed to keep the home insulated, while a shady, green wooden balcony ran along the second story to allow cooling breezes to flow through the living quarters during the hot summer months.

To the left, a traditional three-story Creole Townhouse made of stucco and red brick boasted classic New Orleans decorative black wrought iron balconies on its second and third floors.

"Nothing has changed," Danica softly said.

"Everything has changed," Pat objected behind her. "You've been gone over twenty years, and a lot has happened to the city."

Danica turned back to see Pat struggling with the lock on the gate.

"Since Katrina nothing has been the same. So many people left, I couldn't keep track of the properties we had listed down here. I've never seen so much stuff going up for sale or for rent in the Quarter, and I've lived here most of my life. After that, the taxes, utilities, and insurance went sky high. What the storm didn't drive away, the city government did. Took me damn near a year to get a permit to redo my house in Lakeview, and even then the copper wiring got stolen from the place twice, along with anything else that wasn't nailed down."

Danica moved closer to the gate. "My father was retired from teaching and was living in Florida when Katrina hit. I saw everything on the news in Seattle, but I know it wasn't like being here."

After a swift kick of Pat's black high-heeled shoe, the gate slowly opened with a resistant groan. "What Katrina did to New Orleans was a lot worse than any TV camera could ever capture. I'll never forget the smell after the storm. Damned stench hung over the city for almost a year. Those reporters never talked about that. You know, I still get panic attacks when the lights go out. I spent ten grand on a generator for my house so I would never be without power again." She stepped through the open gate. "I guess we all have some scars after that debacle, but life goes on."

Danica walked behind her. "I wanted to come back and help out after Katrina hit, but my husband at the time was dead set against it."

Pat eyed Danica's dainty nose, carved cheekbones, and porcelain skin. "You're divorced?"

"Two years ago."

"First divorce?"

Danica nodded her head.

"Did you leave him or did he walk out on you?" Pat persisted.

Danica hardened her resolve not to appear flustered by the woman's intrusive question. "I left. It wasn't a very good marriage."

"I know how you feel. I just got over my third divorce. My ex was a plastic surgeon in the city. Great plastic surgeon, crappy husband." She winked at Danica and headed down the narrow alleyway next to the cottage.

Danica turned her attention to the building beside her. She skipped her hand along the cool, yellow stucco on the wall. "It's exactly as it was."

Pat disappeared around the corner of the building just up ahead. When Danica came to the end of the alleyway, she stopped and admired the beautiful courtyard before her.

Around the perimeter of the courtyard a ten-foot-high, red-bricked wall gave the area a feeling of privacy from the bustling streets outside. Just beyond the wall, Danica could see the rear porches of the homes rising up on either side of the cottage. Along the base of the wall were narrow flowerbeds filled with red and white azalea bushes. A small weeping willow tree had been planted in a wider garden located between the wall and the carriage house in the rear. The carriage house was covered in stucco and painted the same pale yellow as the main house. White french doors covered the first and second floors of the square building, while gas lit brass lanterns hung on either side of an oak front door.

"The carriage house is rented by Carl Wethers. He's a big, scary-looking guy, but very friendly. Carl works a lot of nights as a bouncer at a few of the bars in the Quarter, so you probably won't see much of him," Pat remarked, making her way to the back door of the main house.

"Didn't there used to be a pond here?" Danica pointed to the center of the courtyard.

"Mr. Caruso had it removed during the renovations. It was leaking beneath the foundation of the cement floor and into the graves."

Danica spun around. "Graves?"

Pat stopped at the rear entrance and turned to Danica. "You didn't know about the family buried beneath the pond?"

Danica shook her head.

"The original builder of the house was the commander of the local garrison when the city was occupied by the Spanish." Pat waved her hand in the air. "Whenever the hell that was. His wife and three children died of yellow fever and were buried here behind the house. The city had records of the burials in their old archives. The gravestones were left in place when the cement floor for the courtyard was poured almost seventy years ago." Pat gave a nonchalant toss of her meticulously styled blonde hair. "It's one of those things we have to disclose now as part of the renter's agreement."

Danica returned her gaze to the main house. "That would explain a few things," she mumbled.

Her deep blue eyes examined the two tall, dark green french doors on one side of the home, and the long picture window located on the other. Above the doors was a single brass lamp made to resemble a candle. Danica became instantly mesmerized by the lamp's flickering flame.

"What would it explain?" Pat's ascorbic voice resonated throughout the courtyard.

Danica tore her eyes away from the lamp, appearing confused. "What did you say?"

Pat gave her a tolerant grin. "You said 'That would explain a few things.' What did you mean by that?"

Danica shrugged her slender shoulders. "Nothing; just when I was a kid growing up here a lot of strange things happened to me."

"Such as?"

"Oh, it all happened so long ago…and being an only child growing up in the French Quarter, I had a pretty active imagination. But I thought I saw things as a kid."

"Ghosts?" Pat tentatively asked.

Danica waved off her suggestion. “It was just my imagination.”

Pat paused for a minute as she glanced down at the keys in her hand. “You do know this place is haunted, Danica. I’ve talked to a few of the former tenants who will swear to that fact. It’s another of those pesky little disclosures I have to make about the property before you can sign the papers.”

“There are others who think it’s haunted?”

Pat nodded. “Absolutely. But it’s the French Quarter and many houses, I’m told, are haunted. I’m surprised you want to come back to this house after your previous experiences.”

“I never forgot about this place.” Danica surveyed the shady courtyard and smiled. “I loved it here as a kid, and my experiences were never scary.”

Pat snorted loudly as she opened the back doors. “You’d be the first. The other previous tenants I talked to were scared to death. They kept going on about some tall man with dark, angry eyes who would wake them up every night, standing at the foot of their bed.”

Danica felt her heart rise into her throat. “They saw him, too!”

Pat turned to her. “You saw the same man?”

Danica rubbed her hands nervously together. “Every night after I went to bed, I would see a man standing in the doorway of my room. He was a tall, black shadow and sometimes I could see his features, sometimes I couldn’t; but he was never mean or scary. I always got the impression he was standing guard over me.”

“The tenants I talked to had a different experience completely.” Pat stepped inside the cottage doorway. “I personally believe half the people old man Caruso rented to were pretty much out of their minds to begin with, so I never paid too much attention to their ramblings. I don’t give much credence to ghost stories.” She looked over Danica’s long, curly chestnut hair as it encircled her face like a halo. Pat let her eyes travel over her slender figure and casual blue silk dress. “I think you, on the other hand, seem pretty normal. I’m sure you won’t have the same experiences as those other crackpots.” She abruptly turned away and walked deeper into the cottage.

Danica quickly followed her inside. “What did those other renters tell you about the dark man?”

Pat stopped in the middle of an efficiency kitchen. After switching on the lights, she walked past a white cast iron sink surrounded by a wall of white cabinets that climbed all the way up to the high ceiling. Pat folded her arms over her chest and leaned her hip against the white-tiled counter.

"Most of what I heard were stories about knocking and banging on the walls at night. The female tenants said they often heard a man's voice calling to them. But some of the guys had quite a different experience. Most were punched or scratched by something, and when they did hear a man calling to them, they said it was malevolent. It got to where Mr. Caruso wouldn't even consider renting this cottage to anyone but a woman. However, when that gay couple showed up and became desperate to live here, Mr. Caruso relented. Now he regrets doing that. He thinks that the ghost may have had something to do with their tragic murder-suicide. He hasn't rented this place out in over three years." Her brown eyes met Danica's head on. "Still want to live here?" she demanded.

"Definitely. I lived here for ten years with my parents, Pat, and nothing ever happened to my father. My mother had a bad heart condition; if there would have been any activity like what you just described going on around here, we couldn't have stayed. Even after she died, my father and I remained for another year without anything like that happening to either of us." Danica noted the small, white refrigerator pushed into the corner, and the white, electric stove shoved up against it. "The imagination can be pretty scary if you let it take control of your fears."

Pat slapped her jewelry-covered hand down on the countertop. "I knew I liked you." She headed to an arch-shaped doorway, leading deeper into the cottage. "Let me show you the rest of the place," she called over her shoulder.

As the two women traipsed though the arched doorway, two skylights filtered the fading light of the sun into an empty square room. Pat flipped a switch on the wall next to her and an overhead brass chandelier came to life.

"This can be a living room, dining room, or third bedroom if you prefer." Pat motioned to the windowless room with thick, textured white plaster covering the walls. "There is a bathroom with a shower here," she directed as she made her way to a door in the corner of the room. Pat opened the door and flipped on the light. She waited for Danica to approach and peek inside. "Not much room for two, but cozy for one," she added.

Danica inspected the closet-sized bathroom with a sink and vanity not two feet away from a small shower stall. Crammed in between the shower and sink was the toilet.

"This used to be a half bath, if I remember correctly."

Pat nodded. "Mr. Caruso wanted to add another full bath to make it more attractive to renters."

In the far wall to Danica's left, a dark green marble hearth with a black cast iron grate was decorated with chunks of black coal.

"The fireplaces in this room and the master on the other side of this wall are gas. There's an automatic starter to the right of the mantle." Pat pointed to a brass key protruding slightly from the side of the dark cypress mantle.

"Looks the same as when I was a child," Danica told her.

"Probably is. I think the two fireplaces were about the only things that weren't upgraded here." Pat waved to the deep brown carpet beneath her feet. "There's new carpet in this room and both bedrooms. The rest of the flooring is painted cement. Easier to keep clean than the carpet, in my opinion." She walked toward a pair of cypress pocket doors in the center of the far wall. "The living room and entrance to the bedrooms are through here."

"I remember," Danica muttered behind her.

Pat pulled the pocket doors open to reveal another square room decorated with white textured plaster. Along the wall facing the street was an oak, double french door with beveled glass. The doors were covered on the outside by dark green shutters. Above, Danica noticed a shiny six-lighted chandelier, and in each of the four corners of the ceiling were small plaster faces of bearded old men. Their lips pursed together, as if blowing out puffs of air.

Pat followed Danica's eyes to the ceiling. "Aeolus, the ancient Greek god of wind. All of the old homes down here had some ancient Greek symbol or god added into the décor. It was believed to protect the home and its occupants from bad luck." Pat came up to Danica's side. "Those particular pieces go all the way back to the original cottage built in 1789."

"I used to call them my four little dwarfs when I was a girl." Danica turned to her. "Like Snow White's seven little dwarfs, but I only had four."

Pat feigned a smile and then motioned to an archway in the wall to her right. "There's a family room through there with new built-in cabinets for an entertainment system, or the room can be used as an office. The controls for the central air and heating system are in there, as well. Down the hall from that room are the two bedrooms divided by the master bath."

Danica made a move toward the archway, but Pat did not follow her.

"Aren't you coming?"

Pat shook her head. "You go on. I'd prefer to stay here. That part of the cottage gives me the creeps."

Danica furrowed her small brow at the woman. "I thought you didn't give much credence to ghost stories."

Pat shrugged. "I don't. I just know what I feel, and I don't like the feeling those two back bedrooms give me."

Danica gave her a confident grin. "I'll yell if I see anything," she assured her and ventured into the family room.

Relieved to be free of Pat's irksome running commentary on the cottage, Danica relished the opportunity to take in the rest of the old home in peace. She flipped the light switch on the wall and a crystal chandelier, identical to the one in the living room, came to life. The room was wide with a shuttered picture window facing the street. Along the opposite wall were built-in bookcases and cabinets running from the floor to the edge of the twelve-foot ceiling. She inspected the fine oak cabinets and felt a stab of regret at the modern intrusion in the old home's design. Shaking her head slightly, she moved on to the hallway that separated the bedrooms from the rest of the cottage. Just as the slender fingertips of light retreated from the hallway, Danica came to the first bedroom door. She pushed the thick cypress door open and reached into the dark, windowless room for the light switch. When she flipped the switch on the wall next to her, the small room became drenched with warm light from the lamp mounted in the ceiling fan above. The dome over the lamp had been covered with frosty glass, muting the harshness of the bright light. Soft blue paint covered the walls while a matching blue carpet had been placed on the floor. Overhead, the ceiling had been left an austere shade of white.

Danica leaned against the doorframe and reflected on the various stages of childhood and adolescence she had gone through while occupying this room. The rainbow-painted walls her mother had painstakingly decorated for her had been replaced with posters of boy bands and television heartthrobs until her mother had died. After the funeral, Danica had come home and removed all the posters in a fit of rage, wanting to be surrounded once more by her mother's rainbows. The last year she had spent in this room, she had felt comforted by those rainbows, as if her mother's love had been forever sealed beneath the paintbrush strokes on her walls.

"I missed this old place," she whispered.

A sudden rush of cold air moving down the hallway caused Danica to turn away from the bedroom door and peer into the darkness behind her. She took a few steps further down the hall until the aroma of cigar smoke mixed with a hint of brandy wafted in the air around her. Danica remembered that smell. It had always filled her bedroom whenever the dark man would appear.

"Is it you?" she softly called into the hallway. "It's me, Danica. I've come back. Just like I said I would."

Danica walked briskly past the entrance to the master bath to the final door at the end of the hall. Without hesitation, she pushed the cypress door open and walked inside the master bedroom. The light from the large picture window overlooking the courtyard shone into the room, accentuating the deep burgundy color of the carpet beneath her feet. She stepped into the center of the room and observed the ceiling fan above. Danica waited, straining with every breath to hear the slightest stirring.

"Welcome home," a man's wispy voice resonated around her.

A hopeful smile curled the edges of Danica's heart-shaped mouth. "Thank you, Gaston. It's good to be home."

A few minutes later, Danica returned to the living room, where she found Pat scrolling through messages on her cell phone.

"Let's sign the papers," Danica happily announced. "I want to get moved in as soon as possible."

Pat gave her a wary going-over with her brown eyes. "You positive about this, Danica? I need to make sure you're aware that other tenants have had problems—"

"It's fine, Pat. I know you said the place is haunted and people have had some bad experiences, but this…." Danica waved to the room around her. "Just feels right."

Pat gave a skeptical shrug. "I have the papers ready back at the office. The rent is eight hundred and fifty a month. Mr. Caruso wanted me to charge you the same rate he charged your father. He insisted I make this as appealing to you as possible. You must have made quite an impression on the old man when you were a kid. He never cuts anyone a deal."

"Please tell Mr. Caruso I appreciate it."

Pat replaced her cell phone in her front jacket pocket. "Let's turn off all of these lights and head back to the office."

Suddenly, from the shuttered window beside them, three loud knocks reverberated across the room.

Pat grabbed at her chest. "Jesus! What in the hell was that?"

Danica smirked as she watched the color drain from Pat's perfectly made-up face. "Just someone outside on the street banging on the wall…happened a lot when I was a kid. Drunk tourists would often bang on the shutters at all hours."

Pat regained her composure. "Of course, you're right. I didn't think of that."

Danica motioned to the pocket doors leading to the kitchen. "Let's get you out of here, Pat, before you have a heart attack."

"Gladly," Pat offered and rushed to the doors. "I never liked this place. I just hope you know what you're doing, Danica."

"I know," Danica asserted with a grin. "I've always known."

CHAPTER 2

After the last of her furniture had been set up in the master bedroom, Danica escorted the four heavyset men from All-State Movers out the front door. As she stood in the glare of the mid-day October sun and watched the moving van take the turn at the corner down Royal Street, Danica felt her excitement ebb away when confronted by the prospect of unpacking all of her possessions. She wearily reached for the small of her back and stretched out her tired muscles. Just as she was about to step back inside her home, a man's booming voice stopped her.

"Hello there!"

Danica wheeled around to see an older couple coming toward her. The woman had very short brown hair that encircled her thin face, sunken brown eyes, protruding cheekbones, a small pink mouth, and a pointy chin. Her casual jeans and shirt appeared almost baggy on her gaunt figure. To her right, a big man with a round belly, stern face, and sharp green eyes was taking in the curves of Danica's petite figure. She could almost see the snarl of lust on his fat lips when he smiled at her.

"We're the Moutons," the frail woman said in a meek voice that Danica could barely make out over the din of the Quarter around them. "My husband Burt and I live in the house next door." She motioned back to a single story green and white Creole cottage next to Danica's. "We wanted to welcome you to the neighborhood."

Danica wiped her hands on her jeans. "I'm Danica Giles." She held her hand out to the older woman.

Mrs. Mouton took her hand, smiling faintly. "I'm Claire."

Danica turned to Claire's husband and uneasily shook his hand. She could not pull her hand away fast enough from the man's sweaty, thick paw.

"Just wanted to see if you could use any help," Burt Mouton spoke up in a blaring tone that contrasted his mild-mannered wife. "Been waiting for someone to move into the place for quite a few years. Glad to see the old cottage will get some life."

Danica glanced back at her new home. "Yes, the real estate agent told me it had been empty for a while."

"Ever since those two queers died. Paul Caruso spent two years fixing it up and then another year trying to rent it out," Burt informed her.

"Yeah, I heard about that." Danica turned back to him. "Did you know them?"

Burt shook his head. "Nah, never associate with their kind." He motioned to his wife. "Claire used to talk to them about plants and such."

Claire nodded. "Two very nice gentlemen. Never would have guessed in a million years that Elliot and Bob would have ended up like that. They seemed so devoted to each other."

"Devoted? Hell, they were queer, Claire," Burt loudly argued.

"Gay, Burt, not queer," Claire corrected. "They were very quiet and used to do tarot card readings in the front of the cottage. They were very good, too."

"Tarot card readings?" Danica inquired.

Claire's dull eyes briefly twinkled. "Oh, yes, Elliot was exceptionally gifted with second sight. He was very sensitive to impressions. He told me that one day something was going to happen and he and Bob were going to die together. He swore to it. When he I heard he brought a gun to the hospital and made sure they did die together, I wasn't that shocked, but it was still very sad."

"It wasn't that sad, Claire. They were two weirdos, if you ask me. Bound to do something crazy sooner or later." Burt nodded to the cottage. "You going to live here alone, or is there a Mr. Giles?"

"Mr. Giles was my father, Burt, but he died over a year ago. I plan on living here alone."

Claire gave an uncomfortable gasp. "Is that wise, dear? The Quarter isn't a safe place to be, especially for a woman on her own."

Burt hauntingly tugged at the snug waist of his casual dark slacks. "Yes, you need a man around the house to help out, protect you from intruders."

"I had one of those, but since my divorce, I haven't felt the need for another man. But I promise I'll be just fine." Danica shrugged. "I grew up in this neighborhood and know my way around the Quarter. After years of living in Seattle, it will be nice to get back to my Southern roots."

Claire's brown eyes grew in size. "You moved here from Seattle? Alone?"

"Not completely alone. The moving company helped," Danica quipped.

"But that's so brave of you," Claire went on. "I don't know how you young girls do it. Just pack up and move like that."

"I wasn't being brave. I was just ready for a change of pace."

"So, what is it you do, dear?" Claire eagerly questioned.

"I'm a graphic designer. I just got a job at the advertising agency of Morrison and Rau in the city."

"That's wonderful. I always wanted a career, but that wasn't something a woman did in my day. You had to stay home and—"

"Claire," Burt butted in. "Danica's doesn't need to hear that."

"Yes, you're right." Claire patted her husband's thick arm. "Well, just remember, if you need anything, day or night, Burt will come over and help out."

Burt stuck out his chest. "Yeah, you call me. Claire will give you our number. I'm a retired police detective with the NOPD. I've got a loaded arsenal inside. You got a gun?"

Danica nodded. "I usually keep it by my bed."

Burt winked at her. "Good girl. Use it, if you need to. Damn city is crawling with thugs. I should know." He nodded to his wife. "That's how Claire and I met. She was mugged and I was the detective put in charge of her case."

Claire smiled adoringly at her husband. "Some boys stole my purse when I was coming out of the grocery. The police sent Burt to get my statement. Four months later we got married…been married over ten years now. My first husband, Paul, was killed in a car accident and our son, Paul Gaudette Jr., works at Chevron as an engineer, but he—"

"Claire, you're boring Danica," Burt interrupted.

Claire turned her brown eyes sheepishly to the sidewalk. "I'm sorry."

Burt frowned at his wife. "She tends to rattle on." He gave a curt nod to Danica. "If you need any help with anything, let us know."

"I will," Danica told him as she observed the way Claire affectionately looked up at her husband's rigid profile.

Burt's angry green eyes shifted to his wife. "Claire is home most of the time. I have a job as a security guard five nights a week, so it will be nice to know Claire will have someone else around to keep her company."

"Perhaps when I get settled, you two can come over for dinner one night?" Danica suggested.

Burt's plump face sobered. "Thank you, but if it's all the same to you, Danica, I prefer not to spend too much time in your house."

Claire patted her husband's arm. "Burt had a bad experience in there a few years ago right before Bob and Elliot died. He was attacked."

Danica stared worriedly at Burt. "Attacked by whom?"

"More like by what," Burt answered. "I never saw anything. All I know is one minute I was standing up and the next I was on the floor, flat on my back. Elliot was several feet away from me and there wasn't anyone else in the room. I try to steer clear of the place as much as I can."

"I'm sorry to hear that, Burt." Danica refrained from letting a smug grin sneak across her lips. "I know the real estate agent told me people had been hurt before in the cottage, but I didn't realize—"

"Just be careful in there," Burt warned. "Something's not right about that place. I never believed in ghosts until we moved down here."

"You see, we have a ghost, too," Claire jumped in. "A gentle ghost of a man, but nothing like what resides in your house. Our Gaston is a sweet ghost."

Danica's insides twitched at the mention of that name.

Burt gave a condescending snort. "Claire named our ghost Gaston. She wanted to give him a French sounding name. Says he was a French plantation owner or some such nonsense."

"His name was Gaston Deslonde," Claire asserted, sounding unusually resilient. "He owned a sugarcane plantation in St. Bernard Parish. The house we reside in was his city dwelling. He died here of yellow fever in the great epidemic of 1853."

"Claire, for Christ's sake!" Burt shouted. "You just met the girl. Can't you wait a few days before you let her know you're crazy?"

"I'm not crazy. Elliot taught me how to speak with spirits," Claire calmly explained to Danica. "He taught me a great deal about spirits and communicating with the dead."

"All right, Danica doesn't need to hear about your kookiness." Burt warily turned to Danica. "She's harmless, I promise," he added.

Danica laughed lightly, hoping to relieve the growing tension in the air. “It’s all right, Burt, and it’s good to know we have an expert in the occult in case any ghosts wake me up in the middle of the night.”

Burt took his wife’s hand. “Come on, Mrs. Houdini, let’s get out of here before you scare the poor girl to death.”

Danica watched as Burt all but dragged his wife back to their front door. As an image of her ex-husband, Tom, paraded across her mind, her body stiffened while her stomach swirled with disgust. It was the same physical reaction she always had whenever she thought about her marriage

“I was such a fool,” Danica whispered as she turned to her doorway.

When she stepped into her cool air-conditioned cottage, all her heartache from the past melted away. After she shut the front doors, the smell of cigars and brandy permeated the living room.

“And now you’re home,” a man’s deep, seductive voice said in front of her.

When Danica looked up, she saw him leaning against the open pocket doors on the other side of the room. He was very tall with long legs, wide shoulders, a thick chest, and slim waist. Dressed in clothes from another era, he wore a white linen shirt with a high collar, opened at the top, and without the customary tie, waistcoat, or coat. Fitted black trousers hugged the curves of his narrow hips and were tucked into polished black riding boots. His square face had a narrow chin, high forehead, a pale, thin mouth, slightly crooked nose, and was framed by long, dark sideburns. His wavy, brown hair was pulled back with a white ribbon and fell to his shoulders. But when Danica finally took in his eyes, her body quivered with excitement. His sky-blue eyes were still the same, filled with fire and seemingly able to peer into the deepest depths of her soul.

“Gaston,” she sighed as she leaned back against the front doors. “I can’t believe you’re really here.”

“I’ve missed you, my treasure.”

Danica’s body warmed over with delight. “You remembered.”

He moved toward her. “How could I forget? You were always my treasure.”

Her eyes hungrily explored his handsome face. “For years I tried to write you off as a figment of my imagination, a friend I conjured up when life became overwhelming. But you were real. What we had was real, wasn’t it?”

He stood before her, his eyes lingering over every curve of her delicate face. “Yes, it was real, Danica. I am real.”

She longed to touch him, but she knew from experience that her hands would simply pass through him, no matter how solid he appeared.

She nervously reached for her long ponytail of curly, chestnut hair. “How have you been, Gaston?”

His mouth twisted into a sardonic smile. “Still a ghost, as you can see.” He waved a long, muscular arm down his body. “I haven’t changed in all of these years, but you….” His eyes steadily concentrated on her figure, hovering over the swell of her bust. “My God, when did you become this beautiful woman before me?”

Danica glimpsed her grimy white T-shirt, baggy jeans, and dirty tennis shoes. “Still the same old Gaston. Charming as ever.”

He held his hands up in the air, grinning. “I cannot change.” His eyes looked her over once more. “You look good, Danica. How many years has it been?”

She moved away from the entrance. “Twenty years and eight months. I was sixteen the last time we saw each other.” She stepped around him.

“That last night we were together you said your father was taking you out of the state. Where did you go?”

“We went to Florida. I finished high school there and attended Florida State University. I graduated with a degree in graphic design and then got a job offer in Seattle. About a year after I settled there, I met someone…and I got married.”

His high brow furrowed as his bright blue eyes darkened with concern. “And where is your husband?”

“Ex-husband. I’m divorced. Tom and I were not well-suited for each other.”

He crossed his arms over his chest “Divorced? I’m sorry to hear that. What kind of man was this Tom? Would I have approved?”

“No, but you never approved of any of my boyfriends. Tom was…a mistake. I thought it was love, but it turned out to be something else entirely,” Danica whispered, suddenly feeling uneasy about discussing her marriage.

His intense eyes concentrated on her, making Danica squirm with discomfort. “I know you, Danica,” he finally said. “If you had loved him, you would never have walked away. You’re lucky; in my day, divorce was never an option. Marriage was for life.”

Danica cast her eyes to the cement floor. “Times have changed, Gaston.”

“No need to remind me. I may be a ghost, but I still can see and hear the world around me. What I’ve garnered from television and the Internet has been most enlightening.”

She arched an eyebrow at him. “You use the Internet?”

“You’d be amazed what a ghost can do when someone leaves their computer on.”

She chuckled. “I think many would find it pretty scary that a ghost is so well-informed about our tumultuous world.”

“I assure you, I’m a lot less frightful than all of those stories presented on your CNN.” His booming laughter echoed about the small living room.

She noticed the way his face brightened and his eyes glowed with happiness when he laughed. Danica had forgotten how much she had loved his warm, bold laugh. “I kept wondering how you were. I spent a great deal of time thinking and worrying about you after we left. I tried to come back here so many times since then, but then I stopped myself.”

“Why?”

She ran her hand over her face, struggling to find the words. “I thought I was crazy for believing in you. I kept trying to convince myself that I was a grown woman and you could not possibly be real.”

“Then why did you come back?”

She shrugged and slid her hands in the back pockets of her jeans. “Because I was happy here, and I remembered the promise I made to you the night before we moved.”

“You promised you would return to me,” he recalled as he came closer to her. “You crossed your heart and hoped to die on it.”

“Yeah, well, after my divorce, Seattle became rather uncomfortable for me. I started planning on coming back, but couldn’t afford it. When I came into some money….” Her throat tightened. “Dad died last year…I, ah….”

Gaston dipped his head slightly to her. “I know he’s gone, my treasure. I felt him crossing over.”

She desperately searched his luminous eyes. “You felt him? Is he all right? Can you speak to him? Can you give—?”

“You know I can’t do that. Remember what I told you after your mother died?”

Danica lightly sniffled. "That once you cross over to the other side you cannot come back, and you cannot communicate with those you left behind."

"Those of us who have not crossed over stay because we feel we have unfinished business on this earth."

"You've been dead a hundred and fifty-nine years, Gaston. When are you going to finish that unfinished business of yours? Or do you plan on haunting this house for another one hundred and fifty-nine years?" Danica walked over to some boxes sitting on the floor in the corner of the room.

"You know I only haunt this house on Rue Dumaine because it's within close proximity to the place where I died."

"Why do you still call it Rue Dumaine?"

Gaston bowed his head slightly. "Forgive me, but old habits die hard. When I lived the word street was never used, only rue. Our language was a funny mixture of French and English then, something I still miss hearing among the residents of this fair city."

Danica reached for one of the boxes. "You never spoke French with me."

He chuckled behind her. "I tried in the beginning, but you never understood me, so I gave it up. After so many years, I've forgotten much of my French."

"Perhaps I should take lessons so we could speak it together." She placed the box on the floor beside her. "It will give us something to do while you're haunting my house."

"I'm not haunting. I'm merely waiting until I am allowed to cross over to the other side."

"Allowed to cross over? I suspect you don't want to leave. You like it here." She kneeled down beside the box.

"I love it here. Why would anyone want to cross over when they can live in the lively French Quarter instead? Imagine all the fun I would have missed out on if I had left."

"Fun? From what I've been told you've been having a little too much fun." She paused and glared at him. "Why did you scare all of those people away from this house?" Danica probed.

He came up to her side. "I don't scare people. You know me better than that. I'm not spiteful, but I don't like men being in this home, only women." He smirked and bobbed his eyebrows up and down. "Attractive women are always welcome."

"You're a hopeless flirt, Gaston." Danica shook her head. "What about the two men who died here? Bob and Elliot? What did you do to them?"

"Ah, yes, those two gentleman." He let out a perturbed sigh. "Or should I say those disreputable gentlemen."

"They were gay, Gaston, not disreputable," Danica corrected as she tore the tape off the top of the box.

"I may have a great deal of knowledge about your modern way of thinking, Danica, but my morals still reflect my time. Such men were never approved of in my circles, and I pulled out all the stops to get those two to leave. But they enjoyed my haunting…even tried to have séances and such rot to communicate with the dead. It was all very annoying. After a while, I gave up trying to get them to leave. They were too strange, even for me."

Danica began pulling wads of newspaper from the box. "Claire Mouton next door mentioned something about their teaching her how to communicate with you. Is that how she knew your name?"

"Claire Mouton." He rolled his eyes. "There is another person who I find extremely annoying. She talks incessantly about her son, spends too much time watching soap operas, and is always summoning me to come to her side."

"What do you mean summoning?"

He shrugged his wide shoulders. "She uses means that are…impossible for a ghost to ignore."

Danica stopped rummaging through the box and looked back at him. "I don't understand. What means?"

Gaston sat down on the floor next to her. "There are forces on this earth that even ghosts are not immune to. If one knows how to control such dark forces, they can exert their influence over someone like me."

"Are you saying Mrs. Mouton, tiny, mousy Mrs. Mouton, is some kind of witch?"

Gaston slowly nodded. "The Mouton's moved into my former residence about eight years ago. At first, she used to talk to me when her husband wasn't home. I didn't mind because she seemed lonely and unhappy. Then, she began using these spells and incantations to force me to her side. I was able to resist her in the beginning, but soon her magic became hard to ignore, and I had to communicate whenever she spoke some magical words. With every passing day, her influence is growing stronger."

Danica tilted her head to the side. “Stronger? How can it grow stronger?”

Gaston’s intriguing eyes carefully examined her face. “Danica, do you know what black magic is?”

“Of course. Anybody who watches horror movies knows what that is.”

“Then you know there are two sides to magic: good and bad. When Claire Mouton started out with her spells and rituals for calling to me, she only used white or good magic. A few years ago she discovered that harnessing the dark forces of black magic could make her a much more formidable witch. But such power cannot come to anyone without paying a high price. Claire has crossed into a realm from which there is no turning back.”

Danica shook her head, snickering with disbelief. “Black Magic? Dark forces? Jesus, Gaston. I thought you were the only dark force in this house.”

Gaston curiously perused the contents of the box beside Danica. “There are many forces in this house, Danica, some much darker than me. These other spirits do not wish to be known to the living, but they are growing increasingly restless with Claire’s dangerous activities.”

Danica gawked at him. “Others? What others?”

“It’s a very old house, my treasure, with a long history of death.”

“Do you see these others, Gaston?”

He shook his head. “I only feel them, and they are getting angry.”

“Maybe you should talk to Claire, warn her about those dark forces and what could happen. That should scare her.”

Gaston stood from the floor. “I’ve already told her, but she has become too attached to the power of darkness to turn back. Her fate is sealed.”

Danica smirked and went back to unpacking her box. “Her fate is sealed? Now you sound like a normal ghost. All doom and gloom.”

“It’s not doom and gloom I am speaking of. I’m talking about the power of magic.” He gave an impatient sigh “Danica, you have to understand that need is what drives magic. The abject power of need is behind the desire to possess, to love, to be wealthy…oh, any number of needs that are dreamed of by the living. Claire needs to be free. That is where the power for her magic comes from.”

She unwrapped a china figurine from a wad of newspaper. "What does Claire need to be free of?" She put the pink figurine of a ballerina on the floor beside her.

"Not what, but whom." He nodded to the front doors. "You met the despicable man she's married to. What do you think?"

Danica rose to her feet. "Burt? He's obnoxious as hell and probably…."

"Probably what?" Gaston persisted.

"Probably hits her."

He nodded, thoughtfully. "That's very perceptive of you. He does hit her, quite frequently in fact. I've witnessed his abuse."

She paused for a moment as an idea struck her. "Is that why you attacked him?"

"I had just seen him throw his wife to the floor earlier that day. I wanted to give him a taste of his own medicine, so I tossed him to the floor. That was about the time Claire turned to the powers of darkness to help free her of her marriage."

Danica threw a hand angrily in the air. "Why doesn't she just get a divorce, like me? A woman doesn't have to resort to voodoo to get rid of a husband."

"Claire feels trapped. She struggled financially before her marriage and she stays married for the money." He motioned down Danica's body. "She doesn't have your strength or intelligence," he added.

"It doesn't take strength to walk away from an abusive relationship, and it sure doesn't take a lot of brains to know that every time he lifts his hand to you it will not be the last. They may promise never to do it again, but—"

"Danica? What are you saying?" He came closer, his eyes blazing with worry. "How do you know so much about this? Is this why your marriage ended?"

Suddenly, she was ashamed. She did not wish for Gaston to know about all that she had suffered.

Danica quickly lowered her eyes. "No, it wasn't me. I had a friend in Seattle. Her husband beat her and we would talk about it. She shared a great deal with me about her marriage."

He sighed with relief. "I could not bear it if anyone ever hurt you, my treasure. I may only be made of air, but I would destroy anyone who ever laid a hand on you."

"I know, Gaston." She gave him an encouraging smile. "Maybe that's why I came home, because I wanted to feel safe. The only time in my life that I ever felt safe was with you."

They stood gazing into each other's eyes as the growing afternoon light trickled through the cottage front window. For Danica, a long forgotten sense of peace descended over her. After leaving New Orleans, she had forgotten how she had always felt so comfortable with Gaston. Like a favorite blanket in winter, Gaston was a familiar presence that soothed her churning restlessness. It was more than being safe with him; it was as if she were complete with him. She was whole again, and no longer felt as if she had to run at full steam to catch up with life. Her life was here. Her life was with him.

"You should get to your unpacking," he suggested, turning his eyes to the boxes scattered about the living room floor.

Awakened from her trance, she surveyed her scant belongings. She placed her hands on her hips and grinned at Gaston.

"Want to help?"

"Would if I could, my treasure, but you know I'm merely made of air, and moving furniture about takes a great deal out of me."

"I thought you might say something like that." She turned to the box on the floor next to her.

"But I will be happy to give you any decorating suggestions," he commented behind her.

"Thanks, but I think I'll leave the decorating up to my more modern sense of style rather than your outdated concepts." Danica waited for his cocky response, but there was none.

When she turned around, Gaston was gone.

"I always hated it when he did that," she whispered, and went back to her unpacking.

As Danica slowly began to remove the newspaper wrapped around a blue elephant figurine, a satisfied smile crossed her lips. She was home. After years of dreaming of returning to the one place she had known happiness, she was finally back. Finding Gaston waiting for her inside the little cottage had made her homecoming feel almost perfect.

And what would have made it perfect? she silently asked.

An excited tingle rose from deep within the reaches of Danica's belly as she pictured Gaston's arms about her. The handsome ghost she had daydreamed about for most of her life was back, and instead of being content, she was instantly overcome by an unexpected feeling of desire.

Holding the china elephant to her chest, Danica sat back on the floor with a thud. "This is going to be a lot harder than I thought."

CHAPTER 3

Later that evening, Danica emerged from her bathroom freshly showered and dressed in a pink silk robe. She pulled her damp hair back into a ponytail and began spreading her pink sheets on the king-sized oak bed across from the fireplace. When she'd finished making the bed, Danica reached into the drawer of the nightstand and pulled out a .32 caliber Smith and Wesson revolver. She placed the gun at the head of the bed and then put her favorite pillow on top of it. After she had finally piled the last of her numerous pink pillows on the bed, the air in the room suddenly turned colder.

"You're back."

"Didn't I always come to tuck you in?" Gaston said from the doorway to her bedroom.

"You would also tell me a bedtime story, but I think I'm a little old for that now."

He came into the room. "You were a little old for that when you were fourteen, but you always insisted on it." He waved his hand over her pink bedspread, pillows, and sheets. "You still love pink, I see?"

Danica sat down on her bed and undid the clip from her hair, letting her long curls cascade about her slender shoulders. "You know how I feel about pink." She pulled at the belt on her pink robe.

"Yes, I remember. You always said it made you feel like a special little girl." He shook his head slightly. "You remind me of my sister, Yvette. She always loved pink, too." His face became serious, and then he looked away. "Perhaps we should start a new tradition. Why don't you tell me a bedtime story? About your life, the one you lived when you left here so long ago."

Danica fidgeted on the bed. "Not much to tell. I hit the highlights for you earlier."

"What about friends, hobbies…lovers?"

Her eyes shot to his and a jolt of electricity passed through her body. Danica returned her gaze to the bedspread.

"That's rather a forward question, considering the era you came from. I would think it would be ungentlemanly to ask a lady such a question."

Gaston's boisterous chortle bounced about her bedroom. "My God, Danica, when did you become such a prude?"

Her eyes angrily flew to his. "I am not a prude! I was trying to be ladylike. You always taught me to be ladylike when speaking to a man."

"When speaking to other men, not to me."

"Well, how in the hell was I supposed to know that?" She jumped from the bed.

"Why are you angry?" he asked, still amused by her behavior.

"I'm not angry."

"Yes, you are." He folded his arms over his wide chest. "What difference should it make if you had fifty lovers, or waited until marriage to lie with a man? You always said you didn't care what other people think?"

"No, I only care what you think," she blurted out, instantly regretting her words.

He shook his head and lowered his arms. "Then, if that is the case, it does not matter to me if you had fifty lovers or waited until marriage to lie with a man. None of that will change how I feel about you."

Danica paced in front of her bed as she felt Gaston's eyes on her. "It wasn't fifty. I'm not a slut, Gaston."

"The number of men a woman has been with doesn't make her a slut, Danica." He came up to her, interrupting her pacing. "It only makes her more experienced." His eyes scrutinized her face. "So how many was it?"

"Why do you care?"

"Because I'm curious. We always shared so much in the past. Why can't we share this?"

"All right," she stated, trying to stand up to his piecing gaze. "Four."

"Including your husband?"

She nodded.

Gaston raised his eyebrows and turned away. "Did you love any of them?"

Danica's shoulder's sagged and she returned to the bed. "One. His name was William Darlington. We met my freshman year at the University of Florida. He was in engineering." She climbed on her bed and sat down. "He was funny and handsome and…." She looked up at Gaston. "He reminded me of you."

"Me?" He came toward the bed. "What happened to William Darlington?"

"Cheryl Normand, a blonde, blue-eyed cheerleader who stole him away in my sophomore year."

"He was an idiot to let you go." Gaston had a seat on the bed next to her. "Was he the first?"

She nodded her head. "I really loved that guy."

"I'm sorry. I should have prepared you better for the ways of men."

Danica gawked at him. "Why would you have done that? You weren't my father."

"No, but I was your friend. I should have told you how men could be. I was once a man, Danica…selfish, cruel, and blind to the feelings of others. I should have taught you how to avoid men such as myself. I'm sure I could have spared you a great deal of heartache."

"Heartache is part of growing up, Gaston, and you couldn't protect me from that."

He stood from the bed. "Well, maybe if I had taught you more about men, you would have married someone you loved, had a family, and settled into a good life. Perhaps then you wouldn't have felt the need to come back here."

Danica was stunned by his comment. "Are you saying you don't want me here?"

"No, no, far from it." He raised his hands reassuringly to her. "I've wanted you to return to me since the day you left, but I was selfish to make you promise to return. You are alive and should be among the living. I can't give you what you need, Danica, and I'm beginning to wonder if showing myself to you all those years ago was the right thing to do. Perhaps your life would have been better if you had never known me."

"Better?" Danica stood from the bed. "I doubt it. Knowing you has been one of the best things that ever happened to me, Gaston. You don't realize how much you have given me."

His eyes lingered over the slinky pink robe as it clung to the curves of her body. He turned away. “I can’t give you anything, Danica. I’m dead, remember.”

She came up to his side. “You’re more alive that a lot of living people I know. I never want you to think that all the time we have spent together hurt me. You have helped me, because you’re the only one who has always been there for me.”

He stared into her face and that excited tickle in her belly ignited into a deep, burning need.

Gaston turned for the bedroom door. “I should go. It’s late, and you need your rest.”

As Danica watched him walk to the doorway, a thought crossed her mind. “Where do you go when you leave me, Gaston?”

He stopped at the door and turned to her. “I’m still here, floating between my home and yours. Listening to the world and keeping an eye on all things.”

“Will you still keep watch over me at night?” she asked as she pulled back the pink covers on her bed.

“Always.”

Danica reached under the pillow for her gun. She pulled the gun out and checked the safety. “That’s good. Hopefully, I won’t need to use this.”

Gaston rushed toward the bed. “Where in the hell did you get that?”

She was taken aback by his tone. “Tom, my ex, got it for me when we were married. He wanted me to have protection in the house when he was working late. I wanted a dog, but he got me this,” she explained, holding up the gun in her hand.

Gaston stared at the firearm. “I would have preferred the dog, as well. Here I thought you to be a demure and soft-spoken woman, not some female Rambo.”

“How do you know about Rambo?”

Gaston’s eyes shifted from the gun to her. “I watched the movie on television once.”

Danica replaced the gun under her pillow. “Your familiarity with our culture is beginning to worry me, Gaston.”

“You’re sure you’re not going to shoot yourself with that thing? Do you even know how to handle a gun, Danica?”

She smoothed out her pillow. “Tom taught me.”

"That doesn't make me feel any better. Guns were something only men owned in my day, for hunting or for dueling. Women were discouraged from handling guns."

"From what I read of your time, women were discouraged from doing a lot of things," Danica scoffed.

"Women were protected in my day."

"Sheltered, you mean."

"That, too. But you must understand, a woman's honor was a prized commodity. Men had to do whatever it took to defend a woman's honor."

"Like fight in duels?"

He shrugged. "Sometimes, yes."

She eyed him curiously for a moment. "Did you ever fight in a duel, Gaston?"

"Once, when I was in New Orleans, I had to stand beneath the great dueling oak at the outskirts of the city."

Danica had a seat on her bed. "The tree still stands in City Park. I saw it on a field trip in school once. It's not far from the New Orleans Museum of Art." Danica paused and made herself comfortable. "Tell me what happened. Did you fight over a woman?" she excitedly asked.

"Hardly." He waved his long hand in the air. "This fool who handled some business affairs for me cheated me out of a great deal of money. I was going to sue him, but he suggested we duel rather than air our dirty laundry in a court of law. I stupidly agreed. Years of hunting on the plantation had made me a very good shot, so I felt confident I could slightly injure the man, end the duel, and have my stolen income returned to me without having to go through a lengthy court case." He shook his head. "It was neither romantic nor exciting as portrayed today, and the outcome was tragic."

Danica's blue eyes grew in size. "You didn't kill him, did you?"

Gaston lightly chuckled. "No, I merely grazed Gustave Beauregard's shoulder. But when the silly man discharged his weapon, he hit one of the horses pulling his carriage. Poor creature fell dead to the ground. I felt horrible."

Danica sat back on the bed, astonished. "Because the man shot a horse, you felt horrible. What if you had killed this Gustave?"

He grinned at her show of concern. "Men rarely died in duels back then, Danica. It was more for show than revenge. If you stood in a duel and discharged your firearm, you were considered brave according to the standards of my day."

"According to today's standards, you would be considered an idiot," Danica asserted. "He really killed a horse?"

Gaston just smiled and shook his head. "Go to sleep, and make sure you keep the safety on that gun of yours. I would hate to think you might take out a passing carriage horse trotting by the cottage on a midnight tour of the Quarter."

"Yes, Gaston."

He walked to the door, and when he reached the threshold to her bedroom, he turned to her. "I will see you tomorrow, my treasure."

"Goodnight, Gaston."

Danica watched as the solid shape of Gaston's body slowly evaporated in front of her eyes. Once he had disappeared, she removed her robe and reached for her nightshirt at the foot of her bed.

After Danica had slipped under her pink covers and turned out the lamp on her nightstand, her eyes stared out the picture window that faced the courtyard. She gazed up in the sky and marveled at the twinkling stars. She wondered why the gentle ghost who occupied her thoughts had never made it beyond those stars. It seemed to her that Heaven would be a better place with a man like Gaston Deslonde in it. After all, wasn't that where all the good people were supposed to go? As her eyelids drooped, Danica's mind clouded over with images of Gaston, in his black trousers and white linen shirt, standing beneath the great dueling oak and holding a pistol in his hand. Waiting off to the side she saw herself, dressed in a sweeping red velvet gown from the era, with her long hair piled atop her head. She watched anxiously as Gaston raised the pistol in his hand and took aim at his opponent. Fifty feet away from the tip of Gaston's pistol, Danica spied her ex-husband, Tom.

She smiled with satisfaction when Tom's thick, muscular body trembled with fear as Gaston pulled the trigger. Tom's brown eyes then rolled over into the back of his head as Gaston's bullet tore into his cold heart.

"Serves you right, you sadistic asshole," Danica whispered as she turned to her side. "If I had been braver, I would have done the deed myself."

As her vision progressed, Danica saw Tom's body carted off by a group of men, while she walked to Gaston's side. Gaston tossed the firearm in his hand to the ground and reached for her. Danica's heart began to race and her body flushed with desire as she imagined Gaston's lips sampling the delicate flesh on her neck and chest. She pictured his hands undoing the ties on her red velvet gown as she removed the pins from her hair. And as her racy fantasy took her further away from the waking world, Danica sighed with happiness. To Danica, such dreams were her own little piece of heaven on earth.

CHAPTER 4

Danica spent the next two days unpacking her boxes, moving furniture around, and listening to Gaston's endless array of suggestions on where everything should go.

"That brown sofa in the living room needs to be in the center of the room, not off to the side," he told her after he appeared one morning while she was trying to arrange some framed photographs on the mantle in her new office.

She waved off his suggestion. "It's better where it is. No one will run into it when they come through the front doors that way."

"Who will be coming through the front doors?"

"Friends," she insisted, avoiding his eyes.

"What friends? You never had friends growing up."

She turned to him. "I had friends, but the few who did venture over here, you ran off."

He poked out his thick chest, appearing offended by her remark. "I never ran off your friends."

"Betsy Wright," Danica retorted. "She came over here to play when I was ten and you walked into the bedroom and scared the living crap out of her."

Gaston covered the smile spreading over his lips. "I remember her," he mumbled. "She called you selfish, and went on and on about how her Barbie collection was bigger than yours." He frowned at her. "She was not your friend, and I scared her away because I didn't like the way she was bossing you about."

"What about Bobby Woods?"

He gave her a quizzical stare. "Who was Bobby Woods?"

"My date to the freshman dance in high school. You made that candle float up from the table when he was about to kiss me goodnight."

"You had no business kissing that boy," Gaston grumbled. "Your father should never have let you go to that silly dance."

"You did the same thing with Jeff."

Gaston rolled his eyes. "You're not still angry about him, are you? Jeff was not supposed to be coming over to this house when your father was not home. He had only one thing on his mind that night, and I was not about to let him stay and ruin your reputation."

"You set his pants on fire, Gaston," she declared, raising her voice. "My first steady boyfriend and you gave him second degree burns on his ass."

"Can I help it if the stupid boy backed into a candle flame and caught his trousers on fire?"

Danica tried to glare at him, but the charming smile on his face speedily eroded all of her anger.

"I was only trying to protect you," he softly said as he approached her side. "I was a man once, and I knew what all those boys were after. I wanted to keep you from harm."

"You kept me from getting laid," Danica teased.

"You were fifteen. Of course I kept you…." Gaston shook his head. "Do you have to be so crude, Danica?" He turned away from her and walked purposefully across the room. His eyes became distracted by a few drawings she had left on top of her desk.

"I see you're still drawing," he remarked as he gleaned over her work. "These are pretty good, Danica."

"I'm a graphic designer, Gaston. I've made a career out of drawing pictures." She nodded to the sketches. "Those are some ideas I'm playing with for my new job. Tomorrow I start with an advertising firm in town, and I wanted to get a jump on a new ad campaign they're putting together."

He raised his head to her, grinning. "I always knew you would go far."

Returning his eyes to the papers on her desk, she watched as his long hands slowly lifted each sketch and then neatly placed it on a pile to the side. She wondered what those hands had been like when he was alive, and her mind began to drift. Danica imagined those hands caressing her skin, and then she silently chastised her runaway libido. Struggling to find anything to occupy her mind, she recalled something Claire Mouton had said about Gaston.

"How come you never told me about your plantation in St. Bernard Parish?"

He never looked up from the desk. "What about it?"

"Claire mentioned it the other day. I was rather surprised to hear of it because I always thought you lived here in the Quarter. You never told me you had another home."

"Deslonde Plantation was my wife's home, not mine. Clarinda hated the city."

"Yes, Clarinda. You never spoke much about her in the past. I remember you told me about your daughter, Tessa, and your son, Francois, but you never talked about your wife. Why is that?"

Gaston came around to the front of the desk. "You were never interested in Clarinda when you were a little girl. You always preferred to hear stories about my children."

Danica sashayed toward the desk. "I know, but now I'm interested. What was she like?"

Gaston frowned slightly and folded his arms over his chest. "She was very pretty, with dark eyes and black hair. I remember she would always run her fingers through her hair whenever she was nervous or upset, something she seemed to do frequently in my presence."

"You made her nervous?"

He nodded his head. "Her mother died giving birth to her, and when she was five her father sent her off to be educated in a convent until she was fourteen. I don't know if it was me or my being male that always made Clarinda nervous."

"Did you ever ask her about that?"

He had a seat on the corner of the desk. "I did not marry her for conversation, Danica."

Danica wrapped her arms about her body as she moved closer to him. "Then why did you marry her?"

"Her father was a wealthy landowner in St. Bernard Parish and had a few thousand acres adjacent to my plantation. The marriage was arranged to expand my sugarcane farm and secure social prominence for her family." He paused and contemplated Danica as she stood before him. "Clarinda and I had nothing in common beyond the bedroom. After the birth of our fourth child, I didn't feel the desire to visit her bedroom again."

Danica furrowed her brow. "Your fourth child? I thought you only had two children."

"Two children that lived," he corrected with a slight nod. "We had two other sons who never survived the first year of life."

Danica shook her head, suddenly feeling foolish. "I'm sorry. I didn't realize you had lost any children. I shouldn't have—"

"Everyone lost children then, Danica. About half the children born into a family died of different diseases before the age of five. Having a large family was the only way to guarantee there would be heirs. I'd always hoped for more children, but…."

"Was it after you left Clarissa's bed that you moved to New Orleans?"

He took a moment, as if weighing his words, before he answered. "I always kept a place in the city. When I was not managing the plantation, I preferred to be here, seeing to my other businesses. I was often gone for months at a time, but I always tried to make it back to the plantation for the harvest. Unfortunately, I didn't heed the warnings to leave New Orleans that last summer of my life." He sighed and his face dimmed. "I remember lying in my bedroom as the fever tore through me, and wanting to see Deslonde Plantation once more. My mistress, Marna, was taking care of me after I became ill. I kept telling her I wanted to go home, but she would just pat my hand and say when I got better we could go back." He smiled weakly into her eyes. "But I never got better."

"Your mistress? You never told me you had a mistress, Gaston."

"You were too young to hear of such things."

"Where did you meet this Marna?"

Gaston shrugged. "At a quadroon ball. I went with a friend, Jean Henri, who was looking for a new mistress for his home in the city. Marna was there, being paraded around the room by the man she was married to, Judge Joseph Talbot."

Danica gaped at him. "She was married to another man?"

Gaston grinned at her reaction. "It was called a left-handed marriage then, my treasure. Women of color at the time only entered into such alliances with men for a means of support. The term we used was placage. Mistresses were accepted in my day because one did not marry for love, but for family obligations or business."

"So did she leave this judge for you?"

He chuckled slightly. "Not quite. I approached the judge and expressed an interest in buying Marna from him. We came to a reasonable price and then she came to live with me."

"Are you saying she was a slave?"

"No, she was a free woman and could have left him at any time, but when taking such a woman from a powerful man like the judge, it was best to agree on a price or else you could end up at the edge of town, settling the issue with pistols at dawn. Honor was extremely important."

"What happened to Marna's honor? Did you ever bother to ask her what she wanted?"

Gaston stood from the desk. "Yes, I did ask. I would never take a woman who didn't want me. I was not a sadist, Danica. Marna was happy to go with me. It seems the judge did not treat her well. I, on the other hand, was very good to her, and she, in turn, was very good to me."

Danica hesitated before she asked, "Did you love her?"

He waved an impatient hand at her. "Your world is obsessed with love. When the weight of living has been removed from your shoulders and you no longer have to fight the elements and each other for survival, then perhaps all thoughts eventually do turn to love. But that was a luxury my generation could not afford. We were happy enough to find companionship and a few comfortable nights in another's arms, but love? That was something only talked about in fairy tales."

She took a step closer to him, studying his intense eyes. "Did you ever love anyone, Gaston?"

"I loved my children. I still do, even though they have long since turned to dust. But the kind of love you share with someone for a lifetime? No, I never knew that."

"What happened to Marna after your death?"

"I left her my house next door and a small amount of cash so she could be situated. She stayed on in the house for another twenty years until her death. I watched her grow old and eventually mourned her passing to the other side."

Danica peered down at the brown carpet beneath her feet. "That must have been difficult, watching her go to a place you have never been allowed to see. I can't imagine what it has been like for you all of these years, watching as people moved in and out of your home, and you have no say so, no ability to control your fate."

"I'm a ghost. It's what we must endure."

She struggled to find the courage to broach the subject that had been troubling her for some time. "Gaston, what…what's it like to die?"

Gaston seemed taken aback by her question. "You've never asked me that before."

She took a seat on the desk. "When we were last together I was no more than a child. Children hardly think about death. Even after my mother died, I didn't fully understand death. But with age and experience, you begin to question the finality of life."

"There is no finality of life, Danica. Only…transitions. Dying is like walking into another room. I remember feeling so weighted down by my body those last few days. Everything hurt and breathing was so hard; then I began to feel lighter, as if rising up. The next moment I was above my body, looking down at my bed as Marna and the doctor hovered over me. I'm not sure when I actually died; all I know is one minute I was Gaston Deslonde, the man struggling to hang on, and the next, I was Gaston Deslonde, the spirit standing here beside you. There was no trumpeting of angels, no bright lights, no long tunnels like your Discovery Channel talks about. I was alive and then I was…me."

Danica took in his body, appearing almost real except for the pale light radiating from his face and eyes. He always seemed so solid, as if she could reach out and touch him. "Why did you show yourself to me that first night? If you have seen so many people come and go, what made you want to reveal yourself to a six-year-old girl?"

He shrugged slightly. "You were not afraid like all the others. I showed my shadow to you that night in your bedroom and every night after. Instead of growing more fearful, you became even more curious about me. I could sense it. I guess that was the one thing about you that I never had with anyone else living in this house. I could always feel what you were feeling. Still can."

"I was never afraid of you, Gaston, because I knew you wouldn't hurt me. I always felt safe when you came to watch over me at night. And you're right, I was curious." Danica laughed slightly as she rolled her head back. "The first time you spoke to me I was so…relieved. I hoped I had finally found a friend."

"You did."

She gently nodded her head. "You were a good friend to me. You helped me through the toughest times of my life."

Gaston moved closer to her spot on the desk. "I am still your friend, Danica, and I still want to help you, if you will let me."

She tilted her head curiously to the side. "Let you?"

He motioned to the drawings on her desk. "You can do better."

Danica caught sight of the neat pile of sketches he had made behind her. She then turned back to him. "Better? How?"

Gaston went around to the back of the desk and picked up the first sketch on top of the pile. “This ad campaign is for some kind of beverage, I take it.”

She jumped up from the desk and came around to his side. “For an energy drink.”

“Ah, yes, like Red Bull.”

Danica raised her dark eyebrows to him. “You know about Red Bull?”

He nodded. “I watched a special on energy drinks on The Learning Channel.”

Danica frowned. “The Learning Channel? The Internet? Next you’ll be telling me you have a cell phone.”

“I’d never want one of those annoying contraptions.” He placed the sketch in his hand down on the desk. “Perhaps you should be focusing your ideas less on the product and more on its capability. In these sketches you are not telling me very much about what it can do for me if I drink it. I would think by emphasizing the virtues of the product and not the taste, you might garner a wider audience.”

“But they need to know that it tastes good.”

“Danica, they are buying the drink to stay awake, get high, or be able to party until dawn. Do you think your consumers actually care about the taste? From what I have seen of the American diet on television commercials, I’m amazed half the country even knows what taste buds are when all they want is a bucket of hot wings and a gallon of soda for dinner.” He shook his head slightly. “In my time fast-food was an oxymoron, not a way of life.”

“Cute. I’m sure Weight Watchers would love to get that on a billboard.” Danica turned her eyes to the sketches on her desk. “I guess I could bring the graphics on the results out further and make the can smaller.”

“Perhaps some background. Maybe people enjoying the benefits of their added energy. Break dancing on a street corner, perhaps.”

Danica picked up one of her sketches. “Now I know you’ve been watching too much television.”

“If it helps you with this job, then it will all be worth it,” Gaston added as he backed away and pulled her desk chair out for her.

Danica sat down behind her desk and began going through her sketches. Soon she became so engrossed in her work that she did not notice when Gaston simply vanished from the room.

CHAPTER 5

It was after midnight when Danica sat back in her chair and reviewed the new sketches she had made. She hated to admit it, but Gaston had been right. The new design for the advertisement was much better than what she had originally done.

"He may have been dead for one hundred and fifty-nine years, but the man sure knows a thing or two about advertising," she whispered, feeling pleased by what she had accomplished.

She rose from her chair and stretched out her sore back. As her thoughts returned to her conversation with Gaston earlier that evening, Danica smiled. It was good to have him back in her life. She could almost feel her old confidence returning; the confidence Gaston had always given her as a child. After all the trials of her marriage to Tom, and her unhappy times since the divorce, she was beginning to feel like the woman she had been after graduating college; ready to take on the world and embrace life with the enthusiasm of an innocent child.

When she reached to turn out the lamp on her desk, she heard the angry slam of the entrance gate next to her cottage. Curious about who would be coming through the gate at such an hour, Danica went to the kitchen and peeked out the french doors to the courtyard. The lights from surrounding houses shone down into the courtyard, casting a wide array of long shadows across the cement-covered ground. Then she saw the flash of lights coming from the carriage house across the way.

Danica remembered what Pat had told her about the tenant in the carriage house working a lot of nights.

"What was his name?" Danica muttered as she opened the doors leading to the courtyard.

When she stepped into the humid night air, the second floor of the carriage house became drenched in light. Danica slowly walked across the courtyard and stopped when she reached the center, remembering what Pat had told her about the graves beneath the ground. After skirting to the side, she continued on to the small house.

Just as she was about to step before the front door, she heard a great banging coming from inside the home. Then, heavy footsteps could be heard coming toward the door. Suddenly, the front door flew open, and Danica stifled a startled cry.

Standing in the doorway before her, appearing out of breath and white as a sheet, was a very round man with a bald head, thick chest, and large muscular arms covered with an array of bright tattoos. As the formidable man scowled at her, his dark brown eyes traveled up and down Danica's body.

"Who are you?" he snarled in an unfriendly tone.

"Danica, Danica Giles." She motioned to the main house behind her. "I'm the new tenant in the front cottage."

The man's scowl lifted. "Sorry," he mumbled as he waved to the house. "I, ah, heard you had rented the place. I just wasn't expecting you to be at my door at this hour." He looked back inside his home. "Would you like to come in?"

"No, I'm sorry I came by so late, but I heard the gate and then saw your lights and thought…. I probably should have done this during the day," Danica admitted as she nervously ran her hand over her forehead.

He waved off her concern. "I'm Carl, by the way. Carl Wethers." Carl held out his hand to her.

Danica took his hand and gave it a firm shake.

Carl's dark brown eyes softened as he tried to smile for Danica. "I apologize for being rude, but I thought you were…someone else."

"I'm sorry. You were expecting someone else. I should go and leave you to—"

"That's not what I meant," Carl jumped in. "I thought you were one of them."

Danica stared at him. "One of 'them'?"

Carl leaned in closer to her and whispered, "The ghosts. You know, this place is full of them."

Danica feigned an indulgent smile. "So I've heard."

"Probably haven't been here long enough to see any of them yet. Trust me though, you will. Seen a lot of scared people come running out of that house of yours in the middle of the night, yelling about some man standing in their bedroom door."

"I've heard the stories, but I haven't had any experiences like that. In fact, I find the house rather inviting."

Carl snorted with disbelief. "Just wait. Takes a while for them to show themselves. They like to wait and learn your weaknesses. Study you and then…they scare the hell out of you."

Danica directed her eyes to his carriage house. "Do you have any ghosts?"

"Yeah," Carl replied as he wiped some sweat from his brow. "A nun that goes up and down the stairs, and then there are two small children that like to turn on the television and CD player when I'm asleep." He shook his head. "I was going to work tonight and forgot my cell phone. When I came back inside, the television was on and set to The Disney Channel." He patted his chest with his thick hand. "Do I look like the kind of man who would watch The Disney Channel?"

Danica looked over the plethora of tattoos up and down his arms, his black Harley Davidson T-shirt, black jeans, and black boots. "No," she finally said. "You don't look like a fan of The Mickey Mouse Club."

"Creeps me out when they do that. I have to go through the whole place looking for the culprit. Makes me glad I work nights. It's a lot quieter around here during the day. Ghosts sleep during the day, you know."

Danica raised her eyebrows with amusement. "No, I hadn't realized that."

Carl nodded and confidently folded his arms over his chest. "I read several books on the subject after I moved in here. I wasn't going to let the ghosts chase me out of this place. I was a US Marine for six years, so I'm not gonna let nothing scare me. If you ever want to borrow my books to do some research, you're more than welcome, Danica. Best defense against these things is knowledge."

"Have you ever tried talking to your ghosts, Carl? Perhaps ask them nicely not to disturb you. Maybe that would help."

"Nah." Carl waved off her suggestion with a frank scowl. "They don't listen to nobody. They're ghosts. They exist in another dimension and can't communicate with the living."

"Mrs. Mouton next door might disagree with you on that one, Carl. She told me she talks to her ghost all the time," Danica assured him.

"Mrs. Mouton also runs around naked in her courtyard chanting incantations to the full moon," Carl argued with one skeptically raised eyebrow. "I've seen her when I'm going to work. Crazier than a rabid raccoon, that one is. So don't listen to anything she tells you about the ghosts."

"I'll take that under advisement, Carl, thanks."

A sharp trill of musical notes filled the air around them. Carl grabbed for his cell phone in the back pocket of his jeans. He glimpsed the caller ID and frowned.

"Work," he told her, nodding to his phone. "Probably wondering where I am. Drunks start getting rowdy about this time. "

Danica took a step back from his door. "I'd better let you go."

He gave Danica a small smile. "Look, anytime you need to talk about your ghosts or are afraid or somethin' like that, come on over. I usually work midnight to six, five nights a week over at The Dungeon as a bouncer, but other than that I'm home most of the time."

"Thanks, Carl. If I have any problems I'll be sure to let you know."

He replaced his cell phone in his back pocket. "Maybe one night we can get together and go out for drinks. I can tell you the whole sordid history of this place. I've done a lot of online research on the people who lived and died here, going all the way back to Commander Alfonso Carlos Domingo-Castillo, who built the place in 1789. His family is buried under the pond."

"Yes, I heard about that. I think I would like to learn more about the ghosts living here." She paused for a moment. "Carl, have you ever done any research into the other inhabitants on the block? I only ask because Mrs. Mouton told me about a man who used to live in her—"

"Gaston Louis Etienne Deslonde," Carl interjected. "The dark man who haunts your house and Mrs. Mouton's house, as well. Yeah, I know all about him. The guy was a real sleazeball, if you ask me."

Danica inched closer to him, intrigued. "What do you mean 'sleazeball'?"

"Deslonde had a sugarcane plantation in St. Bernard Parish. The remains of the old Deslonde Plantation house are still there, along with the Deslonde family graveyard. The place is reputed to be very haunted. Apparently, Gaston Deslonde never stayed there much. He was in the city most of the time looking after his other business interests. He was part owner of a slave trade company with a man named Charles Lamarque. They had a place on the corner of Common and Baronne Streets in the city's business district."

Danica felt a wave of revulsion rise up in the back of her throat. No, this could not be her Gaston. How could the kind and gentle man she had known been a deliverer of such heinous cruelty in the past?

"Are you sure about that, Carl?"

"Oh yeah. Found a good bit on the man during my research."

"I should go." Danica immediately turned away from Carl.

"Come by and we can have that drink anytime, Danica," Carl called behind her as she headed across the courtyard.

Once back inside her home, Danica slammed the back doors closed.

"Something wrong?" Gaston inquired from her office doorway.

Standing in her kitchen, Danica took a deep breath as his striking blue eyes intently inspected her face.

"You're upset…I can feel it." He came toward her. "What did that cretin Carl say to you? You know he's crazy, Danica."

She tried to calm the flurry of anger swirling in her veins.

Gaston browsed her eyes, and then knitted his brow. "You're angry," he surmised. "At me?"

She let a long hiss of air escape from between her clenched teeth. "You were a slave trader? You bought and sold people for money? You were one of those inhuman, disgusting barbarians that—"

"Before you go on with your tangent, yes," he interrupted with a raised hand. "I was part owner of a slave trading company. Not a full owner, I assure you. I inherited the business from my father's estate. I'm not proud of what I did, Danica. Considering I have existed long enough to see a black man become President of the United States, I know what I did was wrong. But when I was alive, it was what we did. I'm not saying it was right, but the history of mankind has been marked by more wrongs than rights when it comes to the treatment of others. My guilt is no different than the Church's persecution of heretics, Hitler's persecution of the Jews, or Rome's execution of Christians. It was just what happened in that time, and time has corrected that mistake, as it eventually corrects all mistakes. If it makes you feel any better, I have had several lifetimes to consider my mortal sins, and I am truly sorry for what I did."

"Why didn't you tell me about that?" she shouted. "When I was in fifth grade you even helped me prepare my report on the slave trade in New Orleans, and never once did you ever tell me you were involved."

He shook his head. "You were ten. These were things you didn't need to hear about me at that age."

She folded her arms over her chest as she glared at him. "I feel like I don't know you, Gaston. I'm hearing that you fought duels, had a quadroon mistress, and were a slave trader. What other surprises do you have in store for me?"

He lowered his head to her. "What you are learning, Danica, is that I was a man when I walked this earth. Not some knight in shining armor that read bedtime stories to a lonely little girl. I had the same shortcomings as other men. I was not good, I was not free of faults, and I was not wise. I was human, and that in itself means my mistakes were no less worthy of forgiveness than any other soul that has existed on this realm since the days of Adam and Eve." His voice lowered, sounding more menacing than she had ever heard before. "I was going to tell you of my past when I was ready. I'm sorry you had to hear of my shame from someone else." His body began to fade before her.

Instantly, Danica's anger cooled. What was she doing? Yes, she was mad, but for what reason? What she had learned about Gaston had taken place long ago, and whatever his reasons for not telling her, they were his reasons and she should respect them.

"Gaston, please don't go. You're right. I'm acting like a child. I'm sorry."

She watched in amazement as his figure once again became solid.

"I do not want you to be angry with me, Danica."

"I'm not angry, just…all right, I'm disappointed." Her shoulders drooped with the weight of discomfort hovering in the air between them. "I know you tried to protect me when I was little, and I guess hearing all of these things about you makes me realize that you were just like me, human. For a long time I looked up to you. I thought you were perfect. I guess having all my childhood fantasies shattered in the space of a few days is just a bit much for me."

"I don't want to be some childish dream to you, Danica; I want to be more."

"You are more, Gaston. You're my friend."

His face briefly misted over with sadness. "I am that, Danica." He sighed heavily and took a step back from her. "It's late and tomorrow is your first day at your new job. You should go to bed."

"Yes, Gaston." She walked into her office, and when she reached the pocket doors to the living room, she stopped and turned back to see if Gaston was still standing there.

She smiled when she saw his solid form leaning over her desk and inspecting the new sketches she had done.

"These are much better," he commented while keeping his eyes on the drawings. "Your boss will be pleased."

"I'm glad you like them."

He looked up at her. "I don't want you spending time with that crazy ex-marine in the carriage house, Danica. He might get the wrong impression if you have drinks with him."

She pursed her lips together, scowling at him. "Were you eavesdropping on our conversation?"

"I'm a ghost; eavesdropping is our specialty."

"Carl is harmless, Gaston."

He stood from the desk and glared at her. "I don't know if you noticed, but the man's eyes rarely ventured higher than your bustline. In my day, that was considered rude."

"In my day, it's considered male," Danica challenged. "And for your information, the other day when you appeared to me for the first time in the living room, your eyes didn't travel much further than my bustline, either."

Gaston grinned. "I was admiring the way you had filled out since the last time I saw you."

"No, you were being male."

He nodded, still grinning. "That, too." Gaston placed his hands behind his back. "I would hardly be male if I didn't notice the woman you've become."

"I thought that was something you were supposed to leave behind with your body. Ghosts don't have hormones, Gaston."

"No, but attraction isn't about hormones, as you put it. It's about what resides in the soul, not in the…ah…other parts of one's anatomy."

Danica felt a stirring of excitement deep within those other parts of her anatomy. She let her eyes wander over Gaston's toned body and long legs. When she was an adolescent and prone to crushes, she had often dreamed of what it would be like to kiss Gaston. But being young and inexperienced with the opposite sex, she had not imagined more than the PG version of sex. Now that she was a woman, she found her mind becoming preoccupied with fantasies about the kind of lover Gaston Deslonde might have been. There were times over the past few days when her racy daydreams had gotten the better of her.

"Go to bed, Danica," he directed. "What you're feeling right now could be dangerous for both of us."

Danica blushed, raised her hand to her mouth, and quickly turned away from him.

Gaston chuckled lightly behind her. "If it makes you feel any better, my treasure, since the moment you walked through that back door, I've been feeling the exact same thing."

Danica collected herself and faced him. "Why is that dangerous?"

Gaston's face became very serious. He slowly came around the desk and walked up to her. "We are of different dimensions and different times, Danica. What we have now is all we can ever have. Anything else would be…such commingling of a spirit and a person of the flesh cannot happen without paying a grave price." His eyes burned into hers. "I will not have you suffer the consequences for my weaknesses."

"What consequences?"

"Go to bed, Danica. I have said too much already."

"What if we had been of the same time and the same dimension, me in your world or you in mine? Would things have been different between us?"

"In my world you would have been married to another man, mother to his children, and would probably have thought my lifestyle shameful. In your time I think perhaps we would have stood a better chance."

Danica stepped back from him. "Maybe one day, if the gods are kind, as you used to always say."

"If the gods were kind, I would not be here, Danica."

She looked once more into his soulful blue eyes and her heart ached for him. As a child she had never understood the pain he must have had to endure. But now that she had gained some insight into the depth of his suffering, her longing to comfort him began to weigh on her heart. She realized that Gaston was right; the gods were not kind.

Wanting to hide her sorrow, Danica put on a brave smile. "Goodnight, Gaston," she whispered.

"Goodnight, my treasure." Then Gaston Deslonde disappeared.

CHAPTER 6

Danica arrived home from work late the next evening. The streetcar ride from her office building had been crowded with an eclectic mix of professionals and tourists. She had to stand for most of the ride down St. Charles Avenue to Canal Street, and then there was the eight blocks she had to walk through throngs of people crowding the French Quarter streets in order to reach Dumaine Street. When she finally spotted her little cottage glimmering in the last traces of the setting sun, she almost groaned with relief.

She slammed the side entrance gate shut behind her as she pushed the straps to her purse and briefcase higher on her shoulder.

"I have got to get a car," she muttered as she made her way down the alleyway to the courtyard.

"Hey, neighbor!"

Danica turned to see Carl coming across the courtyard. He was dressed in black jeans, a black T-shirt, and black cowboy boots. In his right hand were several papers that he waved at Danica as he came up to her.

"I've got something for you. You just getting back from work?" he asked, eyeing her leather briefcase and conservative gray pantsuit.

"Yeah. Took me almost an hour between the crowds on the streetcar and then the crowds in the Quarter walking back from Canal. Is it always this busy down here?"

"Halloween," Carl admitted. "A lot of people come into town the week before Halloween. They take the ghost tours and stuff. New Orleans is a big stop on the haunted places map."

Danica pushed her back doors open. "Halloween is still a few days away."

"Yeah, but people like to get the party started early around here. Just wait until Halloween night…the place goes wild."

"Great," Danica grumbled as she walked into her kitchen and flipped on the lights.

Carl followed her inside. "Wow!" he exclaimed, taking in the kitchen. "Old man Caruso really did the place up nice. I haven't seen it since before the renovations." He turned to her. "Heard a lot of banging and saw workman coming and going for weeks at a time, but I never got a look at all the updates."

"I would love to invite you in, Carl, but I've got a ton—"

Carl held up the papers to her. "Not to worry. I just came by to drop these off to you." He handed her the thick pile of papers. "I printed up the research I did on your ghost; you know, the sleazeball. I just wanted to bring it over so you could have a look at it and plan your battle tactics."

Danica took the papers from him. "My battle tactics?"

"The best way to deal with these ghosts is to know something about them. Learn their weaknesses, and then you can use it to your advantage."

Danica stared quizzically at the papers in her hands. "But this is research about who they were when they were alive. How is this going to help me deal with them when they are dead? Maybe they're not the same person they once were."

"Once a sleazeball, always a sleazeball," Carl proclaimed.

Right at that moment a loud thump could be heard against the wall from Danica's office just beyond the kitchen. It sounded as if someone was punching their fist angrily into the wall.

"What was that?" Carl asked, moving deeper into the kitchen.

"My cat," Danica answered without thinking.

Carl gave her a doubtful glance. "Old man Caruso let you have a cat?"

She shook her head, silently remonstrating her lie. "No, and please don't tell anyone, but I couldn't just give Oscar up. He's been with me for years and he stays inside. He's very old and I just can't part with him."

Carl smiled at her, a big wide grin that made his plump face look more menacing than childlike. "You're secret is safe with me. I have an iguana. Named him Burt, after Burt Reynolds. He even sleeps with me in the bed."

Danica lowered her gaze to the papers in her hands, trying to hide her amused grin. "Well, thanks for this," Danica said, holding up the papers. "But I really should feed Oscar." She looked back at Carl, hoping he would take the hint and leave.

Carl gave her one last curious look, and then headed to the exit. Once outside, he turned back to Danica. "Don't forget about our drink," he added, and then motioned to the papers. "Let me know what you think of all that stuff. It's real interesting."

Carl gave her one last wave and then headed across the courtyard to his carriage house door.

Shrinking with relief, Danica quietly pulled the french doors closed.

"Meow," she heard behind her.

"Very funny," she said, turning around.

Standing in the arched doorway to her office, Gaston was dressed in his usual white linen shirt, slim black pants, and black riding boots. Danica could not help but let her eyes linger over his tempting figure. It was getting harder and harder not to notice.

"So now I'm a very old cat named Oscar." He frowned at her. "Why didn't you just tell him the truth?"

"What did you expect me to say? 'My ghost is pissed off because you're calling him a sleazeball'? I don't know who would sound crazier, me or him."

Gaston's eyes settled on the papers in her hands. "I hope you plan on burning that."

"Why?" She walked past him and into her office. She went to her desk and placed the papers and her briefcase down. "I would think you would be curious about how history has portrayed you," she added.

"Sometimes too many reminders of what you once were can be a detriment, not a blessing."

She slipped her purse off her shoulder and put it on top of her briefcase. "I think I might like reading up on my ghost."

"Why read about me? I'm right here. No need to do any research. You can go right to the source."

She placed her hand over the pile of papers Carl had given her. "Is there something in here you don't want me to read about?"

He shook his head. "You already know every secret, Danica. You won't find anything that I haven't already disclosed."

"So what upsets you so much about this?"

He walked over to her desk and pointed to the papers. "When I left Deslonde Plantation it was a vibrant place. What is in there are pictures of what is left of my home, pictures of the graves of my children and my wife. Those are things a man should never live to see."

"You've already seen what's in here?"

"Your Internet can be a quick way for a person to catch up with all that has happened in the world." He shrugged slightly. "When the two former residents of this house were not home, I would 'surf the net,' as you say." His intense eyes contemplated the pile of papers on her desk. "My son died of yellow fever a year after me. My daughter grew up and married a man named Arnaud. Her husband took control of Deslonde Plantation from my wife. Many years after the Civil War ended, Tessa's husband passed away and Tessa committed suicide. My grandson was the last of my family to live on at the plantation until they found him dead from an apparent suicide. After his death, the house was sold to a variety of owners who used it as a casino, then a boarding house, and finally a hotel. The place was abandoned in the early 1970's."

"Your daughter committed suicide?"

He ran his hand over his face. "I don't understand it. Tessa and I were always very close. She was levelheaded and practical, like her mother. She was twelve when I died. I was to bring home a new doll for her when I returned to Deslonde Plantation from the city that summer." Sadness blunted the sparkle in his eyes. "I always brought her a new doll whenever I returned from the city. Clarinda would complain that I was spoiling her." He nodded his head slightly to the side. "I did spoil her, but I enjoyed it. She had this wonderful laugh that would lift my heart. I can still hear her laughter echoing through the halls of Deslonde Plantation."

Danica closed her eyes and fought back the urge to scream. She had forgotten about his family, his home, and his feelings.

"You look tired," Gaston said, distracting her.

She opened her eyes and looked over at him. "I am."

"How did your first day at work go?"

"Good." She slid her pantsuit jacket from around her shoulders. "Everyone was very impressed with my sketches."

"Like I knew they would be."

She placed her jacket over the back of her desk chair and then kicked off her shoes. "I have a few changes to make tonight, but my boss seemed pleased. He wants to present them to the client next week."

Gaston stepped back from her desk. “I should leave you to your sketches.”

“I’m too tired to work. I think I’ll just wash the grunge from the streetcar off my body and then get back to the sketches.”

“Why don’t you go and have a hot bath, and I’ll make you some dinner?” Gaston suggested.

Danica snickered at him. “You can’t cook.”

He smiled and his blue eyes beamed with their fiery glow. “I have learned to do quite a few things over the years. I’ve even mastered the microwave. Not bad for a man born in 1818.”

Danica’s smile fell. “You were thirty-five when you died?”

Gaston glided into the kitchen. “I had just turned thirty-five a few weeks before I died. My birthday was in June.”

She followed behind him. “I’m thirty-five. I find it hard to believe that you accomplished so much in your short life. I feel like I have done so little in mine.”

He stopped at the sink. “What are you talking about? You’ve accomplished a great deal. You went to college, have a career, you are educated, successful…all the things that many people only dream of being.” He opened a cabinet above the sink. “I never went to college. I always wanted to go and study science, but my father needed me to stay on at Deslonde. After my brother Pierre died, I was all that was left to take over the plantation.”

“Your brother? I didn’t realize you had a brother.”

He retrieved a can of soup from the cabinet. “Pierre was the eldest, I was the middle child, and my sister Yvette was the baby.”

Danica leaned against her efficiency-sized refrigerator. “Whatever happened to Yvette?”

“She married a doctor in St. Louis, Missouri. We stayed in touch through the years. Yvette was a great letter writer. I don’t know what happened to her after I died. I never could find anything about her on the Internet.” He paused as he studied the can of soup in his hands. “I remember one time my father brought home this expensive fabric he had imported from Paris and Yvette.…”

“Go on,” Danica encouraged.

He slammed the can down on the white-tiled counter. “I shouldn’t remember such things. It’s pointless now.”

“It’s not pointless to remember things that make you happy, Gaston.”

"Yes, it is." He angrily pulled a drawer open. "The people I am remembering are long since gone, and so am I. I'm a shadow of the man I was, and I have to get used to that fact. I need to put my physical life behind me."

He rummaged through the drawer and Danica watched, horrified, as the wooden drawer began to shake inside its sleeve. She rushed to his side and without thinking went to place her hand on his forearm, but her hand simply passed through him.

He stood back from the drawer, holding his forearm against his body. "You may not be able to feel me, Danica, but I can certainly feel you." He wiped his hands over his face. "I should not have appeared to you again. I should have stayed away."

She took a step toward him. "Gaston, what's wrong?"

He backed away from her as his beleaguered eyes searched her face. "This was a mistake." He began to fade.

"Don't you do that!" she shouted to him. "Don't you disappear on me and not tell me what's wrong."

He materialized into solid form again. "You want to know what is wrong, Danica? You're what's wrong." He waved his hand up and down her body. "You came back, looking the way you do, but on the inside you're that little girl I adored, and I don't know how to…." He clenched his fists before his face. "Despite being made of air, I am still a man and I have feelings that are…." He turned away.

"'That are' what, Gaston?"

He twisted around to her. "That are driving me crazy!" he exclaimed. "When I was alive there wasn't a woman I couldn't have. I always got what I wanted, Danica. Now I can't have that anymore. Do you have any idea what that does to a soul?"

Danica retreated from the counter. The tortured look in his eyes frightened her. "I have an idea, Gaston…a very good idea of what you're feeling. Don't you dare think that you're the only one in this room who has desires."

His incandescent eyes burrowed into hers. "I know what you're feeling. I saw your fantasies when your flesh crossed through me. I saw all your hopes for us, and you must know this…we can never be."

"Why?" she whispered, gazing up into his face. "Why is it wrong for two souls who want each other not to be together?"

He went back to the kitchen counter. "Because it is against the laws of nature." He slammed his fist down on the counter and a loud thud rocked the room. "What is dead must only commune with the dead, and the living with the living. It is the way of things, and to cross that barrier is to delve into the realm of darkness."

"Are you saying it's possible?"

"Not for us."

Danica came up behind him and marveled at the way his white shirt clung to his muscular back. "Do you want me, Gaston?" she whispered.

He slowly turned to her. "More than I have ever wanted any woman, I want you, Danica; but I cannot have you."

Danica closed her eyes as a rush of heat surged beneath her skin. When she opened her eyes, Gaston was gone.

"Perfect, just perfect," she roared as she threw her hands in the air. "You leave just when it was getting good."

Danica ran her hand through her hair and walked over to the counter. She picked up the can of soup Gaston had left there and sighed angrily as she placed it back in the cabinet above her head.

"Time for a cold shower." She opened the cabinet below the sink and pulled out a bottle of Johnny Walker Red. "Then I'm going to get good and drunk," she muttered, placing the bottle under her arm.

Danica marched through her office, and as she was making her way into the living room, she heard a light rapping at her front shutters. She placed the bottle of Johnny Walker on a table by the entrance and opened the front doors. After pushing the secured green shutters back, she spied Claire Mouton standing on the sidewalk.

"Claire, how nice to see you," Danica said, trying to hide the frustration in her voice.

"I heard you going through your side gate." Claire waved her hand over Danica's outfit. "Are you just getting home from work, dear?"

Danica fingered with the collar on her white silk blouse. "Yes, I was just about to change."

"Well, I was wondering if you've had dinner yet?"

Danica spied the bottle on the table beside the door and then shook her head. "I'm not eating tonight."

Claire worried brown eyes skimmed Danica's features. "Not eating dinner? Why, Danica, that's not healthy. Burt has gone to work this evening, and I insist you come over and have dinner with me. My son, Paul, will be joining us, and I would love for you two to meet."

A nagging sense of doubt as to Claire's intentions crawled up Danica's spine. "I've got an awful lot of work to do this evening, Claire, and I'm sure your son will want a long visit with you and not want me hanging around."

Claire waved off the suggestion with her bony hand. "Nonsense. Paul would love to have someone his age to talk to. He doesn't want to listen to the blabbering of his crazy old mother." She looked Danica in the eye. "You're too young and pretty to be alone, Danica. I've prepared jambalaya, shrimp cakes with a wonderful remoulade sauce, and for dessert I made Paul's favorite, strawberry cheesecake."

Danica's stomach growled with annoyance at the suggestion of missing out on such tasty food. She turned to the bottle of Johnny Walker and considered an evening alone with only her thoughts of Gaston to keep her company. Her stomach rumbled once more. "Perhaps I could come by for a little while," she finally declared.

Claire jubilantly clapped her hands together. "Good girl. You run along and change, and then come on over." With a final, friendly smile, Claire hastened down the sidewalk to her front door.

As Danica shut her doors, she felt a sense of relief wash over her. Maybe some time away from the oppressive feeling in her cottage might be a good idea. Without further consideration, Danica headed for her bedroom to change for dinner, suddenly revived at the thought of a night out with the living.

CHAPTER 7

"Claire, that was a wonderful meal," Danica announced to her hostess as she sat at Claire's mahogany dining table and sipped on a cup of coffee and chicory. The dining room looked out over a pond in the back garden that was surrounded by a small jungle of potted green plants. As Danica took in the hardwood floors and rough-hewn dark cypress beams in the ceiling, she thought about Gaston living in the home so many years ago.

Claire emerged from a connecting kitchen carrying a silver coffee urn.

"I'm so glad you came over and kept my Paul company." She refilled Danica's coffee cup.

Paul Gaudette Jr. shook his head as he sat in his chair across the antique table from Danica. "Mother, your shameless attempts at matchmaking really need to stop." He turned a pair of deep-set green eyes Danica's way. "She means well, but sometimes…." He rolled his eyes as his mother ventured back into the kitchen.

Danica laughed, entertained by his show of embarrassment. She had been surprised by how handsome he was when they had first met, and had admired his toned body beneath his fitted blue suit. He had fine, light brown hair and a tanned, long face, but his mother's protruding cheekbones and pointy chin. His nose was sharp and turned slightly upward, adding a snobbish air to his countenance. He had long, slender hands that kept distracting Danica. She found herself constantly staring at his hands as he lifted his coffee cup to his thin, red lips.

"Mother tells me you're working at an advertising firm in the CBD," he stated in a surprisingly seductive voice.

Danica tore her eyes away from his hands. "Yes, at Morrison and Rau."

He nodded his approval. “Good firm. I’ve heard them mentioned by a few people I work with.” He took a sip from his coffee.

“What do you do at Chevron?”

He placed his cup down on the table. “I’m a petroleum engineer, but I’m more management than hands on these days. I oversee several other engineers who work in the Gulf finding new sites to drill. They put together reports of estimated recoverable volume of resources, and I present those reports to selection committees who choose new drilling sites.”

“You told me you have an old home on Sixth Street, like to run several miles every morning, and you’re passionate about antiques. Anything else I should know about you?” Danica asked with a flirty glint in her blue eyes.

Paul gave her a charming crooked smile that made her stomach do a nervous flip.

“Paul was on the cross country team in high school, as well as in the honor society,” Claire spoke up as she came back into the dining room. “He was the only cross country state champ ever at his high school. He even got offered a scholarship to LSU for cross country.” Claire’s brown eyes beamed with pride at her son as she took the seat next to him at the table.

Paul turned a slight shade of pink, which captivated Danica. “As you can see, I don’t need a PR firm to help promote me. I have my mother to tell everyone about all of my accomplishments.” Paul’s green eyes lingered on hers for a few intoxicating moments.

“Well, if I don’t brag about you, darling, who will?” Claire admitted, nodding to her son. “That gold digger you were married to never once cared about all the wonderful things you’ve done.”

Paul frowned as he shifted nervously in his chair. “You’ll have to forgive my mother. She and my ex-wife disagreed on just about everything, including me.”

Claire placed her hands demurely on the mahogany dining table. “She was one of those cheerleaders at LSU, looking for a rich husband to set her up for life. She snagged my Paul right after they graduated from college together, but she wasn’t right for him.”

“That’s enough. Don’t bore poor Danica with your ravings against Madison. She had her faults, but being married to me was no picnic, either,” Paul chastised.

An uncomfortable silence hung in the air, and Danica caught herself sneaking a glimpse of Paul's hands as they wrapped around his coffee cup.

Claire suddenly stood from the table. "Well, Danica, would you like to see the rest of the house? I'm sure you're more than curious to see where our Gaston spent his final days."

"Mother!" Paul cried out. "Not your ghost stories again. You don't need to be filling Danica's head with your silly stories about some ghost you think you have haunting the house."

Claire turned to her son. "They're not silly stories. Gaston lived and died in this house, and he haunts Danica's cottage, as well. It would be good for her to see his home."

Paul leaned forward in his chair. "I swear, Mother, if you don't stop fixating on that ghost of yours, that idiot you're married to will have you hauled off to the nuthouse."

"You shouldn't say such things. Burt is a good man," Claire proudly defended. "He was good to me after your father died."

Paul shook his head and held up one hand to his mother. "I shouldn't have said anything. I know how you feel about Burt, but how you feel is not how I feel."

Claire turned her pale brown eyes to Danica. "My son and my husband don't see eye to eye most of the time."

"One of the reasons I try to come and see my mother when Burt is at work." Paul stood from his chair. "All right, Mother, let's take Danica on a tour of your haunted house, and then I will see her back to her front door before I leave."

Claire smiled as she stood next to her son.

Danica rose from her chair. "I'd love to see your home, Claire."

Claire took Danica's hand in hers. "Then come, Danica. Let me show you the room where Gaston Deslonde died."

They passed through a brightly decorated living room, bedecked with rich mahogany antique furniture and an assortment of pictures of Paul at various ages covering the walls. Danica felt the cheery atmosphere in the home change when the three of them came to a tall oak door just at the end of a short hallway.

"I only use this as a guest room out of respect for Gaston," Claire admitted in a hushed, almost reverent tone as she opened the door. "Gaston still likes to visit this room frequently," she added.

"Why would the guy want to visit the place where he died?" Paul dubiously asked.

"Because that's what ghosts do, Paul," Claire explained. "When they have died in a traumatic or cataclysmic way, they're tied to the place of their death. Gaston comes back here to try and reckon himself with his demise, so he can eventually move on." Claire pushed the door open and stepped into the darkened room.

"Guy sounds like he needs therapy," Paul mumbled behind Danica.

A burst of light filled the square room as Danica walked inside, with Paul following close behind.

Painted a bright shade of blue, the room had a single twin bed situated in the corner next to a chest of drawers, with an oak table on the wall across from it. On top of the table were several white candles in various decorative votive jars. Danica turned to a small hearth with a delicately carved cherry mantle. Her breath caught in her throat when she spotted the long portrait of a man above the mantle.

Dressed in a fitted pair of black pants and long white linen shirt, the gentleman had shoulder length dark brown hair pulled back in a white ribbon, and piecing sky-blue eyes that jumped out from the portrait. Looking arrogant and stubborn, he stood before an elegant white plantation home with short, white, square columns supporting a grand second story balcony. The earth below his black boots appeared rich and brown, while the tall oaks and grass in the background surrounding the fine home were a vibrant green.

"That is Gaston Deslonde," Claire enthusiastically proclaimed.

The figure in the portrait seemed an awful lot like Gaston, but the flesh and blood interpretation harbored an almost cruel quality in the subject's countenance, something Danica had never seen in her Gaston.

"How do you know that's Gaston Deslonde?" Danica probed, keeping any hint of emotion from her voice.

Claire came to her side. "I found it in the attic shortly after Burt and I moved in. We were clearing away remnants of an old wall to make room for our things. Behind the wall was a small room, a closet really. In there I found the portrait and a trunk of old clothes. The clothes were all rotted, but this," she motioned to the portrait, "was untouched. We also found a Bible next to an old-fashioned oil lantern. I still have the Bible, preserved in my bookcase. It was the Deslonde family Bible. Their family tree was written inside the front cover, going all the way back to Gaston's great grandfather, Emile, who came here from France right after the city was founded." Claire walked over to the table by the bed and picked up a box of matches. She struck a match and reached for one of the votive candles. "I always leave a candle lit for him," Claire said as she placed the match against the wick.

"That could be anybody, Mother." Paul waved his hand at the portrait. "Something left behind by one of the former owners."

Claire never looked up from the candle. "It's Gaston. He told me it was him."

Danica could hear Paul sighing with frustration behind her. "You're going to burn the house to the ground one day, Mother."

As Danica watched Claire light each of the candles, a heavy feeling descended over the room. An overwhelming sense of sorrow filled her being, as if she could feel Gaston's unhappiness at leaving a life that he had truly loved. Then, a chill pervaded the room, along with a distinctive smell of brandy and cigars.

"He's here," Claire whispered.

"Who's here?" Paul demanded, coming around to Danica's side.

"Gaston," Claire replied. "He heard me call to him."

"Call to him?" Danica asked. "When did you call to him?"

Claire smiled at her, looking almost angelic. "When I lit the candles, I called to him in my mind. I wanted him to join us."

"Mother, really, do you know how crazy this sounds?"

"Why do you call to him?" Danica questioned.

"So he can serve me, and I can help him cross over," Claire calmly told her.

"But you can't help him cross over, Claire." Danica moved toward the woman. "Perhaps you should stop summoning him and let him find his own path. Leave him be."

"You've spoken to him." Claire's brown eyes blazed with an unfamiliar intensity. "You know."

"All right, Mother," Paul said, raising his voice. "Now you are freaking me out. Enough of this foolishness." He placed a protective arm about Danica's shoulders. "I'm going to take Danica home."

The door to the room suddenly slammed shut with a loud bang, making everyone in the bedroom jump. Paul removed his arm from about Danica's shoulders and went back to the door.

"Now he's mad." Claire pointed at her son. "He thinks you don't believe in him and you've made him angry."

"That's not why he's angry," Danica muttered.

Paul opened the door and carefully inspected it. "It was the wind, Mother."

"What wind? We're in the house, Paul, and there are no open windows." Claire placed her hands on her slender hips. "It was the ghost," she insisted.

Paul stepped into the room and grabbed Danica's hand. "Come on, Danica. Let me take you home before she has us both believing that the Easter Bunny is alive and well and hanging out on Bourbon Street."

Danica let Paul usher her from the room as she glanced back at Claire. "Thanks for dinner."

"We'll talk again, Danica," Claire called, and then waved good-bye.

As soon as Danica and Paul had stepped out the front door and into the cool October night, Paul let go of her hand.

"Sorry to be so abrupt," he apologized as he ran his hand through his light brown hair. "But I had to get you out of there before she embarrassed me further." He shook his head. "Next, she would have probably suggested you see her voodoo altar."

"Where does she keep that?" Danica asked.

Paul looked back at his mother's front door. "In the courtyard, out back. She has some crazy stone altar set up next to the pond. She claims she works her magic from there." He ran a nervous hand over his brow. "I know I should be more tolerant of her hobbies, but this ghost and voodoo business has been getting a bit out of hand lately. I never usually come by for dinner, but I wanted to check on her. I've even tried to talk to Burt about it, but he's worthless."

"I think she's just lonely, Paul. Maybe the idea of having a ghost around makes her feel like someone is watching over her."

"My Aunt Louise, Mother's sister, called me the other day and told me she was worried about the way Momma was acting. She insisted I come and check on her. Now I feel even more guilty about not seeing her as often as I should."

"Don't feel guilty. You have a life and can't be here all the time," Danica reassured him. "Perhaps she's just going through a phase. It will be fine."

Paul lowered his eyes to the sidewalk. "When my father died, she was completely lost. He handled everything when they were married. I tried as best I could to help her with the house and bills, but I had to work and couldn't be there every waking moment. I was also married to Madison at the time and was being pulled in several different directions at once." He paused and looked up at her. "Then she met Burt, and I thought she'd be all right. She had a man to take care of her again. Took me several months to figure out what kind of man Burt was. She keeps telling me Burt is good to her, but I'm beginning to doubt it."

An uneasy gnawing settled in the pit of Danica's stomach. She didn't want to get involved in Claire's affairs, but she knew what it was like to be in her situation.

"You should talk about your suspicions with your mother. Let her know you're concerned. It might help her to open up to you."

His eyes candidly searched hers. "You think that could work?"

Danica patted his arm. "It's a start, Paul."

He nodded as he mulled over the idea. "I could take her out to lunch this Sunday, after she goes to church. She always liked to go to lunch after church when I was a boy. We could talk then."

Danica turned for her cottage and Paul quickly fell in step beside her.

"Thank you," he said, leaning over to her as they walked along.

"I'm glad I could help."

"Could you do me another favor?"

Danica gave Paul a wary side-glance. "Another favor?"

Paul stopped and Danica turned to face him.

"Have dinner with me Saturday night? I'd like to get to know you better."

Danica gazed into his handsome face and then Gaston's enthralling eyes crept into her thoughts. His dire warning about the commingling of the dead and the living came back to her. Here was a living man who could possibly make her happy in ways that Gaston could not.

"I would very much like to have dinner with you, Paul."

Paul smiled his delightful crooked smile, setting off a flurry of nervous butterflies in Danica's stomach. He reached into the pocket of his blue suit jacket and pulled out a white business card and a pen.

"Give me your number and I can call you so we can set up a time for Saturday."

Danica took the pen and card from him and scribbled down her cell phone number.

After Paul had replaced the pen and card back in his jacket, he walked Danica the last few steps to her doorway.

"Until Saturday, Danica."

Danica gave Paul one last heartfelt smile. "Goodnight, Paul."

After she had closed the shutters and secured the deadbolt on her front doors, Danica stood staring into the darkness of her living room. Instantly, the room grew colder and the faint hint of cigar smoke and brandy teased her nose.

"You're not seriously considering having a date with him?" Gaston griped as he materialized before her.

Danica switched on a lamp beside her. "I knew when you slammed that door you were pissed."

"He put his arm about you like you were already his," Gaston raved, hovering in front of her.

"I'm not his, and it's just a date, Gaston. One date, and then I will probably never hear from him again."

"You'll hear from him," Gaston growled. "I could see it in his eyes as you were eating dinner together. He wants you."

"At least somebody does," she murmured, and then headed for the archway to the family room.

"Is this what you want, Danica? To give yourself to another man you know you can never love?"

Danica stopped in the family room and examined the wall of bookshelves before her. Her eyes passed over the collection of antique leather bound books she had purposely removed from Tom's prized library in their Seattle home. She recalled how she had hoped to add one last indignity to the already stiff divorce settlement against him. But all the antique books in the world could not make up for Danica's shattered confidence. She knew how it felt to be tossed aside by one you cared about, and she did not want to become like the cruel monster she had been married to.

"I'm not going to go out with Paul to spite you, Gaston. You said we were of two different worlds: the living and the dead. I'm just trying to find my way in my world." She looked back at him through the archway. "This isn't about us. It's about me. I don't have eternity, Gaston. I only have today."

He walked slowly into the room. "Regrets will always feel the same no matter how many days or centuries you have to remember them, Danica. I just don't want you to run into the arms of another man because you can't have this one."

She leaned her body against the wall behind her. "What makes you think I will repeat my mistakes from the past? Maybe I've learned my lesson."

Gaston rested his hands on the wall above her and lowered his face closer to hers. "I feel what you feel, Danica. I always have. Even though you claim not to care what anyone else thinks, you do care, very much. When you are hurt by one person, you invariably turn to another to bolster your belief in yourself."

She obstinately glowered at him. "What other insights into my psyche would you like to share with me?"

"Not insights, my treasure…more like pesky habits you tend to repeat over and over again. If I didn't bring them to your attention, you might not be able to rid yourself of them."

She pressed her back into the wall, suddenly uncomfortable with the nearness of him. "Perhaps I like my pesky habits."

He grinned, entertained by her obvious discomfort. "Close your eyes."

"Why?"

Gaston's brow furrowed with frustration. "I want to show you something. Now do as you are told and close your eyes."

Danica frowned and obediently closed her eyes. The air suddenly grew thick around her, as if she were standing in the middle of a dense fog.

"What is going on?"

"Keep your eyes closed. I can't do this for very long."

"Do what?" But as soon as she said the words, she saw him. In her mind, she saw Gaston leaning over her. He was as clear as when she saw him with her eyes, but there was something different about him. He felt alive, like a living, breathing man.

His face was inches from hers. "I've been wanting to do this for a very long time," he whispered, and then he closed his mouth over hers.

The electrical charge that rocked Danica's body was unlike anything she had ever known. She could feel his lips pressing against hers as his arms slowly embraced her. At first, she didn't know what to do, but as his kiss deepened, instinct took over. Danica hungrily responded to him, opening her mouth and wanting to taste more of him. She could feel the passion escalating between them, and then Gaston unexpectedly broke away.

When Danica's eyes opened, his apparition was kneeling on the ground before her. His form was hazy and his wide shoulders were shaking violently.

She knelt down beside him. "What was that?"

Gaston looked up, and the ever-present bright light in his eyes dimmed. His face was drawn, and appeared exhausted.

"I wanted to show you what you mean to me, but I don't have the strength to do more," he whispered.

"But you can lift things and move objects."

"Objects don't have the same energy as people. It takes a great deal for me to merge my soul with yours." He wrapped his long arms about his body. "I need to rest." Gaston quickly evaporated.

Danica sat in her family room, completely undone by what had just happened. In a few seconds, she had realized an unspoken dream, but instead of being elated, she was even more frustrated than ever before. She stood from the floor and took in a deep, calming breath.

"Is this ever going to get easier, Gaston?" she whispered into the dimly lit room. "I know you want me just as much as I want you, but now what do we do?"

She headed toward her bedroom, slightly comforted by that fact that Gaston did indeed want her, but also painfully aware that their need for each other could never be satisfied.

Maybe it is better this way, she reasoned. So many relationships soured once the blush of passion faded. Danica consoled herself with the knowledge that Gaston would always be her friend, and a good friend to share your life with was a lot harder to find than a lover to share your bed. Danica wondered if she would ever find a man who embodied the best of both worlds, and if she ever did find such a man, what would happen to Gaston?

CHAPTER 8

When Saturday night rolled around, Danica was in her bathroom trying to put the finishing touches on her makeup as Gaston watched from the doorway.

"You have on too much blush," he griped as he stood with his arms folded, scowling at her.

Danica checked her reflection. "I don't think so." She brushed aside a strand of chestnut hair that had fallen from her chic, upswept hairdo.

"You look like a streetwalker," he complained in a deep voice.

Danica ignored him and dabbed a bit more red lipstick on her full lips. "If you can't say anything nice, then don't watch."

"That dress is awfully low cut," he went on, motioning to the scoop neck on her clingy A-line black silk dress.

"What would you suggest, a nun's habit?"

"I don't think this is a good idea. He's Claire's son; if you two don't get along, you'll have Claire to deal with."

Danica put her lipstick away in her makeup bag. "I appreciate the brooding, Gaston, but I'm going out with Paul. Your kiss the other night proved to me that I have to get out into the real world, and being in the real world involves seeing men."

"That's not what I was trying to show you when I kissed you, Danica."

She sighed as she zipped up her makeup bag. "Yes, it was. You were trying to show me that no matter how we may feel, it would never work between us. I'm not happy about it either, but what other choice do we have? Do you want me to sit around this house and wait to die so then we can eventually be together?"

He moved away from the doorway. "No, that was never my intention. I want you to live, enjoy your life, and never take one day for granted. I would just prefer you went out with a different guy."

"Paul is a nice guy." She stepped around him and headed down the hall to the family room.

He followed her into the living room. "Just don't bring him back here after your date and jump into bed with him."

Danica turned to him. "Why, what are you going to do? Set his pants on fire?"

"You never know."

Danica went to the table by the front door and placed her keys on top of her black beaded clutch bag. "What happens if the day comes when I want to bring a man back here? What will you do?"

Gaston went to the brown sofa along the side of the room and sat down. "I suggest you invest in a fire extinguisher," he replied, smirking.

"Sometimes you act just like a spoiled child, Gaston."

He leaned back on the sofa and stretched his long arms over the plush fabric. "All men become spoiled children when they can't have want they want. Get used to it, Danica."

She made an aggravated groan just as there was a light rapping on her front doors.

As she reached for the door handle, she glanced back to the sofa. Gaston was still sitting there with a wide grin plastered on his face.

"Shouldn't you disappear?"

"Only you can see me. You've been the only one who could ever see me."

Danica rolled her eyes. "Then behave, all right?"

Gaston said nothing and kept grinning at her.

A swell of apprehension gripped Danica's gut as she slowly pulled the french doors open. When she saw Paul standing on the sidewalk in front of her home, dressed in a tailored gray suit and pale blue tie, her fears retreated. A gentle evening breeze tossed his light brown hair about his head as his green eyes went over every inch of her dress. When the smell of his woodsy cologne hit her, Danica's excitement stirred.

He waved a hand down her body. "I approve of the dress."

"My God, how utterly gauche he is," Gaston railed from the sofa.

Paul's appealing countenance never wavered, and Danica was relieved that he appeared not to have heard anything.

"Thank you, Paul. I'm so glad you approve," she told him. Not sure of what to do next, Danica stood in her doorway and stared at Paul.

An awkward moment passed between them, and then Paul cleared his throat.

"Do you want to go on to the restaurant, or should I just stand out here and continue to admire the view?" he asked with a playful grin.

Gaston groaned behind her.

"Let's go to the restaurant," Danica hurriedly suggested.

She picked up her purse and keys, waiting on the table by the door, and as she stepped to the doorway, Danica glared at Gaston on the sofa.

"Have a nice time," he added, sarcastically.

Danica said nothing, and slammed the front doors closed behind her.

***

They had just been seated at their table in the lush tropical courtyard at Bayona Restaurant when Paul leaned over to Danica and whispered, "I heard this place was pretty good."

Danica laughed and felt her edgy nerves calm slightly. "Yes, I think I read something about them in the New York Times. The chef, Susan Spicer, is rumored to be pretty good."

Paul nodded approvingly. "Glad to see you know your French Quarter restaurants."

Danica admired the colorful fruit trees and a gurgling fountain not far from their table. "I may have been gone for a few years, but I never really left New Orleans."

"Does anybody? I swore all my life growing up I couldn't wait to get out of New Orleans. After I graduated from college, I spent two years in Houston and hated every minute of it. Couldn't wait to get back home." He rested his elbows on the table. "Funny how this old town does that to people. It gets under your skin and never leaves you."

"Some people are the same way," Danica admitted.

He leaned closer to her. "Yes, you are."

She diverted her eyes to the white linen tablecloth, trying to get a handle on the warm flush rising inside her.

"You're blushing," Paul remarked. "Do you always blush when someone pays you a compliment?"

Danica put her hands against her cheeks. "I haven't gotten a lot of compliments lately...not from a man, anyway."

"Now that is a shame." He sat back in his chair and studied her creamy skin, deep blue eyes, and heart-shaped, red mouth. "I take it your ex-husband didn't compliment you too often."

A busboy dressed in a white jacket and black pants came to the table and began filling their water goblets. Danica fidgeted in her chair as she waited for the busboy to finish. After he had left, she grabbed for her water and took a few sips.

As the cool liquid quenched her unease, she looked over at Paul. "Tom, my ex, wasn't the kind of man to give compliments."

"What type of man was he?"

She banged her water goblet down on the table. "Cruel," unintentionally slipped from her lips.

Paul's handsome face appeared troubled. "Cruel? I hope that doesn't mean he was cruel to you."

Danica shook her head. "I'm sorry. I shouldn't have said that. You don't want to know about my relationship with my ex. It's rotten first date dinner conversation."

"I want to hear about it, Danica. I want to know all about you. That includes everything you have been through, the good and the bad. Don't think of this as a first date; let's just say we're two friends, having dinner and sharing stories about our lives. I don't want you to feel you have to follow some kind of protocol for conversation. I want you to say what you think around me. How else am I ever going to get to know you?"

"What if you don't like what you hear?"

Paul flashed his captivating smile. "That will never happen, I promise." He sat back in his chair. "What kind of man was Tom?"

"Angry," she answered, as she played with a fork on the table in front of her. "When he didn't get his way, he often vented his anger on anybody who happened to be within swinging distance."

"I'm sorry. No woman should ever have to endure such…cruelty." He paused and watched her for a moment. "Did you know when you married him what kind of man he was?"

"No. Before we were married he was the kindest man I'd ever met. But after we returned home from our honeymoon, he changed. For a while I blamed myself, and then one day, I decided enough was enough. I hired a good attorney, sued him for divorce, and threatened to go public with the abuse if he didn't give me everything I wanted." She shrugged. "Tom is an investment broker at a big firm in Seattle. He was afraid that such disclosures would get back to his clients and hurt his business."

"Good for you. I'm glad to see you had the courage to walk away from that relationship." He picked up his water goblet. "Unlike my mother," he added in a gruff voice.

"Don't judge her too harshly for staying with Burt. It's a scary thing to walk out on a marriage."

Paul took a sip of his water and then placed the glass back on the table with a thud. "But you did it. Hell, my ex did it."

"Your wife left you?"

Paul nodded. "She said I wasn't paying enough attention to her. To spend any more time with her, I would have had to quit my job. She was always jealous of my spending time with my mother, as well. Madison was a woman who felt she should be the center of the universe, and everyone else needed to orbit around her."

Danica ran her fingers over the condensation on the side of her water goblet. "Sounds like quite a few women I know."

Paul laughed and his green eyes once again glowed with an alluring heat. "I tried to make it work for three years. One day she came to me and said it was over. She had found someone else."

Danica's smile fell. "I'm sorry. That must have been hard."

Paul folded his hands together on top of the table. "No harder than what you went through. So I guess you could say we are both scarred and a bit nervous about starting over."

"Just a bit," Danica admitted. "But life goes on, and you can either go on with it, or die."

"And then you'll end up being a ghost haunting my mother's place, like that Gaspard character."

"Gaston," Danica corrected.

"Yes, Gaston." Paul ran his long hand over the delicate white fabric of the tablecloth, instantly distracting Danica.

"I'm sorry again about my mother the other night."

Her fingers caressed the stem of her glass. "No need to apologize, Paul. Your mother is a wonderful person. I like her."

He shifted uncomfortably in his chair. "Thank you, Danica, but my mother is not a stable person. I worry that her relationship with Burt may push her to do something rash."

"Claire isn't like that. She's a strong woman."

"Not as strong as you." He gently reached across the table and took her hand.

An unexpected current of electricity surged up Danica's arm when Paul touched her. The feeling almost made Danica bolt from her chair.

"Welcome to Bayona," a thick waiter dressed all in black said as he stood beside their table. "What can I get you two to drink?"

Paul let go of Danica's hand and a cool rush of air overtook her.

"I'll have a scotch and soda," Paul told the waiter, and then he motioned to Danica. "What would you like?"

She looked up at the waiter and gulped back her nerves. "Scotch for me, too, but hold the soda, and make it a double."

***

After dining on sautéed redfish with chanterelle-leeks vinaigrette, mashed potatoes, and chocolate hazelnut torte for dessert, Paul suggested a stroll around Jackson Square to walk off their meal.

Danica was thankful for the fresh air. After two straight doubles of Johnny Walker, she needed to walk off the buzz the alcohol had given her. At least she had quelled her nerves, or so she had hoped, until Paul once again took her hand as they walked down Chartres Street.

"You're awfully quiet," Paul commented beside her.

"Am I? I thought I never stopped talking during dinner."

"That wasn't you. That was the scotch talking. I noticed you got rather animated after you finished your first drink."

Danica felt her cheeks burn. "I'm not used to drinking."

"But tonight you felt you needed two doubles. Do you always drink like that, or was it perhaps…me?"

Danica slowly nodded her head. "I was nervous."

He squeezed her hand. "And now?"

She leaned in closer to him. "Not so much."

Paul let go of her hand and wrapped his arm about her shoulders as they walked along.

The tall spires of St. Louis Cathedral loomed before them, and Danica admired the view of Jackson Square from Chartres Street. Gray slate flagstones covered the street in front of St. Louis Cathedral and The Cabildo, extending out to the black wrought iron fence that wrapped around the perimeter of the square. Originally named the Place d'Armes in 1815, the historic landmark was renamed for the hero of the Battle of New Orleans, Andrew Jackson. The green foliage and towering oaks located in and around the square danced eerily in the pale streetlight as a cool October breeze swirled by. Set up along the thick black fence, artists, tarot card readers, psychics, and street musicians were competing for tips from the small number of tourists still milling about.

Paul kept his arm about her as they walked slowly by an assortment of charcoal drawings and a few tables belonging to tarot card readers and psychics. As they passed a plain wooden table without any decoration or signs on it, Danica felt an odd tingling in her hands.

"You're in trouble, little one," an older woman spoke up from behind the table.

Danica examined the lovely angular face and smooth, coffee-colored skin of the fortune-teller seated regally behind the table. She had long, silky gray hair pulled back in a flowing ponytail around her right shoulder. The simple poncho wrapped around her slender figure was made up of vibrant shades of red, gold, and yellow. When she smiled, showing off her perfect little white teeth, Danica felt her blood run cold.

The older woman motioned to Danica and Paul with a scrawny hand. "Yes, you, Danica."

Paul gave Danica a questioning glance. "Do you know her?"

Danica shook her head. "No. I've never seen her before."

"But I know you, little one. I've heard all about you from the spirits," the woman proclaimed in a rather deep voice. "Come, sit." She pointed to simple wooden chair in front of her table. "We must talk."

Danica approached the table. "I'm sorry, but I'm really not interested in having my fortune told this evening."

"Who said anything about telling your fortune, Danica? I'm here to give you some advice," the woman clarified with a brusque nod of her head.

Her bright hazel eyes had a peculiar glint that momentarily mesmerized Danica. She leaned in closer to the table, never taking her eyes from the fortuneteller's face. "How do you know my name?"

The gray-haired woman glared at Paul, hanging over Danica's shoulder. "He needs to go. This message is only for you."

"What in the hell?" Paul roared indignantly.

"The dark man is in danger," the fortuneteller softly informed Danica.

Danica's heart rose in her throat as she stared in disbelief at the older woman. She immediately turned to Paul. "Why don't you give me a minute here, Paul?"

Paul's mouth dropped open. "Danica, you're not serious—"

"Please," she begged. "I don't want to make her angry. I think I remember her from when I was a child and used to play about the square."

Paul shoved his hands in the pockets of his gray slacks. "All right," he said, looking slightly disappointed. "I'll be right over there." He nodded to the shadows beneath the balconies of the Pontalba Apartments to his right.

Danica waited for Paul to step away and then had a seat at the small wooden table.

"What about the dark man?" Danica anxiously questioned.

The woman's eyes honed in on Danica's face. "He's willing to give up much to be with you, and that could put his soul in great danger. He loves you, has always loved you, but he never knew it until now." She reached across the table and took Danica's hand.

Danica wanted to pull away from the woman's ice-cold hands, but thought better of it.

"You're in love with the dark man, aren't you, child?"

Danica's heart began to thud wildly in her chest. Did she love, Gaston? Perhaps what she had been feeling all these years was love. But was love supposed to confuse and confound you so?

"In love? I…I don't know…I mean I'm—"

"Soon you'll be forced to choose between life and death. If you choose death, you will have love, but you will also have death. If you choose life, you will have what we all do; a life sometimes hard, filled with moments of wonder and sadness, but you will have a life."

Danica shook her head. "I don't understand."

The fortuneteller let go of her hand. "You will soon enough."

"But what about the dark man? How is he in danger? What am I supposed to do?"

The fortuneteller smiled. "When you pass this way again tomorrow night, I'll be here. We can talk some more."

"Tomorrow night?"

"It's All Hollow's Eve," the woman clarified.

"But tomorrow night I will—"

"Tomorrow you will come to me," the older woman cut her off. "Go home now. The dark man is getting impatient."

As Danica stood from her chair, Paul came to her side.

"Everything all right?" His deep-set green eyes worriedly looked over Danica's pale features.

Danica gave his arm a reassuring pat. “Everything is fine, Paul.”

Paul pulled his wallet from his inside jacket pocket. “How much do I owe you?” he asked the fortuneteller.

The noble-looking woman raised her head proudly to Paul. “There’s no charge.” Her eyes turned to Danica. “There were things she needed to hear.”

Paul put his wallet back in his jacket pocket and reached for Danica’s hand. “We should get going.”

Danica let Paul lead her from the fortuneteller’s table, and eventually away from Jackson Square.

“You want to tell me what that was about?” he queried as they made their way through the darkened streets of the French Quarter toward Danica’s home.

“She was a friend of my mother’s,” Danica lied.

“What did she tell you? When I came up to the table you looked like you had seen a ghost.”

The mention of the word “ghost” made Danica tremble with fear.

“Hey,” Paul cooed as he put his arm about her. “What did that woman say to you? You’re shaking.”

Danica’s mind raced with plausible explanations. “She, ah, just told me some things about my mother. She died when I was fifteen and I guess it shook me up a little.”

“What happened to her?” he inquired as they turned down Dumaine Street.

Danica felt his strong arm about her shoulders and her shaking eased a little. “She had a bad heart. As far back as I can remember Mother was always…tired. One morning she woke up with a nasty cough. A few days later, the coughing got much worse and my father took her to the doctor. They found out her heart was failing. She was put on a transplant list, but she did not last long. Momma died a few weeks later.”

“Is that when you left the city?”

“Dad was a biology professor. After Mom died he put in for a position at The University of Florida. He wanted to get out of New Orleans…we both did.”

“Where is your father now?”

“He died last year.”

“I’m sorry.” He looked ahead to her cottage. “When my father died, I had to not only deal with his estate, I had to take care of my mother, as well. It was a difficult time, but I was glad she was with me. It must have been hard losing both your parents when you're still so young."

Danica browsed the charming houses surrounding them. "I guess if we had lived when all of these homes had been built, losing parents at such an age would have been the norm. Did you know that many parents lost half their children to disease in those days? I can't imagine what that must have been like."

"Maybe that's why there are rumored to be so many ghosts down here. All those tragic stories that never got told, yet the memories remain."

Danica spied her cottage just ahead. "Do you believe in ghosts?"

The light above Danica's front doorstep flickered on and off, but Paul did not seem to notice.

"Oh, I'm still holding out before I make up my mind on that one," Paul commented. "I know my mother is into that stuff, but I'm an engineer, and I need to see definitive proof."

Danica stepped out from under his arm and reached into her black beaded clutch bag for her keys. "Sometimes that proof can be staring you right in the face, Paul."

He chuckled beside her as they came to a stop in front of her cottage entrance. "I take it that means you do believe in ghosts."

"I just know I've seen things I can't explain."

Paul placed his hands on her shoulders. "That doesn't mean it's a ghost, Danica."

Danica saw a shadow walk behind her front window. "No, it doesn't."

Paul's eyes noted the few pedestrians strolling along the street. "Perhaps we should go inside," he whispered as he ran his hands down from her shoulders to her waist.

Danica nodded in agreement. She turned to her doors and placed the key in the lock as Paul kept an arm casually draped about her waist. When she pushed the french doors open, she was immediately hit by the smell of brandy and cigars. Warily, Danica entered her home as Paul followed closely behind.

"Kind of looks like my mother's place," Paul commented as his eyes perused her living room. "Same thick plaster walls and high ceilings."

Danica shut the front doors. "My cottage is smaller than Claire's, and not as ornately decorated."

"Yeah, her home has quite a colorful history. Mother did some digging into the local archives, and that is how she found the home was owned by that Garcon character—"

"Gaston," Danica corrected.

"After he died, he left it to some well-known Creole prostitute named Mary something."

"Do you mean his Creole mistress, Marna?" Danica suggested.

"Yes, that's the one, Marna." Paul paused. "How did you know her name?"

Danica cleared her throat. "Your mother mentioned her to me."

Paul shrugged. "Yeah, well, when Marna died she left the house to her nephew, a riverboat gambler named Tristian Lafleur. The house was apparently put up for auction in the early 1900s. It's had several owners since then, but none as interesting as that plantation owner."

The temperature in the living room rapidly dropped, and Danica's eyes nervously searched the shadows for Gaston.

"Are you all right?" Paul questioned. "You've been very jumpy ever since we left that old fortuneteller in Jackson Square."

Danica placed her purse and keys on the table by the door. "Ah, I guess I'm still a little nervous about being here with you."

Paul came up to her and slid his arms about her waist. "I'm just as nervous. Maybe we should get the hard part out of the way, so we can both relax."

Danica's throat went dry as his lips came closer to hers. Her stomach did a few summersaults while her knees trembled. "It's been a while since I've done this," she whispered as she placed her hands on his shoulders.

"Me, too," he admitted as he lowered his head to her.

The instant his lips touched hers, a ribbon of desire ignited in Danica's belly. He felt solid and sturdy against her. As she ran her hands over his shoulders, Paul tightened his arms about her waist. Slowly, Danica became immersed in his kiss. His soft lips pressed harder against hers, begging to be let in. She opened her mouth slightly, wanting to taste more of him.

"You've got to be kidding me," Gaston shouted in her ear.

Danica instantly pulled away from Paul, and when she spied Gaston's tall figure standing right behind him, her hand flew to her mouth.

"What is it?" Paul asked, confused.

Danica shifted her focus from Gaston's scowling countenance to Paul's imploring eyes. "I, ah…." She lowered her hand from her mouth. "This is a little fast for me." She placed her hand on his chest. "I mean you're a really good kisser, a great kisser…really great," she mumbled as she ran her fingers over her lips.

"Thank you," Paul replied, smirking.

Gaston growled behind him.

"I just need a little more time before this goes any further," she explained as she waved a hand between her and Paul.

"Danica, is something wrong?"

"No, Paul. I'm just—"

Gaston raised a threatening hand over Paul's head.

"You should go," Danica shouted.

"Go? But I just got here."

Danica began pushing him to the front doors. "Yes, you need to go before I…." She searched for something to say. "Before I don't want you to go." She cringed as the words left her mouth.

"Danica, please." Paul stopped before the entrance. "You're not making any sense."

She placed her hands on his shoulders and stared into his eyes. "Please, Paul. I need you to go. I'll explain later."

His green eyes were hurt, but he nodded his head in understanding. Danica kissed him on the cheek as he stepped outside, and then abruptly shut the front doors behind him. She stood there for quite some time, keeping her hand on the doorknob, afraid to turn around and face Gaston.

"I can't believe you kissed him like that," Gaston barked behind her.

After taking a deep breath, she turned and spotted Gaston standing beside the sofa with his arms folded angrily over his wide chest.

"Do you have any idea how that made me feel, Danica, watching the two of you kiss?"

"If you didn't like watching us, you could have just left, not screamed in my ear!"

He frowned at her. "Why are you yelling at me?"

"Because he was a nice guy and didn't deserve that, Gaston."

"He was an idiot and totally wrong for you. I can't believe you fell for that line about getting the hard part out of the way. Why didn't you deck him after he said that to you?"

"Did it ever occur to you that I wanted to kiss him?"

He waved at the front doors. “Do you want me to go and get him back for you?”

Her hands curled into fists. “If I can’t be with you, then I’m going to have to find someone to be with.”

“I can’t stand by as you parade a long line of men through this house like you’re trying out actors for a role in a play.” He came toward her. “You’re better than that, Danica.”

“No, I’m not, Gaston. I’m just like everyone else. I want a home, a family, and a man to be by my side. When I was with Paul tonight, I realized those are things I wanted when I married Tom, and they are things I still want.”

He ran his hands over his face, looking as if he was being torn in two. “You’re right,” he softly said, nodding his head. “You are made of flesh and life and you need those things, but I can’t give them to you.” He turned from her and disappeared into the wall.

“Wait, Gaston,” she called behind him.

But the heavy air in the room lifted and the chill that had been there went away. Danica kicked the cement floor with her shoe and silently scolded herself for being such an ass. She was about to turn away when the voice of the fortuneteller popped into her head.

“You’re in love with the dark man, aren’t you, child?”

As Danica stared at the spot on the wall where he had vanished, an uncomfortable realization hit her. She might have been attracted to Paul with his toned body and wicked smile, but it was Gaston who filled her dreams at night. It had always been Gaston. For years she had chased men who reminded her of the ghost she had left behind. When she ran over the short list of men she had been with, she discovered they had all retained certain qualities that reminded her of Gaston. Her first love, William Darlington, had sported a lean and muscular body like Gaston’s. Tom, with his unpredictable anger, had possessed a handsome face like Gaston’s. Even Paul had distracted her with hands shaped like Gaston’s. In every man she had found a feature resembling the one man she could never have. For the first time in her life, Danica Giles knew without a doubt that she was in love with Gaston Deslonde. The only problem was how was she going to love a man who could instantly disappear into thin air?

CHAPTER 9

The next morning Danica climbed out of bed feeling exhausted. She had been up several times during the night checking the house for Gaston, but he had never reappeared. As she stood in her long T-shirt at the kitchen sink and waited for her coffeemaker to finish brewing, her thoughts crept back to their argument the night before and her resulting realization.

All her life she'd waited for love. Armed with the expectations childhood fairy tales instill in the young, she set out for adulthood, waiting with bated breath for those first inklings of love to strike. And when it does, she hoped she'd be confounded, overwhelmed, and undone.

"Not standing by the sink with a hangover, waiting for the coffeemaker to finish," Danica muttered.

She was overjoyed and crestfallen, giddy and depressed. Was this love?

After the timer beeped, Danica grabbed for the coffeepot and filled her mug. When she viewed the calendar on her refrigerator, she saw the little yellow pumpkin highlighting the date.

"Wonderful…it's Halloween." She sighed and added some sugar to her coffee and chicory. "I guess if you're going to discover you're in love with a ghost, then this would be the day for it."

She took her coffee into the office, hoping to get some work done. When she placed her mug down on her dark green blotter, she spotted the pile of papers Carl had given her a few days before. She sat in her chair for several minutes staring at the papers and sipping on her coffee. Unable to stand it any longer, Danica grabbed for an article on the top of the pile. She began reading a detailed history of Deslonde Plantation, and soon Danica became lost in the myriad of stories about people from a long forgotten past.

***

Danica sat in the back seat of a taxi as it drove along a quaint street in the Friscoville subdivision in Arabi. When the taxi stopped at the end of a quiet street, Danica peered out the passenger window at the remnants of an elegant old plantation home.

A tall chain link fence surrounded a four-story rectangular home built in the neoclassical style. Short, square columns supported a sweeping gallery on the second floor and long shaded porch on the first floor. The high-pitched roof had two large dormer windows across the front and a fourth-story octagonal cupola covered with windows was perched above the roof. The massive French windows covering the first and second floor galleries were boarded up, as well as the inset front door. The house had been built of brick, and much of the paint and stucco surface of the home had been stripped away. As Danica inspected the structure and the three-foot high weeds that surrounded the house and property, she sighed. It was disheartening to see such a beautiful structure filled with so much history being left to the elements.

"You sure this is where you wanted to go, lady?" the taxi driver asked as he swerved around in the front seat.

"This is Deslonde Plantation, right?" Danica questioned, taking in the massive oak trees beyond the padlocked gate.

"What's left of it," the driver clarified. "This property has been boarded up for years, but nobody ever wants to visit this place no more. Too haunted."

Danica turned back to the taxi driver. "Haunted?"

"History has it that the former mistress of the plantation, Clarinda Deslonde, was known for mistreatin' slaves that worked the plantation grounds. She used to bury the dead slaves in a field adjoinin' the house. Well, I guess those tortured slaves came back to haunt the family, 'cause one by one all the members of the Deslonde family committed suicide. They say an old woman dressed all in black haunts the back porch of the plantation house and is supposed to be the ghost of Clarinda Deslonde. She always wore black for her husband who died of yellow fever in N'awlins. It was said she loved him a great deal, but he spurned her love and it drove her insane. That's when she started killin' off her slaves. She and her children are buried in a small cemetery off to the right of the house."

Danica cocked a curious eyebrow at her driver. "How come you know so much about this place?"

"I grew up in the Lower 9th Ward on the other side of Jackson Barracks. Everyone in St. Bernard Parish knows 'bout Deslonde Plantation."

"Do you know anything about Gaston Deslonde?"

"Sure do. His family was socially prominent in N'awlins. Their wealth came from the sugarcane they grew here. It was said he kept a quadroon mistress in the Quarter, and that his wife was real jealous of her. Deslonde and his wife were known to have had more than a few very public arguments about his philanderin'. Fed up with his wife, he left the plantation and moved to the city to be with his mistress. A few years later he died at his home in the Quarter. He's buried in the Deslonde family crypt in St. Louis Cemetery Number One." The taxi driver's dark brown eyes looked Danica over. "Why you so interested in this place?"

"I know the woman who owns Gaston Deslonde's former home in the French Quarter. I'm doing a bit of research for her on the family." She held up her cell phone. "I thought I would come out here and take some pictures."

The cabbie pointed through the passenger window to the gates. "The house is boarded up tight, and you best not try and venture inside. It's all run down and too dangerous for a little lady like you. Plus, the owner has a security company that often stops by to chase out trespassers. But if you go to the right of the house, you'll find an iron fence. That's where the graveyard is. You can take a look 'round there if you like." He eyed Danica once more. "You want me to wait for you?"

Danica smiled warmly for the cabbie. "If you don't mind…I won't be long."

The cab driver flashed her a toothsome smile. "I don't mind. It's your cab fare." He tilted his head slightly as he considered her. "You might not want to take too long though." He pointed at the meter. "This thing can add up fast."

Danica looked to his cab license posted above the meter. "Thanks, Miles."

Miles nodded his head. "No problem, miss."

She reached for her door. "Let me just get some pictures and I'll be right back."

Danica left the cab and headed for the gate. She slung her purse over her shoulder as she stepped through a wide hole in the ten-foot-high chain link fence. A light breeze made the Spanish moss on the towering oak trees scattered about the property sway eerily back and forth. As Danica trudged through the high weeds toward the house, she pictured Gaston walking down a shell-covered path to his ancestral home. She wondered what he would have been like, and then the memory of his kiss teased her lips. Danica suddenly found herself longing for the man he had once been.

She stopped before a thick overgrowth of bushes a few feet from the front of the old house. Danica searched through the foliage for the front steps to the porch but could not find any. She climbed her way up the three-foot expanse to the porch. When she finally made it up, Danica kneeled down and ran her fingers over the cool cement. She recalled the rendition of the plantation house she had seen in her research papers. The exterior walls and columns had been painted white to resemble marble, and the red-slated roof was reported to have been seen all the way to the Mississippi River when the afternoon sun warmed the tiles.

"This must have been a grand old place," she whispered.

A bird fluttered out from the thick brush in front of the porch and flew off to the right. Danica's eyes followed the bird and watched as it lighted on an iron fence about a hundred feet away from the house.

By the time she had made her way to the edge of the old iron fence, the bird had flown off, but when she inspected the small cemetery before her, she was stunned. The grass was freshly cut, and each of the fine marble headstones appeared well-cared for. There was no thick brush or even a weed to be seen inside the fence. Then, out of the corner of her eye, Danica spotted a man entering the rusty gate to the cemetery.

He was very tall, slender, and had long, lean legs. He was dressed in a pair of old blue overalls, with a long-sleeved white shirt and a crumpled straw hat that had several holes in it. On his feet were a pair of fine leather boots, and Danica thought the boots seemed a bit out of fashion.

"Excuse me," she called to the man.

He looked up, and when he saw her by the fence he waved. As he came closer, Danica could immediately tell he was an older gentleman with a long, wrinkled face, high cheekbones, and a wide red mouth. His brown hair was speckled with gray and could be seen poking out from underneath the brim of his hat. But it was his eyes that made her breath catch in her throat; they were sky blue.

"Can I help ya, miss?" he asked in a heavy southern accent.

"I was just wondering who takes care of the cemetery? I thought there were no more Deslondes left."

"Oh, there are some still around these parts, but I 'spect I might just be the last."

"Are you the one keeping up the place?" she asked as she waved her hand around the large plot of land.

"Yes, ma'am. That's my job. I promised my grandmother I would always take care of this little cemetery. Keep all the family graves tended to." He stepped over to a tombstone next to the fence and lovingly wiped his hand over the top of it. "It was the last thing she asked of me," he softly said.

"Are you related to Gaston Deslonde? The man who owned this place back in the mid-eighteen hundreds?'

"Yes. I was named after him," the man proudly declared.

Danica gawked at him. "Your name is Gaston?"

He placed his hands about the bib of his overalls and gave her a toothless grin. "Gaston Deslonde Arnaud."

"Arnaud?" Danica shifted her attention to a small tombstone by the fence. "But wasn't Arnaud—"

When she looked back to the spot where the man had been standing, no one was there.

She eagerly scanned the cemetery and surrounding land. She went around to the gate, still looking for Gaston, but he was nowhere to be seen. Stepping inside the cemetery gate, Danica walked over to the tombstone she had seen the older man lovingly caress. When she read the name on the tombstone, she gasped in surprised.

"Clarinda Destrehan Deslonde. Born 1826 Died 1868. Beloved wife, mother, and grandmother."

"Holy crap," Danica cried out as she grabbed at her chest.

She didn't remember running back to the cab, but when Danica reached the back seat of the car, she slammed the door closed and fought to catch her breath.

"Hey," Miles said as he faced her. "You all right there, miss?"

"I think…." Danica gulped in a breath. "I think I just saw a ghost."

Miles laughed as he placed his arm on the seat between them and inspected her with his round, brown eyes. "Well, you wouldn't be the first. Lots of people see strange things 'round here. I told you 'bout the lady in black that haunts the house." He pointed to her hair. "You might want to freshen up a bit."

"Why?"

He swerved the rearview mirror to Danica.

When she caught sight of her reflection, her body recoiled. Her hair and clothing were covered with burrs.

Danica began to pull the burs from her hair. "I didn't go in the house. This happened in the cemetery. There was a man there in a straw hat and overalls, and he—"

Miles began laughing at her.

"What?" Danica asked, staring at him.

Miles turned around and put the car into gear. "Girl, you met old man Arnaud. He was the last of the Deslonde family. He hung himself from the second floor stairway inside the house in 1905. His ghost keeps up that old cemetery. No one ever cuts the grass or sees to the headstones, but no matter who goes there, the cemetery is always nice and clean."

"You could have warned me," Danica admonished as the taxi pulled away from the front gates of the plantation.

"Why?" Miles adjusted his rearview mirror. "I thought that's what you wanted. Why else would you come out here on Halloween? Only people wantin' to see ghosts would come out here on Halloween. Everyone wants to see ghosts these days. My cab is filled with people wantin' to talk to the dead."

Danica sat back in her seat and eyed the fine homes along the side of the subdivision street. "I didn't rent a taxi to come to Arabi and talk to the dead, Miles. That's something I can do at home for free."

***

It was well after five when Miles delivered Danica to her cottage. The afternoon light was beginning to fade over the French Quarter rooftops as Halloween revelers filled the streets. When Danica placed her key in the lock to her side gate, she heard the garbled echoes of laughter mixed with loud conversations drifting over from Royal Street.

"I won't be getting a lot of sleep tonight," she complained as she pushed the gate open.

After securing her back doors, she stopped and smelled the air in the kitchen for any sign of Gaston. But the only aroma she detected was the faint impression of the coffee she had left in the pot.

A sudden rumble from her stomach made her realize she had skipped lunch while on her outing to Deslonde Plantation. Intent on finding relief from her sudden hunger pangs, Danica began rummaging through the kitchen cabinets.

She toyed with the idea of fixing a tuna sandwich, but decided on a bag of potato chips she found above the refrigerator. After further consideration, she grabbed the bottle of Johnny Walker Red from under her sink. As she munched on her chips, she took in the receding light of the sun through the kitchen doors and became entranced as the last bits of orange hastily retreated from the floor of the courtyard. Standing by her back door, Danica observed as the shade of night crept across the ground, and then her thoughts returned to the older man she had seen in the cemetery earlier that afternoon.

"He even looked like Gaston," she mumbled as she picked another potato chip from the bag.

Forcing the ghost of old man Arnaud from her mind, Danica decided the night might best be spent doing some work. She picked up the bottle of Johnny Walker from her kitchen counter, took her bag of potato chips, and headed for her office.

She had not been seated at her desk for ten minutes when she heard a firm knocking on her front shutters. She sat back in her desk chair, considering who could be at her door, and then she remembered the day.

"I don't have any candy, damn it."

But the knocking persisted.

Danica jumped from her chair and went to living room as the knocking continued relentlessly on her front shutters.

"Little bastards," she fumed. "I'll give them a treat they won't soon forget."

But when Danica angrily threw open the shutters, it wasn't children wearing devil costumes waiting on her doorstep, it was a man.

He was dressed in a fitted dark blue suit with a light gray tie. His shoulder length brown hair had been neatly slicked back, and he smelled of spicy cologne. His square face appeared pink and vibrant, but his sky-blue eyes still held their brilliant fire.

"Gaston?" she whispered, looking him over.

He was definitely different, but something besides the new clothes and hairstyle nagged at Danica. This Gaston appeared almost alive.

"Hello, Danica," he said in a deep, dulcet voice.

"What did you do?" She examined him up and down. "Your clothes, your skin…even your voice sounds different."

He held out his hand to her. "Take my hand."

She backed away. "But last time you—"

"Just take my hand, please," he urged.

Danica reached for his hand and touched his warm flesh.

She withdrew her hand and her eyes flew to his. "You're real?"

He took a step closer to the doorway, keeping his magical blue eyes on her. He wavered for a moment and then crossed the threshold of her home. He came right up to her, placed his hands about her face, and lowered his mouth to hers.

When their lips caressed, Danica's legs gave out beneath her. Gaston wrapped his arms about her to keep her from collapsing to the floor. He pulled her body close and kissed her forehead.

"How…?" She ran her hands tentatively over his shoulders. "How can this be?" Her fingers played in his thick, wavy hair. She felt the warmth of his cheeks, the slight stubble on his chin, and lightly traced the outline of his red lips. She laughed and kissed his lips again.

"It's Halloween, my treasure," he whispered into her hair. "The night when the veil between the dead and the living is at its thinnest. The dead can cross over and become one of the living on this night."

She patted her hands against his suit. "But what about the new clothes?"

"I wanted something nice to wear for our date."

"Date?"

He rested his forehead against hers. "We're going out."

She leaned back and leered at him. "You're sure you want to go out?"

He wrapped his arms about her waist and lifted her feet off the floor. "If we go to your bedroom now, we will never leave, and I want to see the city, Danica." He set her feet back down on the ground. "I want to taste food again, drink brandy, maybe even smoke a cigar." He kissed her lips once more. "I want to live again tonight, with you."

She hugged him close and squeezed him with all of her might. "I can't believe this is happening."

"Belief is what makes it happen, Danica." He pulled away from her. "Now go and change."

Before she backed away, Danica kissed his lips once more, anxious to make sure he was indeed real.

"You won't disappear?"

"Not tonight," he assured her as his fingers caressed her soft cheek. "I'm not going anywhere."

Danica turned to the family room and took off at a light jog. When she entered her bedroom, she dashed to her closet and began hurriedly going through her wardrobe. She found a short, pale red dress with spaghetti straps and a tapered waist that was perfect for the evening. She pulled the dress from the hanger, grabbed her black high heels from the floor of the closet, and rushed to her bathroom.

Fifteen minutes later, she walked into the living room, but there was no sign of Gaston. She spotted some movement inside her office, and when she walked into the room, she found him sitting on the side of her desk, holding the bottle of Johnny Walker in his hands.

"God, I forgot how good everything used to taste." He nodded at the bag of potato chips. "Those, by the way, are horrible."

"It's a bit of an acquired taste," she explained, easing up to the desk.

He put the bottle down on the desk beside him as his eyes consumed every inch of her dress.

"I'm going to have a hard time keeping my hands off you," he declared, pulling her into his arms.

He kissed the nape of her neck, then her shoulder, and breathed in the floral aroma of her perfume. "You smell so good." He bit down into her neck.

Danica closed her eyes and pressed her body against him.

Gaston sighed and gently pushed her away. "Not yet. First, I'm going to take you out, wine you and dine you properly before we come back here and…." He took her hand. "Come on. I'm starving." He led her to her front doors.

"Where are we going, Gaston?"

He grabbed her keys on the table by the door. "My favorite restaurant."

"Which was?" she asked as he opened the doors.

He pulled her outside. "Antoine's," he proclaimed as he locked her front doors. "It was the best place to eat, as I remember."

She squeezed his hand. "Still is."

He placed her keys in his front trouser pocket. "That's what I always loved about New Orleans. Nothing ever changes."

They walked to the edge of her property and then Gaston stopped. He stared down at the sidewalk with a mask of apprehension marring his fine features.

"This was as far as I have been able to go since the day I died," he softly said.

Danica took a step in front of him and tugged at his hand. "Let me show you the world."

He raised his head and his eyes melded with hers. He took a step to her and she could see the confidence building in him. Then, he took another step and slowly smiled.

"See, you're not bound to the house anymore."

He came alongside her and placed his arm about her waist. "I can feel my heart beating again. Smell the world again. You have no idea what a gift life can be."

"I know, Gaston. I know exactly what you mean."

He held on to her as they maneuvered through the thick crowds clogging the sidewalks of Royal Street. Some of the people were dressed in costume, some in formal attire, and others in casual blue jeans. But all the faces greeting them in the street seemed lit by an ethereal glow.

"Is it me or does everyone look different tonight?" Danica posed.

"No, it's the energy in the air. You can feel it. All Hollow's Eve has always been magical, especially to my kind." He nodded to a man passing beside them on the street. The stranger was dressed in a dark frock coat over lighter trousers and low-heeled shoes. He carried a soft-crowned brown hat in his hand.

Danica watched as the man walked past them. "Do you know him?"

Gaston turned his lips to her ear. "One of my kind out for a stroll."

"He's a ghost? Do all ghosts on this night become flesh and blood like you?"

He shook his head. "Not exactly. We can be seen as solid by anyone on this day. But of the flesh, no."

"But why can I feel you and touch you?"

He stopped walking and turned to her. "I'm different tonight than all the rest of the ghosts. I am made of flesh, but for one night only. When the sun rises, I will once again become what I was."

Danica moved closer to him and ran her hands along his wide chest. "In that case, we had better make the most of it."

He pulled her into his arms and kissed her again.

"Go for it, dude," someone called out from across the street.

Gaston abruptly let her go and took a step back. "I'm sorry, I forgot myself. Where I come from, a man didn't do something so improper in public."

Danica chuckled at his concern. "Welcome to the twenty-first century, dude, where the improper has finally become proper."

An encouraging smile spread across his red lips as he took her hand. "Let's go eat."

They turned off Royal Street and on to St. Louis Street, where they found themselves standing before the entrance to Antoine's Restaurant.

"This isn't where it used to be," Gaston insisted, motioning to the building. "It was further down the block."

Danica pulled him to a tall leaded glass door set amid a wide wall of french windows. "They moved here in 1868. The restaurant you knew was much smaller than this one."

He stared at her and furrowed his brow. "How do you know that?"

"Don't you remember? My father used to take me here every year for my birthday. He knew all about Antoine's, and taught me about the history of the restaurant."

"I had forgotten about that. You always said you hated this place; perhaps we should go somewhere else."

"I was ten and thought it old and stuffy. Now I'm thirty-five, and I've discovered I like old things." She winked at him. "Very old things," she added.

He opened the leaded glass door for her. "Remind me later to show you what this very old man can do."

Danica stopped in front of him. "I'm counting on it."

Inside, a maitre d' wearing a black tuxedo greeted them behind a high, polished oak podium in the main dining room. The spacious room had classic French décor, high ceilings, and elegant white columns throughout. Several white linen-covered tables were packed with diners. Bursts of exuberant laughter intermixed with the random buzz of conversation hung in the air.

"Good evening. Dinner for two?" the maitre d' asked as he looked them over with his brown eyes.

Gaston nodded. "Yes, thank you, for two."

Danica came alongside Gaston and took his arm.

The maitre d' smiled at them. "I think I've just the place for you two."

He grabbed two menus from a pocket on the side of a podium and nodded at Gaston. “Follow me.”

He guided them through the main dining room to a connecting hallway. Passing the Hermes Bar, they soon turned down another narrow corridor decorated with various autographed photographs of celebrities, until they entered a red-wallpapered room.

“The 1840s room will be quiet and private for the two of you,” the maitre d’ stated as he placed two menus on a table in the corner of the small room. “There’s a pretty rowdy Halloween party being held in the main dining room tonight.”

Gaston helped Danica into her chair “Thank you. We would appreciate a little peace and quiet with our meal.”

After the maitre d’ departed, Danica became fascinated by the beautiful portraits of departed patrons from the past that surrounded a carved walnut mantle. Her eyes rose until she spied the two three-tiered ornate gold chandeliers in the ceiling above.

A busboy attired in a white uniform immediately approached their table. He speedily filled their water goblets, put a plate of butter between them, and then scurried away.

Gaston’s inquisitive eyes inspected the room as he made himself comfortable in his chair. “This reminds me of the old restaurant.”

Danica picked up her menu. “Did you dine there often?”

“It was the place to be seen during my era. Antoine Alciatore was a great host, and his dishes were wildly popular among the aristocratic set. I spent many a late night in his establishment with good friends.”

Danica put her menu down and leaned her elbows on the table. “What was it like, in your time?”

“Harder…and there were fewer comforts like air-conditioning and computers. It was a simpler existence. The people were a lot less demanding and perhaps a little kinder. Sometimes I think that is because we were less stressed than you are today. It was also a lot less noisy.”

“What were the women like?”

Gaston’s fingers traced the edge of the white bone china plate set in front of him. “They were more demure. A woman’s opinion was something she was expected only to express to her husband or to her family. Most men were never interested in what a woman had to say.”

“Why?”

“It was a man’s world. We voted, made the money, and owned most of the businesses. Not to say that there weren’t female business owners, but they were relegated more to the lady of the night profession rather than legitimate businesses. Many people saw any woman who did happen to own a business as something of an oddity."

Danica's anger bristled and she shifted uncomfortably in her chair. "We were the dominated sex, not meant to be heard, and only seen, is that it?"

He rested his arms on the table. "It was the time, Danica. Although I must admit, I like women now more than then. I prefer an equal as a partner, and not a silent mouse who is afraid of speaking her mind."

"Is that what Clarinda was?"

He nodded. "Quiet and subservient. At first, I thought it attractive. But after a year of marriage, I discovered I wanted a partner I could share the burdens of my business with, discuss ideas, and plan a future with. Clarinda would always leave all the decision making to me. She didn't want to know about anything related to my businesses."

"But she didn't like your taking on a mistress, did she? She made it public knowledge that she disapproved of your taking in Marna."

His bright eyes studied her for a moment. "How did you come by that information?"

Danica sat back in her chair. "I met a well-informed cabbie when I went to Deslonde Plantation today, or what is left of it. I wanted to see your home. I saw a lot more than I cared to see."

"What happened?"

"I met your grandson, Gaston Deslonde Arnaud. He was tending to the graveyard not far from your old home."

"But he can't still be alive," Gaston expressed, with a hint of disbelief in his voice.

"He wasn't. You said the veil between the world of the living and the dead is thinnest on this day. Well, he appeared to me as real as you are now. It wasn't until he disappeared that I realized what he was."

"Did he say anything to you?"

She nodded her head. "I asked him about the graveyard. Something about how he promised his grandmother that he would always tend to the graves of his family. I was told he's often seen in the graveyard by your old home."

Gaston sat back in his chair and sighed. "That sounds like something Clarinda would do. Manipulative little bitch she was."

Danica was thunderstruck by his words. "What makes you say that?"

He diverted his eyes from her as he picked up his goblet of water. "When I first took up with Marna, Clarinda spread a lot of nasty rumors about her. Marna couldn't leave the house for a long time without being shunned by many in New Orleans. It took a toll on her. I went to Clarinda and threatened to divorce her if she didn't stop spreading her vicious lies. She begged me to get rid of Marna, but I refused. It wasn't long after that I moved out of the plantation for good."

"What kind of rumors did she spread about Marna?"

Gaston waved an impatient hand in the air. "That she was a voodoo priestess and had cast a spell on me. I was possessed by her sorcery or some such nonsense. Clarinda always was a spiteful vixen."

"I was told that Clarinda loved you a great deal. She wore black for the rest of her life after your death. She killed herself out of despair for losing you."

Gaston snickered with contempt. "She didn't love me, Danica. She needed me. There's a difference."

Danica reached across the table for his hand. "Even though wearing black for the rest of my life would be quite a bummer, I can understand Clarinda's feelings for you. You're a hard man to forget."

He pulled his hand away. "I am a hard ghost to forget."

She reached for his hand once more and held it firmly. "Dead, alive, ghost, or mortal, who cares; we have each other, and I'll take you any way I can get you."

He got up from his chair and kneeled down at her side. "You deserve better."

She traced her fingers along his rough, stubbled cheek. "I deserve you."

Gaston placed his hands about her face and tenderly kissed her lips.

The distinct sound of someone clearing their throat came from behind them.

Danica and Gaston looked to the origin of the interruption. A young waiter, decked out in a pressed black tuxedo, was standing by the doorway to the small dining room, smiling sheepishly.

"I figured I should let you know I was here before things got out of hand," the waiter admitted in an upbeat tone.

Gaston stood and took his chair. "No harm done."

The young man casually ambled up to their table. "May I offer a bottle of our finest champagne on the house to begin with? You two look like you have something to celebrate."

"Yes, we do," Gaston gleefully agreed.

The waiter exuberantly clapped his hands together. "I'm George and I will be your server this evening, and if you would allow me, let me choose your menu. It's an important night for the two of you and I wish to make it memorable."

"I put us in your hands, George," Gaston announced with a dramatic wave of his hand.

George bowed graciously. "Wise choice, sir. I promise you will not regret it."

CHAPTER 10

Throughout the evening, George paraded a host of delectable dishes across their table. Oysters Rockefeller, Creole gumbo, prime tenderloin tips with Marchand de Vin sauce, trout Pontchartrain, and cherries jubilee were all presented with an added flourish by their accommodating waiter. At the end of their sumptuous meal, Danica was sipping on rich coffee blended with chicory while Gaston nursed a snifter of brandy.

"Is there anything else I may get for you?" George inquired when he returned to their table carrying a black bill folder in his hands.

"George, that was wonderful," Gaston declared, smiling up at the round-faced waiter. "You did old Antoine Alciatore proud tonight. Thank you."

"It was my pleasure. May I offer my personal congratulations on your engagement?" George added with a respectful nod.

"Oh, no, we're not getting married," Danica told the sharply dressed waiter.

George knitted his dark eyebrows together. "But I thought when I saw him kneeling beside your chair…."

"I asked," Gaston imparted. "But she never gave me an answer."

Danica swiftly turned her eyes to him. "You asked?"

"I was going to. I know it isn't the best of circumstances between us, but I want to spend the rest of however many lifetimes I have with you."

Danica's heart fluttered as her eyes blurred with tears. "I…I don't know what to say."

George slipped the bill folder on to the table. "I think this is where I came in," he whispered and hastily backed away.

Gaston stood from his chair and went to her side. "I know it isn't conventional, but it's what I feel."

Ever since she had been a little girl she had dreamed of being his. But now that the dream was coming true, she had to wonder, what exactly would she be to him?

"You don't have to say anything right now. Let's get out of here," he whispered as he brushed his lips against her cheek. "There are still so many more things I want to do with you."

He left her side and picked up the bill folder as he returned to his chair. He reviewed the bill briefly, and then reached into the inside jacket pocket of his suit and pulled out a wallet.

Danica watched in amazement as he withdrew three one hundred dollar bills from his wallet and placed them in the bill folder.

"Where did you get that money, Gaston?"

He returned the wallet to his jacket pocket. "I'm not completely inept of what goes on today. What was true in the past is still true today. You need money to do anything or to go anywhere."

"Yes, but how did you get it?"

"You would be amazed at what I had hidden away in my old garden. Burying money and jewels used to be a safeguard against war and robbery."

"Please tell me you didn't break the law to be able to pay for this meal."

He winked at her as he stood from his chair. "Of course I did. I climbed the wall when Claire was at the grocery and dug up my money." He came around to her chair and extended his hand to her. "Stop worrying, my treasure. No harm was done, and it was worth it to have this evening with you."

Danica took his hand. "What if you had been caught?"

He pulled her from her chair. "I wasn't." He slipped his arm about her waist. "Now let's go and have some fun. Like Cinderella at the ball, I want to enjoy the night before I have to turn back into a pumpkin."

They left Antoine's behind and headed for Jackson Square. Gaston claimed he wanted to visit one of his old haunts before returning home.

When they stepped from Chartres Street and on to the gray slate tile surrounding Jackson Square, Gaston breathed in the sweet scent of jasmine in the air. "My favorite spot on earth," he whispered. "When I needed to think or get away, I always came here and watched the people."

"How different is it from when you were last here?" Danica asked beside him.

Gaston gazed up at St. Louis Cathedral, and turned to admire the fancy black wrought iron balconies of the Pontalba Apartments. "Not that different," he admitted.

Danica wrapped her arm about his as she perused the activity in the square. "This was one of the places I missed most when I was away."

Despite the late hour, many people were meandering about. Even many of the trot card readers, psychics, street musicians, and artists who worked the square were still out, trying to make a few extra dollars off the Halloween crowds.

They strolled about, stopping to take in one street performer who was doing magic tricks for the crowd, and then pausing by the black wrought iron fence to admire the paintings an artist had done of some local plantations. When they came to a shadowy corner beneath a live oak, a woman called to Danica.

"You brought the dark man, I see."

Danica halted when she saw the fortuneteller from the previous night, sitting behind her plain wooden table.

Danica left Gaston's side and went to the woman. "It's you."

"Who is that?" Gaston questioned, following her.

"You're the dark man who haunts the houses on Dumaine," the fortuneteller said, never taking her strange hazel eyes off Gaston. "You made your choice then, didn't you?"

"Who are you?" Gaston demanded.

"Madame LeJeune. Priestess, prophet, and spiritual medium."

Gaston's mouth fell open slightly as he looked the woman over anew.

"I come from a long line of women who could speak to spirits. Isn't that right, monsieur?

"Do you know her, Gaston?" Danica asked, placing her hand on his arm.

"Marna's last name was LeJeune," he confessed.

Danica stared at Madame LeJeune. "Do you know of Marna LeJeune?"

She held her head up proudly. "She's one of the spirits who speaks to me, and she has been telling me all about your dark man." She pointed at Gaston. "He's given up a great deal to be with you tonight. Did he tell you what he has done?"

Danica turned to Gaston. "What is she talking about?"

He waved off Danica's concern. "She's a crazy old woman, Danica. Pay her no heed."

"Remember, child, you have a choice to make. Life or death." Madame LeJeune held her hand out to Gaston. "This is death. The man you were with last night is life. You will have to choose one. You cannot have both."

Gaston took Danica's hand and leaned in closer to the woman. "She has chosen me," he growled.

Madame LeJeune never wavered as she stared Gaston down. "She hasn't chosen yet, ghost."

Gaston's face turned a deep shade of red. "Enough of this." He stood back from the table and turned away.

"In three days you will come looking for me, child. I'll be here, waiting for you."

A confused Danica let Gaston pull her away from Madame LeJeune's table. They walked on for a few steps and then Danica tugged at Gaston's hand.

"Gaston, wait," she pleaded. "She said last night you were in danger. We should go back and talk to her."

His eyes flashed with anger as he let go of her hand. "She's a con artist, Danica. A sham. All these people are." He waved his hand about the square. "You can't listen to her. She's just trying to get money out of you."

"But last night I was here with Paul, and she knew my name. She called to me in the crowd, and told me about you."

"She probably knows where you live, Danica, and she has done her homework." His face relaxed and his eyes became soft and caring again. "Don't let that gypsy ruin our night together." He stepped closer to her. "Do you want to go back to her table and listen to her inconsequential ramblings, or do you want to go home and be with me?"

A zing of excitement traveled from Danica's toes up to her stomach and her body heaved with longing. Suddenly, there was no one else around them. There was no Madame LeJeune, no wild revelers filling the French Quarter streets, no noise, nothing.

"Take me home, Gaston," she whispered.

He took her hand and led her toward the shadows beneath the balconies of the Pontalba Apartments. When they finally left the square and headed down Chartres Street toward Dumaine Street, Danica noticed how Gaston's pace quickened.

By the time they reached the front doors to her cottage, they were both breathing hard. Gaston reached into the front pocket of his trousers and pulled out her keys. Danica watched as his slender hands expertly worked the lock like he had done it a thousand times before.

When he pushed the french doors open, he turned to her and held out his hand. Danica smiled and took it.

The living room was dark and Danica switched on a lamp by the door as Gaston pulled the shutters closed and secured them. Then he shut the front doors and drove the dead bolt home. When he turned back to her, his eyes were on fire.

Danica's body burned with an unfamiliar heat as he slowly walked up to her. Gaston brushed his fingertips against her cheek, and Danica closed her eyes as she savored his touch. He placed his other hand behind her back and pulled her to him. When his lips touched hers, Danica instantly opened her mouth, hungry for him. Gaston threw his arms about her as he deepened his kiss. She groaned as his tongue teased her and his hands began to roam up and down her back.

Without warning he picked her up in his arms, still kissing her neck and face. He carried her down the dark hallway and kicked open the door to her bedroom. He did not let her go until he set her gently down on her king-sized bed.

Danica grinned as Gaston stood back from the bed, swiftly peeled off his jacket, and tossed it to the floor. He undid the tie from about his neck and threw it next to the jacket.

She giggled as he struggled with the buttons on his shirt.

She sat up on the bed. "Here, let me," she softly said, and started undoing the buttons for him.

Gaston removed the barrette pinning back her long, curly chestnut hair. "I wish I would have met you in my world," he sighed as his fingers played with a few of her curls.

Danica undid the last of the buttons and slid the shirt over his shoulders. She ran her hands up and down his smooth chest. Her fingers luxuriated over his thick muscles and long arms.

"Perhaps if we had met then you would have thought me bold and rude," Danica suggested as her hands went to the zipper on his pants.

He nuzzled her cheek. "Definitely bold, but never rude. I would have admired your spirit."

Danica eased the zipper down and then pushed the pants over his hips and round backside. "But if I had been raised in that era, taught to be demure and subservient, would I have had any spirit?" She sat back on the bed and admired his bright blue boxer shorts.

"You would have had spirit, my love." He leaned closer to her. "It comes from inside you, not from how you were raised." He placed his hands on her dress and then looked it over. "How do I get this off?"

Danica stood up next to him and slipped the light fabric over her head. She let the dress fall from her hands when Gaston's eyes wandered over her semi-naked body.

"Oh, that makes things very easy. No hooks or corsets, petticoats or long underwear to remove."

Danica swept her hand seductively over her red lace strapless bra and underwear. "Just these."

Gaston glided his fingers over the waistband of her delicate lace panties. "I could get used to this."

She tugged at the elastic waistband of his boxers. "I never figured you to be a boxer man. More like a briefs guy."

"They reminded me of undergarments from my time." He pushed the boxers to the floor. "But then again, I would always do away with undergarments when it got too hot."

Danica's eyes sauntered over his flat abdomen, thick arms, lean waist, and long legs. She moved closer, placed her hands on his erection, and gently began stroking him.

Gaston trembled. "I had forgotten how much I enjoyed being with a woman." He hooked his thumbs inside her panties and slowly pushed them down from around her hips. His hands caressed the smooth curves of her round bottom. "You are so firm," he said in a deep, throaty voice, and gently eased her back to the bed. "Women in my day did not exercise."

Danica removed her bra and reclined on the bed before him. "Pilates three days a week at the health club."

"I have no idea what that is, but I love it already," he professed as he climbed on top of her.

She wrapped her legs about him. "I still can't believe you're real."

He kissed the nipple on her right breast. "I'm real, Danica," he murmured as he ran his hand down the center of her chest, over her stomach, and reached between her legs. "Very real," he whispered.

He began to stroke her delicate folds of flesh, and Danica arched her head back when his fingers slipped into her.

"Yes," she moaned as she reached down and pushed his fingers deeper.

Spurred on by her desire, Gaston spread her legs wide apart and rhythmically moved his fingers back and forth inside her.

Danica rocked her hips against his hand, wanting him to go faster. She could feel the tension mounting in her body as he continued his slow and calculated movements.

"Open your eyes and look at me, Danica," he murmured.

Danica gripped his shoulders as she looked up at him. She bit down on her bottom lip as the pulsations from her groin began to overtake her body.

"I want to see your eyes when you let go, my treasure."

When her release drew near, she reflexively twitched and arched away from him, but Danica dug her nails into his shoulders and fought to keep eye contact with him.

"That's it, my darling," he cooed, and then increased the speed of his motion.

"Oh, God, Gaston," Danica cried, teetering on the edge.

"Look at me, Danica," he commanded.

When the orgasm burned through her body, Danica opened her mouth and screamed, but never took her eyes from his.

She fell back against the bed, panting, just as Gaston kneeled in between her legs. Not yet recovered from her exertions, Danica was startled when he immediately grabbed for her hips and raised them to meet his.

"I'm not done, my beauty," he drawled, and then thrust into her.

Danica sucked in a delighted gasp and closed her eyes when he pushed all the way inside. Resting her arms about his neck, she nestled her head against his wide chest.

"God, I missed this," he mumbled above her as he pulled out and then drove into her again.

Danica wrapped her legs about his hips. "Do it harder," she breathlessly commanded.

Gaston withdrew and forcefully pushed into her folds. "Is that what you want?"

"Yes, that's it."

He gently kissed her lips, pulled out, and entered her harder than before, making Danica moan into his chest. With every penetration, he tried to please her by constantly driving mercilessly into her delicate flesh. She clung to him, slamming her hips into his, forcing him deeper and heightening her pleasure.

"I'm not going to…be able to hold back for much longer," he softly voiced against her cheek.

"Don't hold back."

Gaston quickened his pace, furiously grinding his hips into her. His frenzied thrusts brought on her climax. He was grunting into her hair when her breath caught in her throat and her body shuddered. She jerked beneath him and muffled her cries against his thick chest. Then Gaston tensed, pulled her body closer, and gave a loud, guttural cry.

He relaxed on top of her, catching his breath. When he raised his head, he removed a lock of curly hair from the side of her face.

"I forgot how wonderful it was." He sat up on his elbow and skirted his fingertip along the curve of her jaw. "You are nothing like the women of my time."

"Really? How am I different?"

"You tell me what you want, how you want me to be." He rolled off her and pulled her into his arms. "None of the women I was with ever did that."

She cuddled against his chest. "Not even Marna?"

"Marna enjoyed sex, but I know she always felt she had to please me to keep her position. I never had her heart completely, just her obedience."

She breathed in the traces of his spicy cologne. "What about your wife, Clarinda?"

He snorted with distaste. "Being with that woman was always uncomfortable. She hated sex, and was never receptive to me. I tried to please her in the beginning, but she always saw our being together as a duty and never a pleasure. After the birth of our first child, it just became a formality."

Danica sat up in the bed. "How many woman have you been with?"

He gave a deep, throaty laugh that made Danica smile. "That's not an appropriate question to ask a man."

She lightly punched him. "In your time maybe, but not today. I told you about my experiences, so now it's your turn."

His eyes contemplated her for a brief instant. "All right. Twenty, or maybe twenty-two, I'm not sure."

Danica raised her eyebrows with surprise. "That many?"

"What? Is that not the average for a man today?"

"Not the men I knew," she balked. "What were you, some kind of lothario?"

He snickered lightly. "Well, not after I was married. It was expected of a man to bed a few women before he married."

"Twenty-two is more than a few, Gaston."

"More than most, but I was considered quite a catch in my day. A rich plantation owner's son, who happened to be good-looking and skilled in the social graces, was what all women wanted. Wouldn't such a man be wanted today?"

"Only if he's a good-looking doctor and drives a Ferrari. No one cares about social graces anymore."

"That is a pity," he conceded as he ran his fingers over her soft skin. "Took a lot of study to become skilled in poetry, dance, music, and social manners."

"Sorry to disappoint you, but the only men interested in that stuff today are probably gay. Except for the music part, and only if it's rock."

He tucked his hand behind his head and sneered. "That is one thing I do not understand from your era, the music. Why is singing about a woman's anatomical features pleasing to your generation?"

"What are you talking about?"

"'Baby Got Back'," he answered. "I saw a video of the song on MTV once and thought your world needed a heady dose of wolfsbane."

"What's wolfsbane?"

"In small doses we used it for cleansing or purging the system. In larger doses it was used as a poison to kill off enemies."

Danica leaned over him. "Where did you learn about that?"

His fingers lightly played with a lock of her curly hair. "You had to know about the medicinal properties of plants in case of illness. Doctors were never much help."

Danica frowned at him. "Sometimes they're not much help today, either. They couldn't help my mother."

"I remember how much you cried after she died. It used to drive me mad that I could not put my arms around you and console you."

She curled into his thick chest. "Now you can put your arms around me."

"Only until dawn," he lamented in a disheartened tone.

She raised her head and grinned into his sky-blue eyes. "Then perhaps we should make sure we get the most out of every minute until then."

He sat up on his elbows, cocking one eyebrow at her. "What did you have in mind?"

She let her lips hover temptingly in front of him. "I'll show you." She climbed on top of him and straddled his hips.

Gaston rubbed his hands up and down her slender white thighs. "What do you want me to do?"

She took his hands and pushed them over his head. "Just relax and leave everything to me."

He grinned. "I think I am going to like this."

She tempted his chest with kisses and then let her lips linger on his right nipple. His body quivered as she teased his nipple with her teeth.

"It's my turn to be in charge," she murmured against him.

"I'm all yours, Danica," he sighed. "I'll always be yours."

***

Danica awoke in the early hours of the morning to find Gaston's spot in the bed beside her empty. She turned to the wide picture window facing the courtyard and felt comforted by the darkness outside. Speedily climbing from the bed, she went in search of Gaston. When she stepped out of her bedroom, she saw a faint light shining from the other side of the family room doorway. She followed the light to her office, where she found Gaston sitting in the chair behind her desk, holding the bottle of Johnny Walker Red in his hands.

"I got up and thought that you had left," she admitted, walking up to his side.

He put the bottle down on the desk and wrapped his arms about her naked waist. "I have two more hours yet before the dawn. I didn't want to sleep, and then I remembered that." He nodded to the bottle. "I just wanted to taste the alcohol on my lips once more."

"Whatever magic brought you to me tonight, can you make it happen again?" Danica asked as she sat on his lap and curled into his arms.

"Only on All Hallow's Eve can I come back to you in the flesh."

"Will you come back again next year?"

His eyes turned cold and his mouth twisted into a reluctant half-smile. "I must wait and see what happens."

"What do you mean?"

"There are many things that have to happen before I can come back. Some of the factors are out of my control." He paused and looked away.

"What if I could never come back to you as a man; would you still love the ghost that I am?"

She sat up and turned his face to hers. "Of course. Flesh or air, alive or dead, I'll take you any way I can have you. I just want to be with you."

"You're so young. You have so much life ahead of you. Why would you want to saddle yourself with me?"

"Because I love you, Gaston. I don't care what form you take, as long as we can be together."

"I love you, my treasure. It took death to make me realize what that was, and without you I might never have known such happiness."

She cuddled against him. "I guess it doesn't matter how or when we find it, as long as we do find it."

"Marna once told me that love was the only truth, and to be at one with all things in my world and yours, I had to know love."

"I think Marna was a very smart woman." Danica stood from the chair and eased her hips onto her desk. She wrapped her legs about Gaston and pulled him and his chair closer to the desk. "We have two hours yet before dawn, right?"

"Wasn't three times enough for you?"

She slowly shook her head. "It's going to be another whole year before I can feel you again. So we better make sure we fulfill every fantasy I've had about you. I can spend the next year planning new ones."

He stood from the chair. "What fantasy haven't I fulfilled?"

She leaned back on the desk. "How were the woman in your time? Sexually, I mean."

His eyes instantly perked up and explored her naked body.

"Nothing like you."

Danica sat up. "Were you different with them than the way you were with me tonight?"

His hand caressed her right breast. "I never asked what a woman wanted or needed. I never tried to please her…I just took what I wanted."

Danica tilted her head back and smiled coyly. "Treat me as a woman from your time," she softly said.

Gaston stared into her eyes as if carefully weighing her words. "Take what I want without asking what you want?"

Danica leaned forward. "Just take me."

He reached for her body and lifted her into his arms. After he flipped her over, Gaston forced her facedown on top of the desk. He stood behind her, lifted her hips in the air, and slowly spread her legs apart.

"Tell me you want me to stop."

Danica trembled with desire. "Don't stop." She grabbed on to the edge of the desk.

He rammed into her before she was ready for him, and Danica cried out.

"Is this what you wanted?"

"Yes," she answered in a husky voice.

He drove into her again, forcing her flesh apart. He pressed his back into her body as he leaned over to her ear.

"Why does this excite you?"

She lifted her head a little from the desk. "Because I want you to be in control."

Gaston bit her shoulder as he pulled out and pounded into her again. Her body smashed into the desk as he gyrated behind her. Danica grunted when he lifted her hips even higher and went deeper than before.

Danica's body shook as her orgasm began to hastily build. When the tension was just about to explode, Gaston stopped his vigorous thrusting.

"Oh, God don't stop," she pleaded, pushing up from the desk.

But Gaston threw his body on top of hers, pinning her against the hard surface of the desk. "I am the man and you will do as I desire." He placed his hands over hers on the edge of the desk. "Understand?"

"Yes, Gaston."

"Good girl," He pulled out of her and then ran his fingers between her legs. He teased her folds, making her body heave with need, and then he stopped.

Danica moaned and her knuckles went white against the edge of the desk.

He abruptly entered her again, pushing all the way into her, and then he stayed motionless for a moment. Danica tried to move against him, to encourage him to continue, but he pressed his weight into her back, making her completely immobile.

"You will not move or make a noise. I am in control now."

He pulled out and then entered her once more. His penetrations would at times be hard and fast, and then become very slow and gentle.

At different intervals he would pause, reach between her legs, and stimulate her with his fingers.

"You will take everything I give you and more." He bit into the back of her neck and then rammed into her with all of his might.

Danica's body arched beneath him and he stopped once more, staying perfectly still inside her.

"Tell me you are mine," he whispered to her.

She sucked in a ragged breath. "I'm yours; just don't stop."

Gaston pushed his hips into her, and then he started to move very slowly. When Gaston suddenly stopped, Danica let out a throaty, painful moan. Her arms were trembling and her muscles were getting tighter. A small trickle of sweat poured from her brow.

"Are you ready to finish this?" he murmured.

"God, yes," Danica cried out.

Gaston roughly dove into her once more, but this time he did not hold back. He grunted into her hair as he pushed into her faster and faster. Danica was holding on to the edge of the desk as her body exploded with pleasure. Soon she began bucking beneath him, and then Danica's scream filled the room. As she began to settle down, Gaston's orgasm ripped through him, making him groan against her back.

As they lay across the desk, panting, Danica began to giggle. "Where in the hell did you learn how to do that?"

Gaston wiped his hand across his sweaty brow as he rolled to the side and reclined across the desk. "Many of those twenty-two lovers I told you about were prostitutes. They taught me a thing or two about sex."

"You were an apt pupil." She leaned against his wide chest. "It's never been like that with anyone."

"That is a shame. You need a lover who will satisfy you, Danica."

She rubbed his smooth chest. "Now I have you."

He pulled her into his arms. "You have me for about another hour and a half."

She sat up next to him. "That's time enough."

He sat up on his elbows and knitted his brow. "Enough for what?"

She grinned. "For you to do that again."

CHAPTER 11

The sun was shining through the picture window in her bedroom when Danica's eyes opened. She rolled over and felt for Gaston next to her, but he was gone. She heaved a heavy sigh and ran her hands over her face.

"I don't know if I can wait another whole year."

Danica eyed the alarm clock on the nightstand next to her. "Damn it! I'm going to be late for work."

As soon as she stood from her bed, her body began to ache. Her thighs, back, and even between her legs hurt with every step she took. Once in her bathroom, she flipped on the lights and reached for the shower faucet. But when she passed before her vanity mirror, she stopped and stared at her body.

Her stomach, thighs, and hips were covered with bruises. She recalled how Gaston had pinned her against her desk, and then again against the pocket doors to her office. She closed her eyes and fought back a frustrated groan as her body began to ache for him.

"This is ridiculous." She fought to regain control of her lust, and then she smiled. "No, this must be love," she softly reasoned.

After a quick shower, Danica headed for the kitchen in search of coffee and Tylenol. When she entered her office and saw the papers tossed about her desk, she blushed. Never had she known such a man, and spending one night with him had only intensified her desire for him. Unexpected beeping from the kitchen made Danica turn away from her office.

When she entered the kitchen, she found the reason for the beeping. Her coffeemaker alarm had gone off, signaling that a pot of freshly brewed coffee was waiting for her. She walked up to the coffeemaker and saw that a white coffee mug had already been placed on the counter next to it.

"Thank you, Gaston," she whispered. "Thank you for everything."

***

The trolley ride home from work was less crowded than Danica had expected, and the French Quarter seemed unusually quiet for a Monday evening. But remnants of the festivities from the night before were still readily apparent on every street corner, where debris had been neatly swept into piles for pick up by the sanitation department. A refreshing cool breeze was winding its way through the Quarter as Danica wandered down Royal Street. With her briefcase and purse slung over her shoulder, she strolled along in no particular hurry as memories of the night before preoccupied her thoughts. She lingered over flashes of Gaston eating dinner, walking with his arm around her, and making love to her. As her mind became swept up in their frenzied moments on her desk and in her bed, she made the last turn down Dumaine Street.

The sight of two police cars parked outside Danica's cottage immediately roused her from her happy memories. She picked up her pace, alarmed that something terrible may have happened.

When she reached the side entrance gate to her house, a police officer was coming out of Claire's front door.

"Is something wrong with Burt or Claire?" she asked the stout man dressed in the standard blue uniform of the New Orleans Police Department.

"Are you family?" he questioned in a snappish tone.

"I live next door," she replied just as Paul came bounding out the front door.

"Danica," he called to her. "You're home."

He came up to her as the police officer stood by watching. Paul placed his arm about her waist and guided her back to her gate.

"What's going on, Paul?" She pivoted her eyes from Paul to the policeman standing close by.

"Burt's dead," Paul calmly informed her. "They found him in St. Louis Number One Cemetery early this morning."

Danica's hand went to her mouth. "Oh, my God."

The officer stepped away and walked over to one of the white police cars parked in the street.

Paul's deep-set green eyes turned to her. "The police aren't sure how he died yet. He was found early this morning by some people placing flowers on the graves for All Saint's Day."

Danica turned to the front door of Claire and Burt's home. "How is Claire?"

Paul wiped his face in his hands. "Not good. She's just sitting in her chair by the front door and not saying a word to the police. The police are the ones who called me at work this morning to come and keep an eye on her. They said she was screaming one minute and laughing the next after they told her about Burt. She kept telling them it was her fault, that she sent him to the cemetery."

"Why would she send him to a cemetery?"

"I have no idea. She told the police it had something to do with that damned ghost she's always going on about."

Danica's gut twisted into a knot. "What would any of this have to do with Gaston Deslonde?"

"They found Burt in front of his family tomb. Police think she may have sent Burt there for some weird Halloween thing. Who knows? You know how my mother is into all of that crap. Maybe she talked Burt into going there to place something before the guy's grave and something happened to him." He paused and shifted his attention to the police cars on the street. "The police say they won't know what killed Burt until the autopsy tomorrow."

Danica placed her hand on his arm. "I'm so sorry, Paul. Is there anything I can do?"

He shook his head. "Thanks, but I've got a call into a doctor that has seen my mother in the past for her bouts of depression. I'm waiting for him to call me back."

"I didn't realize Claire was seeing anyone for depression."

"She hasn't seen Dr. McKay for a few years. I thought she had beaten that demon, but I guess I was wrong."

Paul's cell phone started ringing from the inside pocket of his black suit jacket. He pulled the phone from his pocket and checked the number. "I've got to take this."

He stepped away from her side and Danica looked over at the two police cars parked along the curb. Sensing there was nothing else she could do, she walked to her gate.

When she stepped into the rear entrance of her home, the air was thick with the aroma of cigars and brandy.

"He must have told you," Gaston said as she shut the back doors.

He was standing beside her kitchen counter, and his luminescent figure was once again dressed in black fitted pants, a white linen shirt, and shiny, black riding boots.

"Do you know what this is about?" she asked.

He cast his eyes to the floor. "No."

Danica immediately grew suspicious. "You know something, Gaston. Tell me."

He turned away from her. "I know she was unhappy and wanted out of her marriage. She would often ask me to get rid of Burt for her, but I told her I could not." He paused and showed his profile to Danica. "There were times when I saw him hit her, and it would pain me to watch her go through that, but there was nothing I could do. I never understood what he got out of beating her."

"Control," Danica whispered. "It makes them feel as if they are in control." She smiled weakly. "Such men like their woman meek and subservient."

Gaston came closer to her. "You spoke before about such things and said it was your friend who was beaten by her husband. But it wasn't, was it?"

She tossed her purse and briefcase onto the white-tiled kitchen counter. Leaning her hip against the counter, Danica took a moment to collect her thoughts.

"The first time Tom hit me was right after we came home from our honeymoon. We argued about going out to dinner. I didn't see the blow coming until it was too late. He got me right across the jaw." Danica simulated the blow lightly on her jaw. "I had never been hit like that before and it knocked me off my feet. Of course, he was very sorry after, and begged me to forgive him, which I did. I thought it was my fault. I should have wanted to go out to eat with him. I figured it was just one of those things and tried to put it out of my mind. Two months later he came home from work and I was at my desk, trying to finish a project for the PR firm I worked for. I hadn't cooked dinner and Tom went crazy." She paused, closed her eyes, and shook off her frightful memories. "By then I knew our marriage was a mistake, but I was too afraid to walk away…ashamed and afraid. Took me almost two years to file for divorce, but when I did I finally felt like I was back in control. After the divorce, I knew I needed to put Tom and Seattle behind me for good. Then Dad died, and when I was packing up his things I decided to come back to New Orleans. I thought I could start over here." She pushed her body away from the counter. "I have started over, with you."

Gaston lowered his head and said nothing for a very long time. When he raised his eyes to her, they were brimming with tears.

"I'm sorry. I should have paid attention. I should have asked before now." He wiped his face in his hands. "I shouldn't have done what I did last night on the desk. If I had known you had gone through—"

"Hey," she said, coming up to him. "Last night was wonderful. All of it was wonderful, and I don't regret a second of it. You have been more of a man with me as a ghost than my husband ever was as a flesh and blood person."

"How did you end up with someone like that? You are a smart, beautiful woman who could have any man."

"I ended up with Tom and all the rest of the men in my life because I was looking for something in each of them that I desperately wanted but knew I could not have."

"What was that?"

She waved her hand up and down his figure. "You; every man I've ever been with had traits or pieces of you in them. I didn't realize any of this until the other day. I knew what I had been searching for was simply a substitute for what I thought I couldn't have."

Gaston walked around her and headed into her office. "I have ruined your life. I've kept you from finding happiness with a man. I knew I should never have come to you last night, but I wanted you so much. I wanted to touch you, to hold you against me, but now I know that was a mistake."

"How can you say we are a mistake? What we feel isn't wrong."

He stopped in front of the fireplace. "But what we have isn't normal. It isn't natural." Gaston slammed his fist into the dark cypress mantle, making the wall next to them shake.

She wanted to reach out to him, to console him in some way. But Danica held her hands to her sides and fought to control her urge to touch him.

"Gaston, who's to say it isn't right or normal? Whatever god determines our fate puts such deterrents in our way not to punish us, but to bless us. When we struggle to overcome the most difficult of obstacles, we learn to appreciate every facet of our lives. We realize that everyone around us, whether they're made of air or flesh, are precious. All love is precious and never a mistake."

He turned to face her. "But love should be something that makes us happy, Danica. Love should never scar or maim our hearts. Just like Tom scarred you, our love will eventually hurt you as well. I don't want to let that happen."

Danica threw her hands in the air. "So what are you going to do? Just walk away and hurt me even more?"

Gaston shook his head. "I can't leave you, ever. I am bound to you. I've always been tied to your side. Even though I may regret my mistake, I felt compelled to make it. Sometimes I think you are the reason I stayed behind when I died. Fate must have determined this existence for us. I will stay by your side, until you become a spirit just like me."

Danica grinned into his bright eyes. "Can we haunt this house together?"

Gaston chuckled. "If you like."

"I would very much like to spend eternity with you, Gaston."

He sighed as his eyes hungrily lingered over her red lips. "I want nothing more than to be with you, forever, my treasure." He raised his hand as if to touch her face, and then lowered it to his side.

A shrill beeping suddenly came from the kitchen.

"I put a some soup in the microwave for you," Gaston explained as he motioned to the kitchen. "I wanted to make sure you had something warm to eat when you walked in the door."

"How are you with microwave dinners?"

"As long as it doesn't come with a whole lot of directions, I'm fine with microwave dinners."

She walked toward the kitchen archway. "I'll keep that in mind next time I'm at the grocery."

"You may want to get another bottle of Johnny Walker for next Halloween," he suggested over her shoulder. "I finished up your bottle before I left this morning."

Danica faced him. "Next Halloween?"

"I figured we could start planning our next night together."

Danica slowly smiled. "I'll put it on my list."

"And get a good bottle of brandy, too. I promise you next year, we will not be going out." He looked her body up and down. "We'll be staying in every Halloween from now on."

CHAPTER 12

Later that evening, Danica was sitting on the floor in her family room with Gaston, watching a program on television.

"That is all a hoax." Gaston waved at the intrepid ghost hunters on television using their digital recorders to speak with the dead. "No ghost would ever want to put on such a display," he informed her.

"Why? Is it written in a handbook somewhere that you guys can't be seen on camera?"

"No, of course not," Gaston balked. "But no ghost I know would pull such theatrics. Imagine if one of us did come out of the closet; then their quiet home would be inundated with ghost hunters, the avidly curious, and the generally insane."

"Do you know other ghosts?"

"A few. Ones I see passing on the street, or in the neighboring homes. We talk occasionally."

"What do you talk about?"

He shrugged as he watched the flat screen television before them. "People. Dead or alive, gossip is still gossip."

An insistent knock at the front doors made Danica flinch. "Who could that be?"

Gaston rose from the floor. "Let me get it."

Danica jumped to her feet. "God, no. Can you imagine the lunatics who would be knocking on my door if the world found out about us?"

"You would be famous," he asserted with a chuckle.

"I would be locked up and they would probably throw away the key."

When Danica walked into the living room, she saw Paul standing outside her cottage doorway.

"Is everything all right?" she asked him as she opened her doors.

Paul's light brown hair looked disheveled and his eyes had dark circles beneath them.

"I have to ask you a big favor. Can you watch my mother for a half an hour? Dr. McKay dropped off a prescription for her a little while ago to help calm her down, and I need to get it filled, but I'm afraid to leave her alone."

Danica nodded her head. "Absolutely."

Paul sighed, sounding relieved. "Thank you, Danica. I owe you for this."

"You don't owe me, Paul. If anything I owe you an apology for the other night. I shouldn't have been so…rude."

He gave a crooked smile and Danica's toes curled in her tennis shoes. She didn't understand why she felt that way. She was in love with Gaston, right? So why should a simple smile from Paul make her feel so…special?

"Maybe when things settle down we can try again? What do you say?"

Danica thought of Gaston. She wanted to tell him that any possibility of a relationship was out of the question, but she just couldn't. She wasn't quite ready to walk away from a chance with Paul. "I would like that," she finally admitted. Frustrated by her lack of resolve, Danica turned from her doorway. "I'll just get my keys."

She darted inside to find a menacing Gaston looming in the arched doorway to the family room.

"Why did you agree to see him again?" he all but shouted.

She ignored him and grabbed her keys from the table by the door. "We will talk about this later," she whispered.

She stepped outside to find Paul waiting with his hands in his black trouser pockets.

"I really appreciate this. I promise not to be long. I was just going to walk over to the pharmacy on Royal Street."

She locked her front doors. "I'm glad to help, Paul."

Paul stepped up to her side and then placed his arm casually about her shoulders as they walked back to his mother's front door.

"Have the police told you anything else about Burt's death?" Danica inquired.

"They said they're following up on some leads, but they don't suspect foul play. There were no signs of trauma on Burt's body, and he still had his wallet on him with all of his money and credit cards. The only odd thing the police said was he was wearing a suit. I didn't think Burt even owned a suit."

An unsettling feeling gripped her as Paul opened the front door to his mother's cottage. When they stepped inside, Claire was sitting on an antique mahogany and red velvet love seat in the corner of the ornately furnished living room. She was gazing up at the two-tiered chandelier hanging from a delicate medallion of intertwined roses situated in the middle of the white plaster ceiling. The odd white robe she was wearing had dirt stains around the knees, and was tied at the waist with a black cloth belt. Her dirty feet were bare and her short brown hair looked as if she had not washed it in days. Her face was haggard and she seemed to have aged decades since the last time Danica saw her.

"Mom," Paul softly said to her as he approached the love seat. "Danica is here from next door to stay with you while I go and get your pills. All right?"

Claire's empty brown eyes turned to her son and then she smiled, but never said a word.

Paul gave Danica a worried frown and then patted his mother on the shoulder. "Maybe Danica can help you get out of your robe and into your nightgown. I promise I'll be back shortly."

Claire's eyes turned to Danica and immediately the serene smile on her face morphed into an angry scowl.

But Paul did not seem to notice. He kissed his mother's cheek and abruptly headed for the front door. When he reached the door, he turned to back Danica.

"My cell phone is programmed into her house phone. So you can just pull it up and call me if you need to." He paused and silently mouthed, "Thank you."

Danica's heart went out to him and she wished she could do more. He looked as if his world was about to come crashing down around him.

Paul hastily retreated from the house and quietly shut the front door behind him.

When Danica turned back to the love seat, Claire's pale brown eyes were glaring at her. The air in the room turned thick with hostility.

Danica sucked in a steadying breath and walked up to Claire's love seat. "Claire, you should get out of this outfit," she instructed in a firm tone. "You need to clean up and change."

"These are my ritual clothes," Claire squawked in an unsteady voice. "I committed myself to the powers of darkness. I was anointed with their magic."

Danica was stumped and not quite sure how to proceed. She could either entertain the woman's babblings, or she could get her oriented back to reality. She decided on the latter.

"Claire, you're covered with dirt, not magic. You have to clean up before Paul comes back. He's worried sick about you." She placed her hands on her hips and frowned. "You had better start making sense again before he has you and your powers of darkness committed to the psych ward."

"He likes you, my boy. I can see it in the way he looks at you. But you don't see him…you only have eyes for Gaston."

Danica kept her face calm and collected. "Claire, stop talking nonsense."

"It's the truth." Claire pointed an accusatory finger at Danica. "You and I both know it." She paused as she placed her hand back in her lap. "Did you have as much fun with Gaston last night as you had with my son?"

A twinge of dread whipped through Danica. "Last night?"

"On your date, your Halloween date with a very real Gaston." Claire slyly smiled. "Oh, he had such plans for the two of you. Did he take you to dinner at Antoine's like he talked about? Did he bring you home after and tell you that he loved you?" Her brown eyes turned into two black beads. "Did you spend the night naked in each other's arms, only to find him gone at the break of dawn?"

As Claire spoke, a wave of nausea rolled through Danica. "What are you talking about?"

Claire sat back on the love seat, looking very smug. "How do you think he became flesh again, hmm, Danica? Did he tell you that the veil between the living and the dead is thinnest on Halloween and that he could return to you because he simply willed it to happen?" Claire uttered a cold cackle that made Danica's heart shrink. "He could not will such a thing, you silly girl. He needed magic to make that happen, and he needed someone who could make that magic happen for him. He needed me." Claire stood from the love seat appearing tough and resilient. "I made him yours for one night. I gave him life so he could touch you and lie with you. I joined myself with the powers of darkness so he could walk this earth for one night to be with you."

Danica took a wary step back from her. "What have you done?"

Claire's face showed not the slightest hint of emotion. "He loves you. He has always loved you, and it was driving him mad not to be with you. I told him there was a way to fix that…to call on the powers of darkness to help him, but he refused. When you went on a date with my boy, he changed his mind. He came to me and begged me to help him. I gave him one night in the flesh with you, and he gave me freedom from Burt."

"Burt?" Danica hesitated. "What do you mean Gaston gave you freedom from Burt?"

Claire played with the black belt on her robe. "The first time he kissed you, he told me you saw what it did to him. Being entwined with your life force weakened him considerably. It's the same with us. If we allow a ghost to inhabit our bodies, we are drained in the very same manner. But a person has to volunteer for such a possession, and it takes a great deal of meditation to open up for a ghost. Even when it does happen, the possession can only last a few minutes. But there are spells that can weaken the will of a person, make them almost like a zombie, so a spirit can possess them without resistance. That's what I did to Burt. I turned him into a vassal for Gaston. To you he appeared as Gaston, but to the rest of the world he was Burt."

Danica recoiled in revulsion at the image of Burt lying naked next to her in bed.

"But Burt had a weak heart," Claire went on. "You wouldn't know it by looking at the man, but he was on several medicines to keep him going. I knew one night of being possessed by an old and powerful spirit, such as Gaston, would be too much for Burt. And it was."

Danica moved closer to her. "What did you do?"

"Do? I didn't do anything. I simply allowed the dark forces to work their magic and get rid of a problem for me. Burt was a cruel pig who enjoyed beating women. He got off on it. After he beat me, he would want to have sex. He would tell me how sorry he was and that he would never do it again, but he always did."

Danica wrapped her arms about her body as the memory of those same words from Tom came crawling back from the past.

"For years I asked Gaston for help, but when you returned I knew I'd finally found something to force his hand."

Danica boldly faced her. "I will not stand by and let you hurt Gaston. He didn't kill Burt, you did. You're the one who planned this whole thing, to do what? Get out of a bad marriage? Free yourself of an abusive husband? Why did you involve Gaston, Claire? Why didn't you walk away from Burt? I've been in your shoes. I know what you went through, but I divorced the abusive man I was married to. You could have left Burt and no one would have been hurt."

"And be poor?" Claire howled with laughter. "When Paul's father died, he left me with a mountain of debt and a house I could not afford to keep. Burt was there, like some knight in shining armor ready to step in and take care of me, and he had money, lots of money. His mother was a very rich woman who came from an old New Orleans family, and Burt was her only child. When she died, she left him everything. So I showed him how to spend his money. We bought this place and all of this furniture." She waved her frail hand about the room. "Not long after we moved in, I discovered Gaston. I read up on everything I could about ghosts. Eventually, I started to learn about spells and rituals to gain control over them. But in order to control a spirit, you must first give them something they desire. When you moved in next door, I discovered his feelings for you. That's why I introduced you to Paul. I knew Gaston would come to me after seeing you with another man. Jealousy can be a very powerful incentive." Claire sighed and turned for the doorway behind her. "Now Gaston is bound to me. I can make him do my bidding at any time I choose. His soul is mine."

"Bound to you?"

"He had to submit to me in order to enter Burt's body. By allowing me to control his soul, he became bound to me. I'm the puppet master, pulling all of his strings. He has to do what I say until I set him free."

"You will set him free, now," Danica demanded. "You will not enslave Gaston. I won't allow you to do that. I love him."

"You love a ghost, you stupid girl." She waved her hand gracefully in the air. "Why love air when there's a real man wanting you. My Paul fancies you, and I want my boy to be happy. He will make you a fine husband, and you will be his obedient wife."

"Stop it, Claire," Gaston's deep voice filled the room. "Leave Danica out of this. She is mine." He instantly manifested in front of Claire.

"Ah, there he is now." Claire's eyes eagerly searched the room.

Danica realized that Claire could not see him.

"I told you Danica was never to know," Gaston growled.

"She needs to know, Gaston. She needs to know the price of your love." Claire settled her gaze on Danica. "If you ever betray me, Gaston, I will destroy her."

"No," Gaston yelled as he rushed toward Claire.

But as he reached her side, a dark shadow enveloped her and stopped him dead in his tracks.

Danica felt the room's temperature plummet. "What's going on?"

Gaston turned to her. "She's protected by black magic. It covers her like a suit of armor. Nothing will hurt her."

Danica's blue eyes wildly explored Claire's body. "Are you kidding me? How long has she been like this?"

"Since sunset on Halloween," Claire informed her. "When I performed the ritual to bind him to me, I also gave myself to the dark side of magic. Now it protects me."

Danica stepped closer to Claire. "This has to stop, Claire. You can't get away with this. I'll go to the police."

Claire's maniacal laughter chilled Danica to her very core. "And tell them what? Burt died of a heart attack. The autopsy will back up that fact. He was not robbed and had no marks of violence on his body. You go to the police with stories of ghosts and black magic, and you will be the one getting locked up in the psych ward, Danica." She turned away and moved through a doorway behind her. "I will never free Gaston. He's mine forever," she added, and then disappeared into the darkness of the next room.

Danica glared at Gaston. "You should have told me!"

He floated to her side. "I couldn't tell you because you would have tried to talk me out of it."

"One night together was not worth this, Gaston. You are bound to her? What does that even mean?"

He sighed and ran his hand through his wavy, brown hair. "It means I must do her bidding. I'm hers to command."

"How could you go along with that?"

"I wanted you. I was desperate…and I don't regret it, Danica. Claire will make it so we can be together, always."

"Claire will pull us apart, can't you see that, Gaston? She controls you now, and she wants me for her son, not you. She will use her power over you to push me together with Paul, and keep you as her minion."

"But you don't love him, you love me!"

Suddenly, the jingle of keys in the heavy front door made Danica spin around. The thick oak door burst open and Paul stepped inside. His eyes immediately went to the love seat.

"Where is she?"

"Taking a bath," Danica calmly assured him. "What are you doing back so soon?"

He went to the decoratively carved walnut coffee table in front of the love seat. "I was in the pharmacy when I realized I forgot the stupid prescription." He picked up a slip of white paper from the table. "You're sure you're going to be all right with Mom?" he asked, worriedly taking in her face.

"Fine." She gestured to the front door. "Go and get her medicine,"

"I really hate that guy," Gaston snarled, standing beside her.

"At least you're getting Mom to clean up." Paul folded up the prescription and put it in his trouser pocket. "That's more than I could get her to do all afternoon. She must be calming down."

"We talked for a little while, and she seems to be doing better," Danica lied.

"You're a very good actress," Gaston joked.

"She talked?" Paul appeared amazed. "Then she is doing better." He ran his hand over the back of his neck. "Maybe she doesn't need the pills after all."

"Why don't you let me get her medicine?" Danica offered, suddenly wanting out of Claire's home. "You look like you could use a break."

He nodded. "I could use a drink."

"We all could," Gaston mumbled.

Danica motioned to the back of the house. "Go and fix yourself one while she's in the bath, and I'll get her medicine."

Paul pulled the prescription from his pocket and gave it to Danica. "Thank you," he added, reaching for his wallet. "Here. That should cover it." He handed her four twenty-dollar bills.

Danica took the money and turned for the door.

"You're really special, Danica," Paul said behind her.

"You're not really going to buy that line," Gaston snapped in her ear.

When she turned and saw Paul and Gaston standing side by side, staring at her, she noted the similarities between the men. Both had tall, lean figures, sharp features, and long, tapering hands; but it was the eyes that held the most striking differences. Gaston's light blue orbs appeared intense and ethereal, but Paul's deep green eyes were filled with warmth and understanding. She had never noticed before how calm Paul's eyes made her feel. Shoulder to shoulder with Gaston, he was suddenly the one who appeared familiar and comfortable.

"I think you're special too, Paul."

Gaston crossed his thick arms over his chest and glowered at her. "He's not the one for you, Danica."

The room began to close in on her and she grabbed for the door handle. When Danica stepped onto the street, Gaston followed her out the door.

"You're not actually falling for this man, are you?" he questioned.

Danica shut the front door and shoved the prescription and money into the front pocket of her blue jeans. "What was I supposed to say?" She started down the sidewalk toward Royal Street before he could reply.

"I felt what you felt in that room when you were looking at us," Gaston told her as he walked beside her. "If you allow yourself to fall for that man, you're letting Claire win."

She stopped in front of her cottage. "I'm not going to let Claire win, and I'm not going to let her keep you on a leash like some trained monkey."

"There is nothing you can do, Danica. What's done is done. I don't want you trying to take on Claire; she's too powerful."

Danica headed down the sidewalk again. "Then I'll have to find someone just as powerful to help," she muttered over her shoulder.

He fell in step beside her. "Who?"

"I don't know," she replied with a note of aggravation in her voice.

Gaston suddenly pulled up next to her.

Danica looked back and saw him staring down at the sidewalk below his feet, marking the edge of her property.

"When you come home, we need to talk about this," he asserted, and then disappeared.

Danica shook her head and walked on. "Now you're beginning to sound more like a husband and less like a ghost."

CHAPTER 13

All the next day, Danica was distracted and unable to concentrate at work. As she sat in her cubicle and stared at a rough draft for a new ad campaign on her computer screen, she kept thinking of Gaston.

Claire's disclosures from the night before had been eating away at her. Why had Gaston committed himself to the woman, and what did Claire have planned for him? Perhaps the most unsettling part of the entire situation for Danica was that she was the reason for all the trouble. If she had not returned to her childhood home, Gaston would never have allowed Claire control over his soul.

When five o'clock finally rolled around, Danica rushed from her office building and to the nearby trolley line, anxious to get home. As she stood in the crowded trolley and a cool November breeze wafted through the open windows, Danica's thoughts strayed to Paul.

The comparisons between Paul and Gaston the night before had taken Danica by surprise. For most of her life, she had compared every man she had ever met to Gaston. But for the first time, she had found someone to measure Gaston against, and the differences, more than the similarities, had riveted her. As she remembered the way the two men had looked, standing side by side, it became readily apparent that Paul had possessed something that Gaston had lacked…the glow of life. The energy shining from Paul's green eyes had comforted her last night. Amid the chaos of everything swirling in her head at the time, she had only felt peace with Paul.

While exiting the dark green trolley car on Canal Street, Danica pondered what Claire had told her. The possibilities ahead for Gaston were daunting, and Danica knew she was out of her element. Black magic was something that was talked about on ghost tours or in voodoo shops, but not a topic that she knew anything about, let alone knew how to fight.

"I've got to find someone who knows what to do," she mumbled as she walked down Royal Street, heading for home.

When she reached the corner of Royal Street and St. Peter's Street, her eyes wandered over to St. Anthony's Garden. A black iron fence enclosed the secluded green oasis behind the stately towers of St. Louis Cathedral. Always a welcome spot amid the noisy surroundings of the French Quarter, the garden was named for St. Anthony, but dedicated to the memory of a Spanish curate, Antonio de Sedella, also known as Pere Antoine. The garden's western exposure had always attracted artists in the community wanting to display their works along the iron fence. As the last tendrils of the setting sun shone down along the array of paintings hanging from the old black fence, Danica stopped for a moment and peered down the shaded recesses of the famous Pirate's Alley next to the garden. She saw Jackson Square on the other side of the alley, and then she remembered the old fortuneteller, Madame LeJeune. Suddenly, an idea overtook her, and Danica turned into the alley, making her way speedily toward the square.

It did not take long for Danica to find the old fortuneteller sitting behind her plain wooden table beneath the shade of an oak tree along the edges of the black fence. Madame LeJeune was curled up in her chair with her arms crossed over a light blue shawl. Her head was tilted slightly to the side and her were eyes closed. But when Danica stood before her table, Madam LeJeune's disconcerting hazel eyes opened.

"I knew you'd come back."

Danica took a seat in the brown chair before the table. "I need your help, Madame LeJeune." She placed her briefcase down on the gray slate at her feet.

"Ah, then it has begun," the older woman whispered.

"What has begun?" Danica questioned. "How do you know about any of this? How did you know about Gaston?"

Madame LeJeune proudly raised her head as she pulled her bright blue shawl closer around her shoulders. "Did he tell you that Marna LeJeune was regarded as a great medium in her time? It was one of the reasons Gaston Deslonde wanted her. It is a gift she passed down to all the women in her family."

Danica sat back in her chair. "Are you telling me you're related to Marna?"

She dipped her head. "She was my great, great aunt. Her spirit talks to me, and that's why I took her last name, out of respect. She was the one who first warned me about your dark man."

"Has she told you what has happened to him?" Danica asked, folding her arms over her chest.

"He has become trapped with black magic, and sold his soul to another in order to be with you. But this can't last. The one he belongs to is dangerous. You must help to free him."

Danica leaned forward and rested her folded arms on the wooden table. "How do I do that?"

Madame LeJeune closed her eyes and sat very still for a moment. Danica skeptically watched her performance. Con artists and those wanting to part eager tourists from their money filled the French Quarter streets on any given day of the week. Trusting one of the street performers was difficult enough for Danica, and Madame LeJeune's theatrical display was not helping bolster her confidence. When Madame LeJeune finally opened her eyes, she placed one hand over Danica's arm.

"Return home, now. They're looking for you. Something has happened," Madame LeJeune stated in an ominous voice.

"What has happened?"

"Go," Madame LeJeune ordered. "The man from the other night needs you."

"Who? Gaston?" Danica rose from her chair.

"No, the other one. The man with the eyes that bring you comfort."

Danica picked up her briefcase and was about to go when Madame LeJeune stood from her chair. "Be careful, child. You're about to enter the lion's den, and I'm afraid all you have to protect yourself is a dead man's love and nothing more."

Danica slung the strap from her briefcase over her shoulder. "I thought love conquered all."

"Only in the movies, child." Madame LeJeune nodded back toward Chartres Street. "Now go, and when you need me again, I'll find you."

Danica gazed once more into the woman's odd eyes and then took off at a brisk pace across the square. When she came to Chartres Street, she turned right, rushing toward Dumaine.

It did not take long for her to reach the street leading to her cottage, and when Danica turned the corner for home, she froze. Parked outside Claire's cottage were two police cars and a black windowless Suburban with "New Orleans Parish Coroner's Office" posted along the side.

Danica ran to the front door of Claire's home. As she reached the entrance, the heavy front door opened and a uniformed police officer walked outside. He waved for her to stop as she sprinted for the door.

"Ma'am, you can't go in there," the short policeman declared as he held his hands out to her.

"But I know Claire Mouton. Is she all right? What has happened?"

"Danica?" Paul stepped out the door and immediately pulled her into his arms. He held her for a moment, squeezing her tight.

"Paul, what's wrong?"

Paul stood back from her and glimpsed the police officer. He took Danica's arm and slowly led her to her side gate.

"Mom's dead," he disclosed in a wavering voice. "I came back from making arrangements for Burt at the funeral home and I found her in the bathroom. She had taken one of Burt's guns and…." His voice caught in his throat. Paul ran his hand over his brow. "She shot herself."

"What?" Danica almost screamed. "But Claire was fine yesterday afternoon. I know you were worried about her, but she—"

"She has attempted suicide in the past, Danica," Paul admitted with a pained expression. "After my father died, she took a bottle of pills. I found her then, too, only this time she meant to die."

Danica put her arms about his shoulders and hugged him. "I'm so sorry, Paul. I know how hard it is to lose your mother."

Paul stood back from her. "You do know, don't you?"

"Mr. Mouton?" A police officer motioned to Paul from Claire's front door. "Can we speak with you for a moment?"

Paul took Danica's hand. "I have to finish up with them."

Danica nodded and gave his hand an encouraging squeeze. "Is there anything I can do?"

"Be around in a little while?" He sighed and then let go of her hand. "I think I'm going to need a drink," he added.

"I'll be here," she whispered to him.

Paul turned and walked back to his mother's house.

Danica slipped through her black gate and made her way down the narrow alleyway to her back doors. After she had placed her briefcase and purse down on the kitchen counter, Danica called into her darkened cottage. "Gaston?"

"I'm here," he answered, and his image emerged from the arched doorway to her office.

"Did you see what happened?"

Gaston looked glumly at the floor. "She began cooking breakfast this morning like she did every morning. She was in the middle of making Burt's scrambled eggs when she realized he was gone. It hit her very hard."

"But I thought she wanted to be rid of Burt. You said that was her grand plan. It was why she worked her magic on you and why she set me up with Paul."

"It may be what Claire thought she wanted, but when she was confronted by the reality of him being gone, she became undone."

Danica rubbed her hands over her face. "Paul told me she tried to kill herself after his father died."

"She mentioned that to me. She kept going on and on about the pain she felt in her heart. I guess in the end she really loved Burt."

Shaking off thoughts of Claire, Danica slid her light green pantsuit jacket from around her shoulders. "Well, at least now they're together."

"They're not together, Danica."

She dropped the jacket on top of her briefcase. "She's dead, of course they're together."

Gaston stood defiantly before the arched entrance. "Burt crossed over, but not Claire. She committed suicide, and such acts have a way of blurring the doorway to the other side for spirits. I've seen it before here in this cottage. When those two men were living here, the one that was killed moved on, but the one who killed himself stayed behind."

Danica recalled what she knew about the former residents as she stared at Gaston. "Are you telling me that Elliot is here in this house?"

"Elliot is in the air here, but he has never taken any form. He chooses not to."

She ran her hands up and down her bare arms, staving off the chill in the kitchen. "But what difference would suicide make? Death is death, isn't it?"

"Death is not as clear-cut as you think. The issues you had in life still manifest themselves after you die. Leaving the physical body doesn't relieve the pain of the soul, only the pain of the body. Sometimes a soul can't leave until they have worked through their issues, or have made amends."

Danica knitted her brow. "Amends? To whom?"

"To those who suffered because of their death. Taking your life is a selfish act because you only think of what you must endure. But when someone does what Claire did there are emotional scars embedded on the ones who are left behind. It's to those individuals that the spirit must make amends."

Danica shook her head, feeling overwhelmed. "How does a spirit make amends?"

"Your world is filled with my kind, Danica. You may not see us or hear us, but we are here: mothers and fathers who will not part from their children, family members who remain behind to keep an eye on other family and friends. Many times those who were there for you in life are still there for you in death. The only divide between us is not an emotional one, but a physical one."

"Are there a lot of souls who have not crossed over?"

He slowly nodded his head. "Crossing over for many means letting go."

"Letting go of what? This life?"

"No, letting go of fear. Fear can keep us from a great many things, Danica, both in life and in death. Fear of moving on ties many a ghost to a certain place." He pointed to his chest. "Like me. I feared moving on because I had not experienced all I had wanted in my life."

"What did you feel you had missed?"

"Love," Gaston answered with a slight grin. "All my life I searched for it, but never found it. When I died, I felt cheated that I had not experienced that once in a lifetime kind of love. And because of those feelings, I didn't cross over."

Danica took a few seconds to consider everything that he had told her. "But what of your children, and Marna? Didn't you want to see them again?"

Gaston ran a hand through his hair and his face grew dark. "Sometimes what we leave behind is a stronger pull than what we have waiting ahead. I loved my children, but my love for them wasn't as great as my selfishness. My desire to discover true love kept me weighted to this plane like an anchor moors a ship to depths of the ocean. I can't describe what or how this happens, but for a brief second you have a choice, and what is inside your heart decides for you, not your brain or thoughts. What you feel, have always felt, that's what determines your ability to move on. Those who have known love move on because they believe love continues on the other side. I've never known such depth of emotion, and my doubt held me back. That was until I met you. Ever since the day you first entered this home, with your long-pigtails and gap-toothed smile, I fell in love with you. I watched you grow and waited for you after you left. I knew you would come back to me, and I knew you would one day love me, too."

Exasperated, she threw her hands up. "But how does that change anything?"

"It has filled in the blanks from my life and answered questions left lingering after my death. I now know that I am worthy and capable of loving someone with every inch of my soul, and that has given me a sense of peace, and a desire to move on."

"Then why don't you go?"

"There's more to it than that, Danica."

She marched directly up to him. "I saw that fortuneteller at Jackson Square on my way home, Madame LeJeune. I think she knew about Claire killing herself, and she said something to me about your being tied to her black magic."

His dark scowl loomed in front of her. "Why did you go back to that old fool?"

Danica folded her arms over her chest, unflustered by his furor. "She's not a fool, Gaston. She knows things."

"She's a con artist and a charlatan, out to take away your money."

"She's also a distant relative of Marna's. Did you know that?"

Gaston eyes burned with rage. "Did she tell you that?"

"I think you already suspected; I could see it in your eyes the other night."

He turned away from her. "I sensed it. I could feel a connection with her, and she looks like Marna. Her eyes are the same."

"Why didn't you say something to me?"

"What difference would it have made?" he argued over his shoulder.

"It would explain how she knows so much about you and me. She told me Marna was a medium, and it was the main reason you took her into your home."

Gaston let out a weary sigh as he eased around to face her. "It's true, Marna had a gift. The judge who kept her before me used her talents as a medium to his advantage. He was never interested in her as a lover. However, I was very interested. Marna was a beautiful woman, and many men sought her affections, but I was the only one she wanted to be with."

"Was it the challenge or the woman you wanted?" Danica scoffed.

Gaston shook his head. "In the beginning, it was the challenge. In a time where a man was judged by what he possessed and not what he did, keeping Marna was important to me. After a while, I grew very fond of her. She taught me a great many things about life and death."

"What did she teach you about death?"

"Marna taught me about the other side, how to speak with the dead, and how to break through the veil between the living and the dead. Marna made me see beyond the physical world."

Danica became intrigued by his words. "How did she do that?"

"She opened my mind. I watched her when she went into trances to speak to the dead, listened to what she said, and believed her. That's all it takes to change a mind…the power of belief."

A sudden knock on the back entrance to the cottage interrupted them.

Danica turned from Gaston. "That might be Paul."

"You care for him, don't you?"

She reached for the doorknob. "His mother just committed suicide, Gaston. Of course I care."

When Danica opened her doors, she was rather surprised to see Carl standing in the courtyard. Wearing his usual black biker attire, his bald head glistened beneath the late afternoon sun.

"Did you hear what happened? Claire blew her brains out in her bathroom," he declared with all the enthusiasm of a nine-year-old child.

Danica ran her hand over her brow as she reigned in her desire to throttle him. "Yes, I know, Carl. Her son, Paul, told me earlier."

Carl casually stepped inside Danica's back door. "I knew that old lady had a screw loose. Mr. Georges, on the other side of the street, told me about poor Burt this morning. See what happens when you sleep all day? You miss all the mini-dramas."

"Carl, perhaps we could discuss this another time. Right now I'm a little—"

"He's here." Carl scanned her office doorway.

Danica's heart dropped. "Who's here?"

"Can't you smell that? It reeks of cigars and brandy. They were the two favorite things of Gaston Deslonde. He must be here." Carl paused for a moment, and then smirked at Danica. "I think he likes you."

"Tell that obnoxious cretin to get the hell out of here!" Gaston shouted.

Danica was startled by the harshness in Gaston's voice.

"You can't smell that?" Carl questioned, staring into her face. "It's so strong."

Danica shrugged and tried to exude an air of disinterest. "Maybe you're just one of those sensitive people. I can't smell a thing."

"He feels pretty angry. Which should be no surprise. From what I read, the guy had a hell of a temper."

"Get him out of here, Danica!" Gaston howled.

Danica took a step closer to Carl, ignoring Gaston. "He had a temper?"

A rush of wind blew past Danica and one of the french doors to the courtyard slammed against the kitchen wall.

Danica and Carl both looked to the door. But only Danica could see Gaston standing by the open doorway, pointing outside to the courtyard.

"Oh, yeah, he's pissed," Carl affirmed. "Just goes to show you, angry man, angry ghost."

Danica turned to Carl. "What are you talking about?"

Carl clucked, expressing his disappointment. "You didn't read those papers I gave you, did you? Otherwise, you'd know about the rumors."

Danica swiveled her eyes to Gaston. "What rumors?"

Carl's brown eyes lit up, seeming pleased to be able to tell her of his research. "After his death, a lot of people in the city began to believe he didn't die of yellow fever, but at the hands of his mistress. She was supposed to be some kind of witch. Many thought she made up his will and then killed him after he signed it. I saw an old copy of his will down at the hall of records, and it was dated two days before he died. His wife contested the will in court, claiming his mistress, a woman named Marna LeJeune, had forged it. His wife produced a separate will signed two years earlier by Gaston Deslonde, leaving everything to her, including his New Orleans property. The entire court case was covered by the local newspaper at the time."

"But that wouldn't mean she killed him," Danica pointed out.

"No, but it would explain why he still haunts his place. He was murdered by Marna, and somehow his spirit seeks revenge."

"Enough!" Gaston screamed.

"Did you hear that? It sounded like a man's voice." Carl grinned at her. "Or maybe it was your fictional cat?"

Danica rubbed her hand over her forehead. "Yeah, about that…."

"Don't worry about it," Carl assured her, shaking his head. "Who wants to admit they have an angry ghost?"

Gaston knocked an impatient fist into the wall, sending a loud thud throughout the kitchen.

Danica frowned at Gaston. “Perhaps you should go, Carl. Maybe all of this talk about murder and his will is upsetting the poor ghost.”

“Cool, I understand. You’ve got to live here, not me. Don’t need a pissed off spirit banging around the place at night.” Carl turned to the doorway and stopped. “Were you close with crazy old Claire?” he added.

“I think I’m closer with her son than I was with her,” she admitted.

Gaston gave an incredulous snort. “Oh, now you’re admitting you like him.”

“Wow!” Carl exclaimed, gazing about the kitchen. “I think I just heard your ghost again.”

Danica hurried him out the doors. “I’ll let you know what I find out about Claire,” she told him, motioning to the courtyard.

“Yeah, yeah,” Carl admitted, looking a little distracted as he stepped out the doorway. “I guess this means we’ll have another ghost around the place.”

Danica’s stared at his thick back. “Another ghost? What are you talking about, Carl?”

“Claire killed herself, and from what I’ve read about ghosts, that pretty much guarantees a haunting.” Carl stepped further out onto the courtyard and glanced back at Danica. “You gonna be all right?”

“Fine, Carl. Don’t worry about me.” Then she hastily smacked the back doors closed.

“Impossible man!” Gaston roared. “Don’t you dare believe any of that crap he told you about Marna. She was good to me, and I wanted to leave her my house. I wanted to sign that will.”

Danica kept her eyes peeled on the french doors in front of her. “But did she make the will out?”

“At my request,” he admitted behind her. “I was growing weaker and I knew I was going to die. I asked her to write it out for me. The physician who was tending to me, Clarence Dupuy, witnessed my signature. Marna had nothing to do with it.”

“Then why the rumors?”

“Because Marna was misunderstood and she was labeled as a witch by many who knew me, including my wife. Clarinda hated Marna and tried to do everything in her power to separate us.”

“So Marna never poisoned you?”

He shook his head and walked to the kitchen counter. “If anything, she saved me from a very painful death.”

Danica moved closer to him. “How did she save you?”

Gaston did not answer right away, and Danica patiently observed as the light drained from his face.

"I asked her to end my pain. Those last few days were agony, and I lingered for so long. The doctor believed I would recover, but inch-by-inch the fever took my strength. I was a very healthy man, and I had survived quite a few afflictions in the past. But as the days went on, I was tired and done with the pain. I asked Marna to make me a potion to end it. At first she refused, but when I told her I would leave her everything in New Orleans, then she agreed. The day after I signed the will, she mixed a sleeping draught and added poppy seeds to it. I remember it was bitter, very bitter, and I chased it with brandy. Not long after I felt my body become heavy with sleep. I was dreaming about going back to Deslonde Plantation and seeing my children again, and then I felt my body get lighter. I rose up from the bed and looked down to see Marna weeping over me, and that was when I knew I was gone. The next thing I remember, I was standing in the parlor of my home and watching the funeral director come to collect my body."

"You committed suicide?"

He banged his fist down on the white-tiled countertop. "Yes, I took my life, is that what you needed to hear?" He kept his eyes from looking at her. "Marna helped me, but I was the one who drank her death draught."

Danica ran her hand over the back of her neck. "Why didn't you want to tell me this before?"

He lowered his head. "Because I was ashamed, Danica. Ashamed I wasn't strong enough or brave enough to hold on until the end. I had to take the coward's way out."

"There's nothing wrong in wanting to end your pain, Gaston. We do that for patients dying of cancer or other horrible diseases. Some states even allow assisted suicide."

"But those are laws. Man-made laws. Not the laws of nature," he maintained.

"What about free will? Don't we have a choice to end our lives when we wish?"

"Not according to the eyes of the church," he declared.

She shook her head. "That's religion, Gaston, not nature."

"It's belief, Danica. I believed I sinned, and that sin has damned me to this earth."

"I think you damned yourself, Gaston. Is that why you haunt this place, because you feel guilty about what you did?"

He began pacing back and forth in the kitchen. "I was supposed to be a man. Strong, determined, and able to face whatever destiny was chosen for me. But I was afraid, afraid of suffering and…."

She stepped in front of him. "What were you afraid of?"

He stopped pacing and leveled his bright blue eyes on her. "Have you ever seen someone who survived yellow fever, Danica? They are frail, weak, and have to be cared for always. I didn't want to become like so many other men I had seen who survived the outbreaks in the past. They were but pitiful shells of their former selves. I couldn't live like that, and I never wanted to burden Marna with a broken man."

"Did you ask Marna what she wanted, or did you just tell her what to do?"

He raised his head haughtily. "It was not her place to offer an opinion on the matter. It was my choice."

"But did you ask her?"

"No. She begged me not to leave her, but I did not listen. I wasn't concerned about her feelings, only my pain."

Danica mulled over his words. "What if it had been me taking care of you and not Marna? Would you have disregarded my feelings as easily as hers?"

He waved his tapering hand at her. "That question is irrelevant, Danica. It happened over a hundred and fifty years ago. You're the woman you are now because of the time in which you were raised. Marna was a product of her time. The question has no merit."

"She was a woman, just like me, Gaston. If I had been there, if you had loved me then, would you have left me, too?"

His bold eyes stared into hers as the corners of his mouth stretched into a disapproving scowl. "Yes," he finally answered. "I would not have wanted you to care for me. You would have eventually hated me for tying you down, and our love would have vanished." He turned away from her. "That's something I could not bear, then or now."

"Love is for the good times and the bad times, Gaston. In sickness and in health, for richer or poorer…." Danica purposefully did not say the rest.

He faced her. "Until death do us part. I know the words, Danica. How does that apply to us? I'm already dead. What bond can unite us?"

"The bond of love," Danica countered. "I thought that mattered to you."

He let out a long sigh and ran his hands over his face. "It does mean something to me. My question is…what does it mean to you? You're the one with life still left to live. Are you prepared for what loving me can mean?"

A loud rap on her front shutters made Danica turn away from Gaston.

"It's him," Gaston muttered.

Danica hurried from the kitchen, grateful for the opportunity to avoid answering Gaston's question. She hated to admit it, but the idea of spending the rest of her life waiting for Gaston had been consuming her thoughts. She didn't know if she was strong enough for that kind of relationship. And now with Claire dead, she wondered if another Halloween night would even be possible.

When she pushed back her front shutters and saw Paul standing before her home, the growing doubts she had about a future with Gaston began to take hold. As she took in the attractive man waiting on her doorstep with his rumpled suit and disheveled hair, her body suddenly yearned to reach out to him.

"You're falling for him," Gaston calmly stated behind her. "I can feel it."

Paul stepped inside her open doors. "Hey, Danica," he said, sounding every bit as fatigued as he looked. "The police are just finishing up next door."

"How are you holding up?"

His shoulders sagged forward, burdened by his grief. "I think I could really use that drink about now."

"Don't even think about it, Danica," Gaston warned. "I will not have him in our home."

"How 'bout we go down the block to Harry's Bar and I buy you a drink?" She turned back to Gaston. "I don't have anything stronger than tea in the house."

Paul's dull green eyes flashed with disappointment. "Fine. I'll meet you out front in about ten minutes."

Danica worriedly considered the deep lines etched into his wide brow. "I know you may not want to go to a bar with a lot of—"

He held up his hand to her. "No, it's fine. I think a bar might be better for me right now. More distractions and less opportunity to think about everything."

The guilt gnawing at Danica's insides won her over. "I could go to the market around the corner and pick up something. Scotch, perhaps?"

Paul's face brightened with relief. "Yeah, scotch." He paused and gave her a hint of his crooked smile. "Thanks for understanding."

"I know how it feels, Paul. I've been there before."

"I'll come over once I get the police out of my hair."

She put her hand on one of the open doors. "Is there anything else I can get for you?"

"No, just the scotch," he admitted. "And to be able to spend some time with you."

Danica stomach fluttered with anticipation. "I'll see you in a little while." Then she turned away and closed the doors.

"I will not have him in my house!" Gaston objected next to her.

Danica secured the deadbolt. "It's my house, Gaston. He needs a friend right now. Don't you dare try and pull anything!"

As she hastened to the kitchen for her purse, she expected Gaston to follow her and continue his tirade against her seeing Paul. But when he never showed himself again, Danica became alarmed. His stubborn silence was beginning to worry her more than his bitter remonstrations.

CHAPTER 14

"I still can't believe this is happening," Paul uttered as he sat on Danica's sofa and cupped a half-empty glass of scotch in his hands.

"When my mother died, I think I just walked around in shock for a week," Danica told him as she sat next to him on the sofa, holding her glass of the amber-colored liquid. "My father tried to be brave, but when I wasn't looking, he cried. I remember how we cleaned this cottage from floor to ceiling when we came home from the hospital that day. The funny thing was, one minute she was there and the next she was gone. It was as if she just stepped into another room."

"Hardly like stepping into another room, Danica," Gaston offered as he stood above the couch, staring at the two of them.

Danica glared at him.

"Must have been hard to lose your mother at such a young age. I think a girl needs her mother to help her through the difficulties life throws at women."

Danica turned back to Paul. "I don't think what women go through is any different than what men experience."

"But women have children, raise them, and always have that nurturing way about them." He lifted his drink to his lips. "I think that's what you missed sharing with your mother." He took a long pull from his glass.

"He can't be serious," Gaston howled. "Women are made for such things."

"You're right." Danica eyed Paul's long hands. "It would have been nice having another woman to talk to about things. I'm so glad you're aware of the challenges of being a woman, Paul. Some men are completely oblivious to that fact."

Paul stared into his glass. “My mother taught me a great deal about women.”

“And what about your ex-wife? What did she teach you?”

“How a woman ought not to be,” Paul commented with a slight smirk. “Everything about Madison makes me cringe with regret. I should have seen the kind of woman she was. My mother saw and warned me, but we never listen to our parents, do we?” He paused for a moment as his eyes stared into hers. “I hope you had some good friends or close relatives to confide in when you were growing up.” He took another sip from his drink.

Danica rolled her glass in her hands. “I did have this one friend. He was around a great deal after my mother’s death, before my father relocated us to Florida. I got to share a lot with him. He helped me through a tough time.”

“Who was he?” Paul probed.

“An older man who was a close neighbor. He listened to my troubles and made things easier for me.”

“Does he still live around here?”

Danica’s eyes found Gaston. “No, he should have moved on a long time ago.”

“Are you suggesting I leave you two alone?” Gaston huffed.

“He was also a rather ornery older man who was always very protective of me. I guess he felt I needed to be taken care of, but I was a little girl then, and not a grown woman.”

Gaston folded his arms over his broad chest and sneered at her. “I’ll go then, but if I hear anything remotely sounding like kissing, I’ll come back and set his pants on fire.”

“Must have been nice to know someone cared about you so much,” Paul remarked.

Danica watched as Gaston’s figure dissolved before her eyes. “It was comforting at times, and then sometimes suffocating.”

“I heard that,” Gaston hollered as the last vestiges of his form faded from view.

Danica breathed a sigh of relief to be out from beneath his dissecting gaze.

Paul emptied the last dregs of scotch from his glass and reached for the bottle on the coffee table beside them. “My mother was the over-protective type when I was a kid.” He began to fill his glass. “Thank God for my father. He kept her doting at bay. He insisted I be a man, and not a momma's boy."

"What was he like?"

Paul shrugged slightly as he put the bottle back down on the dark coffee table. "A no-nonsense kind of man, but with a big, gentle streak. He tried to put on a stoic outward appearance, but once you got to know him, you could tell it was all for show. On the inside he was a gummy bear: soft, flexible, and very sweet."

"Sounds like a great guy."

Paul nodded. "He was. He held it together for our family." He leaned back against the sofa. "As you can probably guess, my mother wasn't the most resilient of individuals."

Danica placed her glass on the coffee table. "I think your mother was very resilient, Paul. She lived with a Burt for a long time, and probably put up with a great deal."

Paul tilted his head back and sighed. "Did that make her resilient, or a fool for putting up with that man for as long as she did?"

"She wasn't a fool, she was afraid. There's a difference. Sometimes it's easier to stay where you are than to face the world on your own. I know I felt that way for a while with Tom. Then there comes a point when you've had enough. We can never walk in another's shoes no matter how close we may feel we are to them. Sometimes a person's justifications for staying in an abusive relationship are difficult to explain. You can never understand a person's reasoning, but you must eventually learn to accept it."

"What about her reasons for killing herself?" Paul slammed his glass down on the coffee table. "I can never accept that. No matter what her excuses for staying with Burt, when she is finally free of that man, she puts a bullet in her head and leaves me…."

Danica put a comforting hand on his arm.

"I'm sorry," he whispered. "I'm angry and not used to a lot of alcohol."

"Maybe you should stay here for the night. I don't think you should be driving home after three straight glasses of scotch."

Paul shirked off her hand and stood from the sofa. "No, I'm fine."

Danica slowly rose to her feet. "You're not fine."

He turned to her. "I can't impose."

She gently brushed away a comma of hair that had fallen into his green eyes. "You're not imposing. I don't think you should be alone tonight."

Paul stepped closer to her. "I'm all right, Danica."

"I won't argue with you." She held up her outstretched hand. "Where are your car keys?"

He furrowed his brow. "Why?"

"I can't allow you on the roads. You could kill someone. Now give me your keys."

Paul shook his head and reached into the pocket of his trousers. He pulled out his keys and placed them in her waiting hand. "Happy?"

"Very." She motioned to the sofa. "It may not seem like much, but this is a very comfortable sofa. I'll get you a pillow and some extra blankets." When she turned to go, Paul reached for her hand.

"When all of this mess is over, after we have put their funerals behind us, I want to see you again."

The hint of lust in his eyes made her body pulse with desire. She wanted him. She wanted him just as much as she wanted Gaston. But Paul was real, and there were no curses, or spells, or special nights when the veil between life and death was at its thinnest required for them to be together.

Danica smiled for him. "I would like to see you again, too."

"We could have dinner at my house. I am particularly good at spaghetti and meatballs," he added with a proud grin.

"You hate Italian food," Gaston's voice intruded.

"I love Italian, Paul. That sounds wonderful."

Paul let go of her hand. "Then it's a date."

She nodded in agreement. "It's a date."

"Should I light some candles and put on romantic music for the two of you?" Gaston's deep voice echoed in her ear.

Danica blushed. "I'll just go and get your blankets." She abruptly bolted from the room.

When she entered her bedroom, Gaston was already waiting, pacing back and forth in front of her picture window.

"I can't believe this. The man comes over, flashes you his crooked smile, and you melt like ice on a hot summer's day. Are you that easily swayed by the opposite sex, Danica? In my time you would have been labeled a flirt."

"In your time I would have been married off and made into a breeding machine by the age of fifteen. What am I supposed to do, Gaston? Shoot down his ego right after his mother just killed herself? I can't crush him like that. I'm not you."

His eyes turned to her, fuming. "What is that supposed to mean? Are you saying I am insensitive and uncaring?"

She went to her closet. "Yeah, that's what I'm saying."

"What, now he's turning you against me?"

"Jesus, Gaston, were you this insecure when you were alive?" She pulled the closet door open. "For the tough man you keep telling me you were, you sure are exhibiting an awful lot of insecurity right now."

"Because I am a man—"

"Were a man," she jumped in.

"I'm still a man, and I know how men operate. He's toying with you, Danica. Playing on your sympathies to get you into bed."

She grabbed a pale pink blanket from the top shelf of her closet. "What did you play on to get me into bed?"

"What?" he shouted.

She calmly turned to him, holding the blanket against her chest. "You came to me that night in the guise of another, something I'm still having a hard time getting my head around." She paused and forced the image of Burt's body making love to her from her mind. "Then you professed your feelings for me, seduced me, and told me after the fact that if we're lucky we can get together once a year and screw like rabbits."

"I didn't hear you complaining that night."

"Of course not. I was in awe that you were with me, but since then I've had time to think."

"You've changed you mind about me, is that it?"

She hugged the blanket closer to her body. "No, I haven't changed my mind. I'm just…afraid, Gaston. What is to become of us, of me?" She turned away. "I know that sounds selfish, but there have been times I wanted you to hold me or to feel your hand, and I couldn't. It's not about the sex, Gaston. It's about support. How can you support me when you aren't even real?"

He floated around in front of her. "I'm real, Danica."

"Are you?" She stepped around him and went to the door. "I'm beginning to wonder, Gaston."

Danica returned to the living room to discover Paul had already removed his suit jacket and tie and was unbuttoning his shirt. When she glimpsed his tanned, muscular chest beneath his white shirt, she swallowed hard.

"Here's your blanket," she said, placing the neatly wrapped blanket on the corner of the sofa closest to her.

Paul pulled his shirt out from his pants and continued undoing the last of the buttons. "Thanks." He nodded to the blanket. "Do you have a pillow?"

Danica tore away from gawking at his toned body and went back to her bedroom.

"He excites you, doesn't he?" Gaston's voice asked as she headed down the hall to her bedroom once more.

"Shut up," she muttered.

After she retrieved an extra pink pillow from her bed, she hurried back to the living room. Paul was spreading out the blanket on the sofa. His shirt had been discarded on a chair to the side, along with his tie and jacket.

"Here," Danica said, trying not to stare at his smooth chest.

"I really appreciate it," he said softly.

"There's a new toothbrush under the sink in the bathroom if you want it. You're welcome to anything in the kitchen." She shrugged. "Make yourself at home."

"I don't want to be a bother."

"You're not a bother, Paul." Overwhelmed by her attraction to him, her eyes nervously darted about the living room. "Well, I'll see you in the morning. The coffeemaker is set for seven."

"That sounds good. I'll need to get out of here early tomorrow." He gave her a weak smile.

Danica turned on her heels and scrambled for her bedroom door. She was anxious to put a little space between her and the alluring Paul Gaudette.

***

The following afternoon when Danica returned from work, Paul was sitting on her shuttered front doorstep. Leaning against the wall next to him was a large, rectangular object covered in a blue padded blanket.

"Hello," he said as he stood up. "I was hoping to catch you."

Danica looked over his blue jeans and white T-shirt with ocean waves printed on it.

"What are you doing here?" she asked, glancing over his shoulder to Claire's front door. She spied the large white van parked in front of the home.

Paul waved back to his mother's house. "I had to meet the cleaning people here." He paused for a moment. "They needed to get in and…."

Danica placed a steadying arm on his shoulder. "You all right?"

"Not yet, but I'll get there." He pointed to the blanket next to him. "I wanted to give you this. Sort of as a thank you for all that you've done for me and for my mother. I know she would have wanted you to have it."

Danica stared down at the blanket-wrapped object. "That really wasn't necessary, Paul…what is it?"

"The portrait of that guy…you know, Mom's ghost, Garland."

"You mean Gaston."

"Yeah, him." He nodded to the painting. "I remembered how you admired it that night when you came to dinner, and I thought…."

Danica gestured to the thick blanket resting against her house. "I can't take this, Paul. It must be worth a fortune."

"Please, Danica, take it. It would make me happy to know that something my mother cared so much about has a good home."

A lightning bolt of guilt rumbled through Danica. "All right," she finally said with a nod of her head. "I'll just go around back to the kitchen, and then I can open the front shutters so you can bring it inside."

Paul smiled happily. "I'll even help you hang it."

Danica reached into her purse for her keys as she thought of how Gaston would react at seeing Paul lugging the portrait into her cottage. "That's really not necessary, Paul. It's very big and I don't want—"

"I insist," he said, leaning in closer to her.

Danica's stomach unexpectedly tingled with excitement as she felt the heat from his body brush against her skin.

She pulled her keys from her purse. "Perhaps in my office, above the mantle," she stated without thinking. "It might look nice there."

Danica rushed through the gate and down the narrow alleyway to the courtyard. When she reached her back doorway, she hesitated before she placed the key in the lock. She remembered what Gaston had said about feeling her emotions.

"Just pull it together, Danica," she mumbled. "Whatever you do, don't think of what the guy looks like naked."

She had just opened the rear door to the kitchen when Gaston suddenly appeared. "You are not serious about that stupid painting?"

She rolled her eyes. "What are you, a spy or a ghost?"

"I could hear you two talking through the front door," he snippily replied. "You can't hang that piece of crap in your office."

"Why?" She placed her handbag and briefcase on the kitchen counter. "It's a very good portrait of you." She waved her hand over his semi-solid body. "Or at least of who you used to be."

"My wife had the stupid thing commissioned after I settled in my house in the city. Clarinda said she wanted to remind me of what I had left behind. I wanted to get rid of it, but Marna insisted I keep it."

Danica walked through the kitchen. "Then how did it get in your attic?"

"I placed it there soon after it arrived," he explained as he followed her into her office.

She stopped and looked above the fireplace to the empty wall above the mantle. "I think it would look nice there."

"Danica, I insist you let the fool take the picture back to his mother's house."

She glared at him. "I can't do that, Gaston. I won't hurt his feelings because you're upset about a painting."

"Careful, my treasure," Gaston advised in aggravated voice. "You are getting too attached to this man."

Danica said nothing and turned away from him, heading toward the front of the house.

"Why won't you tell me the truth?" Gaston pleaded behind her.

As Danica reached for the door handle, she tried to think of something to tell him, something to soothe his jealousy, but her mind was blank. Lying to Gaston about her feelings for Paul would only make things worse between them. She did not want to hurt Gaston, but then again, she did not want to hurt Paul, either.

She turned back to Gaston. "Be nice."

"I make no promises, Danica."

Sighing with frustration, she turned the doorknob and pulled the doors open. As she reached for the bolt holding the shutters in place, a cool breeze brushed against her skin.

"Just remember, I'll be watching," Gaston whispered in her ear.

Danica angrily slammed the bolt back. "I know, Gaston. You're always watching."

***

"I think that's the perfect spot for it," Paul announced as he admired the portrait from the top of the stepladder in front of Danica's office mantle. "Gives the room a touch of aristocracy."

"Aristocracy?" Danica almost laughed as she reached for the hammer on the dark cypress mantle. "You mean class."

Paul climbed down from the stepladder. "No, I meant aristocracy. The guy exudes this superior aristocratic vibe from the portrait." Paul stepped to the floor. "He must have been one hell of an asshole."

"Danica!" Gaston shouted from the corner of the room where he had been quietly observing the pair. "Shut him up before I shove that hammer up his—"

"Paul," Danica said, cutting off Gaston's threats. "I seriously doubt Gaston Deslonde was…what you called him. From my research I discovered he was a pretty decent fellow and—"

"Your research? Please tell me you are not getting obsessed with this guy like my mother was?"

Danica shook her head. "Actually my neighbor, Carl, in the carriage house out back, did the research, not me. He brought over some articles he pulled off the Internet to help me deal with the ghosts."

Paul laughed as he folded up the stepladder. "Ghosts? What ghosts?"

Danica shrugged. "He insists Gaston Deslonde is haunting my house, as well as your mother's place."

He placed the stepladder against the wall and turned to Danica with a worried expression. "Do you think he is haunting your home?"

"Damn right I am," Gaston bellowed.

"No, of course not," Danica said, struggling to appear sincere.

Paul frowned slightly. "I thought you said you believed in all of this ghost stuff?"

Danica eyes drifted to Gaston in the corner of the room. "No, I believe in people and the emotions they impart on a place."

"Emotions?" Paul chuckled. "This building is brick and mortar. It was meant to house people, not emotions, and certainly not ghosts."

"Closed-minded ass," Gaston snarled.

"Perhaps the emotions, good and bad, people felt while living in a place leave some kind of imprint on a structure," Danica suggested.

"Danica, I'm an engineer. I have never heard of anything like that or studied such theories in school. It's a building. It has no life of its own, no energy field that keeps the past alive inside it." He paused and lowered his gaze to the floor. "If that were the case, there would still be feelings…emotions…left in my mother's home after…."

Danica's stomach fell to the floor as she remembered Paul's loss. "Oh God, I'm sorry…that was thoughtless of me."

Paul shook his head. "No, I'm the one who should be sorry. I shouldn't scoff at your beliefs. It's just that I keep thinking of my mother and what happened, and…." Paul perused the framed family pictures Danica had placed on the mantle beside him. "I should get back to the house and check on that cleaning crew."

"Of course, Paul, and thank you for doing this." She raised her eyes to the painting. "You're right; it does look wonderful there," she hastily added.

"It would look even better above your bedroom mantle, overlooking your bed," Gaston offered with a grin.

Paul moved toward the pocket doors that led to the living room. "The cleaning guys are probably wondering what happened to me." When he reached the living room he turned to Danica. "I know this might be out of line, but with everything that has happened, I feel like I am coming and going in all directions right now. I was wondering if you might consider lending me a hand with some of the funeral arrangements. I just got started on Burt's funeral, but now I guess I'll have to have one for Mom, too."

Danica came up to his side. "Are you sure? I mean, I would be happy to help you in any way I can, but I'm almost a stranger."

Gaston came up to her. "He's playing off your sympathy, trying to get closer to you."

"You're not a stranger to me, Danica," Paul declared. "I was never any good at planning such things. Even after my father died, I left most of these details to my mother. I figured I should have something small with immediate family and a few friends, but I'm not sure where to begin. Should I bury them together in our family crypt?"

"Why don't you get in touch with your mother's church and plan a service there for her and Burt before their funerals?" Danica suggested.

Paul nodded. "Yeah, I should do that today."

"After, you could have a small reception at your home."

Paul's brow crinkled with concern. "I don't know anything about catering or what to serve at something like that."

Danica placed her hand on his arm. “Why don’t you leave the reception to me?”

Paul clasped his hand over hers. “Thank you.”

“Do you know what you are doing?” Gaston softly questioned.

“I know exactly what to do,” she avowed as she removed her hand from Paul’s arm.

Danica walked to the entrance and opened the french doors for him. When she turned back to him, Paul kissed her on the mouth. The tingle that surged through Danica’s body was completely unexpected. But before she could return his kiss, Paul pulled away.

“I’ll call you later,” he whispered, and then darted out of the house.

“You should have slapped him,” Gaston shouted as he slammed the doors closed.

“Why would I do that? It was just a friendly kiss, Gaston.”

“It was more than that and you know it.” He came up to her, his eyes simmering with jealousy. “I felt your reaction, and your desire to kiss him back.” Gaston leaned over her petite figure. “Where I come from a woman sporting with two men at once would have been called a whore.”

“You son of a bitch. Need I remind you, you arrogant, egotistical asshole, that you’re not a man, but a ghost?”

His face contorted with anger. “Every time I long to pull you into my arms I am bitterly reminded of that fact, Danica.”

Danica instantly regretted her harsh words. He was right. It was cruel to flaunt her feelings for Paul in front of him, but what could she do? As long as she remained in that house, Gaston would be forever watching her every move.

“I’m sorry. I should have pushed him away,” she told him after a few uncomfortable seconds.

“No, it’s my fault.” Gaston came around to her side. “I’m asking too much of you. I’m a ghost and you’re a woman with…needs.”

“Gaston, please, it was just a kiss.”

Gaston shook his head and then began to fade away. “No, Danica. It was a beginning.”

CHAPTER 15

Four days later, Danica was standing on a red-bricked walkway and staring up at a wide, dark green double-gallery home in the Garden District of New Orleans. Swirling black wrought iron encircled a second-floor balcony, while a sweeping portico wrapped around the first floor, all supported by thick, white, round columns. White french windows beckoned from the first and second floors, with an arched oak doorway situated at the entrance. Tastefully decorated gardens done in white gardenias and pink azaleas curved around the red-bricked steps that led to the front door. Close to the entrance, an immense oak, blanketed in ivy vines, cast long shadows over the eastern portion of the home.

Danica luxuriated in the cool, crisp air and smelled the greenery around her. She loved living in the French Quarter, but there were times when she desperately missed having a lawn and garden to enjoy.

"I told you I would come and get you," a deep voice reprimanded from the doorway.

When Danica spotted Paul standing on the wide portico, she could not help but smile. He looked dashing in his double-breasted black suit, but the vulnerable look that had haunted his face for the past few days was still there.

He came down the steps toward her at a brisk pace. "Danica, I told you I was going to pick you up before the service. I didn't want you riding the streetcar," he said as he stopped before her. When he spied her face, his expression changed. "Are you all right? You look beat."

Danica rubbed her hand over her forehead, wishing she had applied more make up under her eyes to hide the dark circles. "I, ah, haven't been sleeping very well the past few nights."

Paul put his hands on her shoulders and carefully examined her eyes. "What's wrong?"

"Just these weird dreams that keep waking me up at night. It's nothing."

"What are your dreams about?" he asked.

"That's the funny part, I can't remember. I wake up, my heart is racing, but I can't remember what I was dreaming about."

He stepped beside her and rubbed his hand up and down her back. "I've probably been working you too hard. I know you've been busy getting that big presentation together for your client at the ad agency, in addition to helping me with this memorial service and reception stuff. I should not have asked so much of you."

"I wanted to help," Danica insisted.

"I know, but now I really feel guilty for not picking you up this morning. I can't believe you didn't wait for me."

She playfully punched his arm. "Don't be ridiculous, Paul. You don't need to do all of that driving today. You have to go to the airport for your Aunt Louise and Uncle Bob and then bring them to the service, and then bring them to their hotel after the reception. You didn't need the added worry of picking me up as well."

"It's bad enough I'm corralling you into helping me with the reception, but to have you take the streetcar here from the Quarter…you know I wanted to come and get you, Danica."

She patted her hand against his chest, feeling his strong muscles beneath the jacket of his suit. "I know, but I didn't want to be a bother. Besides, it's a beautiful fall day, and I really enjoy the streetcar."

"You're hardly a bother." He slipped his arm casually about her waist and guided her down the red-bricked walkway toward his home. "I don't know what I would have done without you these past few days."

"You've had a lot on your mind with the investigation and all," she assured him as they slowly made their way to his door.

"I had no idea there was so much involved in a police investigation. Between Mom's death and Burt's death, I haven't had a moment's peace from the NOPD."

"They have any news on what happened to Burt?"

Paul shook his head. "Nah, but they don't suspect foul play anymore. The coroner determined it was a massive coronary that killed him, and he did have a history of heart trouble. Now they're convinced he just wandered into Saint Louis Number One Cemetery with some late night Halloween tour group and got lost. Kind of odd he ended up in front of the Deslonde family tomb though."

Danica thought of the ghost she had left pacing in her living room. "Yes, that is odd."

Paul stopped in front of his door and removed his arm from about her waist. "Are you sure you don't want to go to the service? I know I asked you to help out with the reception, but it was never my intention to keep you from the memorial service."

"No, you go on, and I'll take care of everything here. It will be easier this way. I can have everything laid out and ready for your guests, and you won't have to rush back here after the service."

He clasped his arms about her waist. "You don't know how much this means to me." He lowered his head to her. "The past few days you have been my rock."

A swarm of butterflies tickled Danica's stomach. She blushed as she tried not to stare into his eyes. "I was just being a good friend, Paul."

"You were being a hell of a lot more than that." He leaned forward and kissed her lips.

At first, Danica was surprised by the touch of his lips, but then the heat from his body made her instantly forget about the neighbors who might be spying from their windows or the traffic passing by on the shady street. Slowly, she ran her hands up the front of his suit as his arms curled around her back. Danica's toes tingled, her heart raced, and her lips parted for him.

Paul pulled away. "Oh God, forgive me." He placed his forehead against hers and sighed into her cheek. "Here I am about to go to the memorial service for my mother and stepfather, and I am practically attacking you on the front doorstep of my home."

Danica ran her fingers down his cheek. "I wasn't exactly putting up a fight, Paul."

He slowly grinned. "You weren't, were you?"

She shook her head while flirtatiously smiling up at him.

He surveyed the gardens of his home and his eyes traveled to the street just at the edge of his walkway. "Tonight, after everyone has left, I want you to stay here with me." He turned back to her. "Say you will stay with me, Danica."

Danica pictured Gaston at home, waiting for her throughout the night. What would he say when she walked in the door the next morning? How would he react, knowing where she had been?

"I don't know, Paul." She pushed down her overwhelming yearning to stay. "You have a lot to get through today and you may not feel like having—"

"Is there someone else?" he interrupted.

She stepped back from his embrace. "What?"

He reached out for a tendril of her curly, chestnut hair that had fallen from her barrette. "I just get this feeling, like I'm not the only one vying for your affections. Is there another man?"

Danica's stomach clenched and she let out an uneasy breath. "No," she finally admitted. "There is no other man in my life."

A white van with Novelty Caterers emblazoned on the side pulled up to the curb in front of Paul's home.

"The caterers are here," he stated as he let her lock of hair fall from his fingers. "Do me a favor…wait until everyone has gone before you answer, and if you choose not to stay, then I will take you home. I don't want you riding that damned streetcar at night, or walking around the French Quarter alone. It isn't safe, Danica."

She nodded. "I promise I will wait for you to bring me home tonight."

He gave her a cocky grin. "That is if you decide you want to go home. I'm hoping I can get you to change your mind."

Paul started down the steps to the caterer's van before Danica could respond. She silently prayed for the strength to go home later in the evening. Every second she spent with Paul, the harder it was getting to push him away. She knew there would be hell to pay with Gaston if she did stay, but suddenly the idea of appeasing her ghost seemed inconsequential when compared to the allure of satisfying her burgeoning desires.

***

Paul's offer lingered in the forefront of her thoughts for the remainder of the afternoon and evening. Distracting her mind with the perils of empty food trays and clearing away dirty dishes, Danica rushed back and forth from Paul's gourmet kitchen, with its dark Italian tile counters and black appliances, to his beige-painted living room, with its grand mahogany inlaid mantle. Hoping to avoid Paul as much as possible, Danica tried to blend in with the numerous guests milling about the first floor of the home. But Paul was constantly checking on her whereabouts, often following her back and forth from the kitchen, and begging her to leave the domestic duties to the caterers.

"You're not the hired help," he chided as he took her elbow and guided her away from the kitchen entrance.

"I thought you wanted me to manage the food?" She fought back the flush of warmth she felt whenever he was near. "I didn't realize your mother and Burt had so many friends," she added, taking in the large group of people spilling over from the living room and into the white-tiled foyer and hallway.

"Most are friends from their church, and the rest are family." He paused and let go of her elbow. "You need to relax. I never intended for you to oversee the reception. I just wanted you to make sure the caterers didn't burn the place down while I was at the service." He turned to the living room and observed a small crowd of people standing beside the mahogany mantle. "Come, I want you to meet my Aunt Louise. She keeps asking me about the beautiful woman in the black dress."

"Paul, every woman here is wearing a black dress."

He leaned his lips closer to her ear. "Yes, but none of them are as beautiful as you."

Danica's legs almost gave out beneath her.

Paul took her hand in his and pulled her into the living room. "Now let me introduce you to everyone here, so they can go home and gossip about the two of us, plan our wedding, and decide what we should name our firstborn."

Danica was introduced to a slew of relatives from Claire's side of the family, as well as a few distant cousins related to Paul's late father.

But when Paul coaxed her across the living room to meet Aunt Louise, Danica felt her body grow cold when she absorbed the woman's pale brown eyes. They were exactly like Claire's, and even though Aunt Louise had a heavier build than Claire's delicate frame, it was obvious from the sharp cheekbones and slender mouth that Aunt Louise was Claire Mouton's sister.

"Claire often spoke of you," Aunt Louise said in the same soft voice as Claire. In fact, Danica found the woman's mannerisms almost identical to her dearly departed sister.

"I'm so sorry for your loss," Danica offered. "Claire was a good neighbor, and even though we did not know each other very long, I felt we had become friends."

Those pale brown eyes zeroed in Danica's face with all the intensity of a cat about to pounce on its prey.

"My sister was a kind soul, but not the wisest of individuals. Her taste in men left a lot to be desired." Aunt Louise swirled a glass of strong-smelling gin in her svelte hands.

"Now Auntie L," Paul jumped in. "Please don't bring up Burt again. It's over and done with."

"Burt Mouton drove my sister to her death. If he had not bought her that silly haunted house, none of this would have happened. I told you I was worried about the way she kept going on and on about that ghost of theirs."

"Ghost?" Danica looked from Paul to Aunt Louise. "You mean Gaston Deslonde?"

Aunt Louise nodded. "She researched the house before they had even purchased it. My sister was into ghosts. All her life she wanted to commune with the dead. That's why Burt bought her that damned place. She wanted to live in a haunted French Quarter home and have a ghost. She always talked about being some kind of medium with the dead."

Danica's eyes never wavered from Aunt Louise's face. "Did your sister ever talk about…witchcraft?"

Aunt Louise laughed, a funny cackle that sounded nothing like Claire's light, tinkling twitter. "She spent a small fortune buying books on spells for speaking with the dead, or raising the dead, or some such rot. She even went to a few voodoo priestesses in the Quarter, wanting to learn about incantations. Dragged me with her to one of those charlatans last time I came in for a visit. I told her then to get therapy, but all she talked about was wanting to get closer to her ghost, Gaston." Aunt Louise shook her head. "I swear she was besotted with the man."

"Are you saying she was in love with her ghost?" Danica asked, suppressing a sudden rush of dread.

"Claire was always impressionable. But after she did some research on the former owner of that house, she became infatuated with him, like he was going to rescue her from her life and lead her toward a new path. That is what she said last time I spoke with her."

"When was that?" Danica probed.

"Right before Halloween. She told me she was waiting for the magic of Halloween to awaken her powers and bring Gaston to her." Aunt Louise snorted with disgust. "Can you believe that? I even called Paul and told him to get her in to see someone. I warned him that she was about to lose it."

"That's why I was having dinner with Momma the night we met," Paul chimed in. "I wanted to check on her after Aunt Louise phoned me. I should have known something wasn't right when she insisted on showing you the room where that man died. Then when she talked about calling to him and…I should have taken her to get help."

Aunt Louise shook her finger at Paul. "Don't you do that, Paul. Don't blame yourself. Your mother made her own decision to leave this earth, and all we can do is abide by it. I always knew my sister would do something crazy like this in the end."

Paul's body wilted slightly and Danica could tell the events of the day were weighing on him more than he was letting on.

Aunt Louise rested a supportive hand on his shoulder. "I think when something like this happens, you can't judge a person. You can never know their pain or their thoughts at that moment when they decide to…leave. You just hope they have finally found peace."

Paul raised his eyes to her. "Peace?" His lips curled in a funny grin. "I hope so. I hope she has finally found that. God knows she never had it in life."

Aunt Louise offered an encouraging smile. "She's fine, Paul, and she is at peace. I promise you that."

But as Danica listened to the exchange between Paul and his aunt, she could not help but wonder if Claire Mouton was at peace. It just seemed to her that a life filled with so much bitterness might never find peace, even in death.

"Paul tells me you're a graphic designer, Danica," Aunt Louise commented, snapping Danica away from her thoughts. "So how do you like drawing pictures for a living?"

Danica could not help but smile. "I love it. Ever since I could pick up a crayon, I have been drawing pictures. It was an obsession when I was little. Now I get paid to do it."

Aunt Louise winked at her nephew. "I must say I've heard a great deal about you from Paul. Poor boy can't stop talking about you."

Paul rolled his eyes. "Thanks, Auntie L."

She coyly grinned at him. "Anytime, Paul." She handed him her glass. "Be a dear and get me another gin with a splash of tonic. I want to interrogate this young woman without you hovering over us."

Paul took her glass as he looked to Danica. "Ignore anything she says."

Danica smiled. "I'll try."

As Paul walked away, Danica ogled his powerful body hidden beneath his black suit.

"Boy, do you have it bad," Aunt Louise commented. "I may not know a lot, but I can still recognize desire, Danica, and you have definitely got it for my nephew."

Danica blushed, lifting her hands to her cheeks. "I'm sorry…I just don't know what to say except that I care—"

Aunt Louise raised her hand, silencing her. "Spare me. I'm not an idiot, and I can see my nephew is just as crazy about you."

"We've just started seeing each other, and right now we are good friends. I'm not sure if it will go any further than that, but—"

"So who is he?" Aunt Louise asked, cutting her off.

An uncomfortable burst of adrenalin jolted Danica's body. "Who?"

Aunt Louise studied Danica's eyes for a few moments. "There's someone else. Someone you're not quite sure about."

Danica said nothing but kept her polite smile glued into place.

"You care for this man, but there's a problem. If it were otherwise, you'd be telling me about him and not watching my nephew's fine ass as he walked out of the room."

Danica sighed. "It's complicated."

"Is he married?"

Danica nervously rubbed her hands together. "He has other obligations that keep him from being able to commit to me."

Aunt Louise snickered under her breath. "Is he a priest?"

Danica shook her head. "No, but it isn't going anywhere."

"You care for this man, and yet you have feelings for my Paul, as well. I'd say you have a dilemma, dear girl."

Danica stared steadily into Aunt Louise's pale eyes. "Do you think that makes me a bad person?"

"No, it makes you human. You don't know me and you may think me an old fool, but may I give you a bit of advice, Danica?"

Danica slowly nodded her head.

"If whatever this man is involved with is a more powerful draw than you, leave him. A woman has enough trouble trying to keep a man interested these days. We live in a world filled with distractions. If you can't be the distraction that pulls this man away, then you pull away. Find someone who makes you his world. I'm rather prejudiced, but I watched my nephew suffer through one bad marriage to a woman who wanted the universe to revolve around her. Paul spent most of his time keeping Madison happy, but she never did the same for him. She was too selfish, kind of like that man who is holding you back. When it's love, you give up everything to be with someone, you don't make excuses."

Danica shrugged. "In a way he has given up a great deal to be with me, but it just isn't enough. I guess I want more."

Aunt Louise patted her hand. "Don't chase rainbows, Danica. My sister was always chasing rainbows, thinking that the next relationship, the next man, would be better than the one she had, but they weren't. You can't live on what ifs and what might be. Life is real, hard, and sometimes happy; if he can't be there one hundred percent to get you through every day of it, then walk away. Don't get so caught up in your dreams that you let happiness pass you by."

Danica spotted Paul coming toward them, carrying his aunt's drink in his hand, and her heart skipped a beat.

"I think you've already made up your mind." Aunt Louise whispered as Paul approached.

"So what horrible things did my aunt say about me while I was gone?" Paul inquired as he handed Aunt Louise her drink.

"We were just talking about men," Aunt Louise told him. "You know, the usual…how difficult you are to live with and all your bad habits."

Paul suspiciously eyed Danica. "You don't believe anything she told you, right?"

Danica grinned. "Not yet."

Paul put his arm around Danica's shoulders. "Don't trust a word she says. She hates men, and never let my mother forget she had a son and not a daughter."

Aunt Louis lifted her glass to Danica. "Thank God I never had any of those, either. I had four husbands, and they cured me of my desire for kids." She knocked back a large sip of her gin and tonic, and then nodded to her glass. "Good booze makes a bad marriage bearable."

"You've been married four times?" Danica asked, rather surprised.

"Bob is my fourth husband. My first husband, Elliot, shot himself. My second husband, Trent, died in a hunting accident, and my third husband, Byron, ran off with his twenty-two-year-old legal secretary and then died of a heart attack. Luckily, I wasn't suspected in any of my former husbands' deaths."

Paul chuckled. "Yes, everyone in the family refers to Aunt Louise as 'the black widow.'" Paul winked at his aunt. "Speaking of which, where is your next victim? I haven't seen Uncle Bob around here."

Aunt Louise nodded to the hallway that led to the kitchen. "Packers are playing the Colts. He's watching it on the television in your office."

Paul appeared surprised. "I don't have a television in my office."

Aunt Louise snickered. "Of course you don't. Bob brought his handheld one. He takes it everywhere with him." She took another long sip from her drink, almost downing the rest of the contents in one gulp.

"Should I get you another, Aunt Louise?" Paul nodded to her glass.

Aunt Louise finished the last dregs of gin and tonic and handed him the glass. "Good boy. Bring two when you come back. Remember to put less tonic and more gin in them this time. "

Paul took her glass. "Of course, Auntie L." Before he turned away, Paul raised his eyebrows to Danica.

Aunt Louise nudged Danica with her elbow. "You're a lucky girl. Just promise me you won't hurt him. When that silly wife of his up and left him with this big old house and a hole in his heart, I never thought he would recover. That's a good man who deserves a good woman."

Danica nodded. "I know."

"I can see why Claire wanted you to get together with Paul. She told me you two were well-suited for each other."

Danica furrowed her brow. "She said that?"

"One of the last things we talked about before she died. She told me how much she hoped you two would make it. Claire thought you were the perfect girl for her son."

Danica thought back to the night before Claire died and her horrid admissions about Gaston, Burt, and her plans for Danica. "I find that surprising. I thought Claire Mouton didn't care for me."

"Nonsense," Aunt Louise chided. "If Claire Mouton didn't like you, you'd know it. You could never tell by looking at my sister, but beneath her mousy demeanor was a woman as ruthless as a cornered lioness."

Danica stifled a sudden urge to laugh out loud. "Great," she muttered. "Now you tell me."

***

Danica was in the kitchen loading the last of the glasses into the dishwasher when Paul walked through the door.

"Danica, I told you to leave that for my housekeeper. Melba is coming by in the morning to take care of everything."

She shut the dishwasher closed. "There wasn't much left. The caterers cleaned up most of the dishes and glasses already. I just wanted to make sure it was all put away."

He came up to her side. "The way you scurried around that reception, making sure every food tray was full and every guest had a drink, made me feel very guilty."

She leaned her hip against the kitchen sink. "Sorry, but my mother always pounded into my head that you have to be an attentive hostess, even if it isn't your party."

"Sounds like your mother and my mother would have had…." His voice cracked.

Danica trailed her fingers along his brow, pushing the comma of brown hair out of his eyes. "You all right?"

"Just tired." He turned to a cabinet above the sink and pulled out two old-fashioned glasses. After placing the glasses on the black granite countertop, he walked to the pantry door and pulled it open. When he stepped from the pantry, he was holding a bottle of Johnny Walker Black in his hands.

"I think we deserve this," he reasoned, coming back to her side.

He unscrewed the cap and began to pour three fingers of scotch whiskey in each glass.

"How do you plan on driving me home after this?" she questioned, pointing to the bottle of scotch.

Paul picked up one of the glasses. "I don't."

Danica folded her arms over her chest. "Should I call a cab?"

He picked up her drink and handed it to her. "I'm not asking you to sleep with me, Danica. Just drink with me. Tonight I really don't want to drink alone." He looked up toward the ceiling. "I've got two guest bedrooms upstairs where you can pass out, and in the morning I will bring you home. Just stay with me, talk to me, and help me to forget about…everything."

Danica took the glass from his hand. "All right, Paul, I'll stay."

He tipped his glass against hers. "Thank you."

Danica watched as his slender hands lifted the glass to his lips. He took a long sip from his drink and then closed his eyes as he swallowed back the alcohol. When he opened his eyes, he reached for the bottle on the counter.

"Now, why don't you tell me the story of your life?" He turned toward the kitchen door. "We've got all night to talk and drink."

"Sounds like a plan," Danica admitted.

As she followed Paul out of the kitchen, Danica felt a pang of regret. Gaston would worry when she did not come home, but then again he knew where she had gone. But the curve of Paul's trousers over his tight, round butt as he walked in front of her, magically distracted Danica from her concerns about Gaston. A more pressing flurry of thoughts began to occupy her mind. How was she going to get through an evening alone with Paul without ripping his clothes off? And more to the point, how could she keep him from slowly inching his way further into her heart?

CHAPTER 16

It was a little after two in the morning when Danica was startled awake from a sound sleep. She scrutinized the dark bedroom and stifled a thread of panic teaming through her when she did not recognize any of the furniture or decorations. Then, slowly, it all came back to her. Her body relaxed against the king-sized sleigh bed as she remembered helping Paul up the stairs to his bed after the four glasses of scotch he had downed earlier in the evening. After taking the bedroom next to his for the night, she had discarded her clothes on a burgundy wingback chair and crawled under the covers to sleep.

Her eyes took in the outline of ornate antique furniture captured in the beams of moonlight pouring in through the long windows on either side of her bed. She swung her legs over the side of the bed and rubbed her face in her hands. Her stomach rumbled slightly, and then she recalled how she had skipped eating anything all afternoon and evening because she had been too busy with the reception. The scotch she had consumed with Paul had given her a slight headache, and her mouth tasted like cotton.

Knowing she would never be able to get back to sleep with her discomforts, she went to the chair to retrieve her clothes and go in search of a late-night snack. When she approached the chair and saw her formfitting, black dress neatly spread out, she dreaded having to pull the garment over her head just to raid the kitchen. Curious to see if she could find something else to slip on, she went to the closet next to the bathroom door. Inside, Danica was surprised to discover a full wardrobe of men's suits, slacks, and dress shirts. Danica pulled out one of the shirts and smelled the hint of Paul's woodsy cologne lingering on the fabric. She smiled and then held the shirt against her face, breathing in the intoxicating aroma.

She giggled as she realized what she was doing and then remembered Gaston and the distinctive scent of cigars and brandy that always filled the room whenever he appeared. But this smell was different, more vibrant, more overpowering, and felt…real.

As she slipped Paul's long-sleeved shirt around her naked body, an image of his firm backside danced across her mind. Her belly ignited with an intense white heat and her loins suddenly ached. Danica grabbed on to the doorframe of the closet.

"Aunt Louise was right. I do have it bad."

Shaking off her lust, Danica exited the bedroom while buttoning up the shirt. Once out on the second-floor landing, she quietly padded her way to the stairs and tiptoed down to the first floor. Halfway down the old, white oak staircase, one of the steps moaned loudly beneath her weight. Danica stood frozen for a moment, hoping she had not awakened Paul. After a few seconds, she heard nothing coming from upstairs, and then rapidly progressed down the steps. She figured all the scotch he had put away the previous night world probably keep him out until well after morning.

On the first floor, she turned right at the quaint entrance foyer decorated tastefully in gold brocade wallpaper, and headed down a short cypress-paneled hallway toward the kitchen. She passed the spacious dining room that seated twenty, with its oval walnut table and three-tiered brass chandelier, and turned into the arched doorway that marked the entrance to the gourmet kitchen.

After flipping on the lights, she headed to the built-in Sub-Zero refrigerator and peeked inside. Danica's eyes browsed the selection of food trays left over from the reception until she decided on the finger sandwiches. Pulling the tray from the shelf, she walked over to the island in the center of the kitchen, pulled out one of the iron and leather stools, and had a seat.

As she munched on a triangle-shaped sandwich of egg salad, Danica's eyes scanned the wide kitchen. She noted the collection of shiny stainless pots hanging from a curved rack along the wall next to the black Viking oven. The dark Italian tile countertop on the island gleamed under the overhead lights, and Danica decided she liked the feeling of the open kitchen, unlike her cramped little efficiency. In fact, Paul's home had been a nice break from her almost austere living conditions. She didn't realize how little she had until she stepped into the man's huge house. She wished she had fought for more from Tom, but then again, it would have only dragged out the entire divorce process. Danica had walked away with a nice chunk of Tom's belongings, but after the glow of winning such a hefty divorce settlement had dimmed, she realized having a few of his prized possessions had been a rather hallow victory. Tom had taken more from her than she would ever be able to collect in a divorce.

"Sometimes getting over the pain inflicted by a bad marriage is harder than getting over the marriage itself," she mumbled.

"I thought I heard a prowler," a man called from the kitchen entrance.

Danica careened her head around to see Paul, resting his shoulder against the doorframe, grinning at her. He was wearing only a pair of dark blue pajama pants, and his arms were folded over his naked chest.

Danica gulped back the last bite of sandwich when she saw his wide chest taking up the doorway.

"I, ah, was hungry and figured…I'd raid your fridge," she said, stumbling over her words.

Paul slowly walked up to her, eyeing his half-buttoned dress shirt hanging loosely about her figure.

"You raided my closet, too." He came alongside her chair as he reached out and caressed the collar of her shirt.

As Danica watched his hypnotic hands, she desperately tried to suppress an image of those hands traveling along her naked body.

"I found it in the closet in my bedroom," she confessed to him. "I hope you don't mind?"

He gave her a crooked smile. "Nonsense. You look good in it." He inspected the sandwich tray before her. "Any roast beef left?"

She pointed to a few finger sandwiches on the far right of the tray. Paul eagerly grabbed one of the meat-stuffed snacks. He had a seat on the stool next to her and took a hearty bite of one of his sandwiches.

"So what woke you up?" Danica asked as Paul munched on his roast beef sandwich. "I thought you would sleep until morning after all that scotch you drank last night."

He shrugged. "I had this weird dream, more like a nightmare." He tossed the last of his sandwich into his mouth.

Danica looked over the tray, scouring for another egg salad sandwich. "Really? About what?"

Paul leaned over and explored the tray of sandwiches. "I think my mother was in it. She was floating around me and seemed really mad. She kept asking me questions." He reached for a turkey sandwich.

Danica sat back on her stool, intrigued. "What kind of questions?"

Paul wrinkled his brow, recalling the dream. "I can't remember. I think they were about you and that ghost, Garfield."

"Gaston. What did she have to say about him?"

He let his eyes linger on the sandwich in his hand. "You know, it's odd how that guy's name creeps into almost every conversation we have." He shifted his deep-set eyes to her. "Do you want to tell me why that is?"

Danica bit down on her lower lip, knowing she had come to a turning point with Paul. She either told him the truth, or threw away any chance she had with him by compounding her lie. "There's something you should know," she declared.

Paul put his sandwich down on the tray. "That doesn't sound good."

Danica fortified her resolve with a deep breath. "Gaston Deslonde really does haunt my house, just like your mother said."

Paul briefly chuckled. "You're not really buying into those crazy stories my mother told us about her ghost, are you?"

"Paul, it's true. I didn't want to say anything before because I didn't want you to think I was crazy."

"Have you seen this ghost?"

Danica slowly nodded. "When I was a little girl, living in that cottage, I saw things, heard a man's voice, and smelled cigars and brandy everywhere."

"Wow." Paul sat back on his stool, looking slightly awestruck. "I've smelled that cigar and brandy thing at my mother's a lot. I thought that was just something related to the building being so old. "

"I think that smell is Gaston's trademark. Perhaps it was something he was fond of in life."

"You sound like my mother." Paul snickered. "So you really think you have a dead guy living in your house?"

"Not a dead guy, but maybe some form of energy that once belonged to him. I believe we're all made up of energy, and I think that energy can be left behind when the body dies. All I know is that I've seen and experienced things I can't explain." She tilted her head slightly to the side and smiled. "Besides, having a ghost around makes you feel like nothing is wasted. Life goes on in some form or another."

Paul caught a tendril of her long, chestnut brown hair in his hand. He felt the silky hair between his fingertips and sighed.

"I like the way you describe it. Gives me some hope that my mother is at peace." He let her hair fall from his hand.

"She is at peace, Paul. I know it."

His eyes grew dark with doubt. "Can someone who was so tortured in life have peace when they die?"

"Once we are free of our bodies, all the pain we suffered in them is released. We can start over and heal."

"That's a nice philosophy, Danica, and I wish I could believe in it, but my mother was never a happy person. As far back as I can remember life was about keeping Momma comfortable. I always avoided making too much noise when I was a kid. Making sure I got good grades and excelled at school, so she would be proud and happy; checking on her moods, dancing on eggshells when she was upset or depressed, and spending every day of my life worrying about whether today would finally be the day when she tried to kill herself again."

Danica rested her hand on his forearm. "I spent every day of my childhood living under the same cloud, only my worries were about my mother's health. I had to watch over her when she was sick, make sure she took her medicines every morning, and spent hours drawing pictures for her. She loved my pictures and seemed to take such pleasure in them. It made me believe that I could have some control over her illness. If I drew pictures for her, it would make her better. Silly isn't it, to believe in such a thing. I guess that's why I still do it. I'm trying to make sure she is happy with me." Danica pulled her hand away from him. "I should never have said that."

Paul stood from his stool. "Hey, it's all right. I want you to tell me everything. I want you to share all of your secrets with me."

"But I've never told anyone that before. Not even—" She covered her mouth with her hand.

"Tom? Is that what you were going to say? You've never shared such an intimate detail with your ex-husband, did you?"

Danica slowly lowered her hand from her mouth and looked down at the dark-tiled floor beneath her stool. She realized there were some things she had not told Gaston; things she had felt comfortable enough to share with Paul.

Paul placed his hand under her chin and raised her face to him. When their eyes met, Danica trembled.

"I want you to always tell me what you're thinking or feeling, Danica," he whispered as he embraced her. "Good, bad, weird, or angry, I don't care. I want you to know you can talk to me about anything. I won't judge you or scold you. I care too damn much about you to ever want to hurt you."

Danica leaned back in his arms. "I care about you too, Paul, but…." Her mouth went dry.

Paul tightened his arms about her. "I keep getting these mixed signals from you. I sometimes wonder how you really feel about me."

Danica felt the heat of his skin through her thin shirt. "I'm just so afraid of making another mistake."

"You won't make a mistake with me."

"How can you be so certain?"

He lowered his head to her. "Do you want me, Danica?"

She never took her eyes off his as she slowly nodded her head.

"Then it isn't a mistake," he whispered right before his mouth covered hers.

The passion in his kiss instantly snuffed out any concerns Danica had about the two of them. She wanted Paul like she had never wanted another man, even Gaston. With Gaston there had always been questions and lingering doubts, but with Paul there was only desire.

As his lips encouraged her, she pressed into him while her hands began to explore the muscles in his chest. She could smell the scent of his woodsy cologne on his skin and the remnants of minty shampoo in his hair. Her hands swiftly developed a mind of their own as her fervor rose. When she reached down and cupped his erection, Paul moaned into her cheek.

"Christ, you're driving me crazy." He picked her up in his arms and began carrying her to the kitchen doorway.

Danica pointed to the island counter. "What about the sandwiches?"

"To hell with the sandwiches."

Paul didn't even switch off the lights as he practically ran with her in his arms to the stairs. Climbing the steps two at a time, Danica giggled into his chest.

"In a hurry?" she murmured, kissing his neck. "We've got all night."

"You're distracting me," he complained as he rounded the second-floor landing.

He approached his bedroom door and kicked it open with his foot. When he carried her to his antique captain's bed, Danica tempted his neck and chest with kisses. After setting her down on the bright blue comforter, Paul grabbed at the shirt she was wearing and tore at the buttons. Once he had freed her of the clothing, his hands eagerly began caressing her hips and breasts.

"I can't stand this," Paul muttered, and hurriedly wiggled out of his pajama bottoms.

Danica kneaded the taught muscles in his round behind as Paul pushed her back on the bed.

"Tell me what you like," he murmured against her neck.

"What I like?" Danica ran her hands down to his erection and stroked his shaft. "Don't ask and don't be gentle. Just take what you want."

Paul grasped her hips in his hands and flipped her over onto her stomach. He pinned her hands above her head and then spread her legs apart. As he fondled the sensitive valley of flesh in between her legs, he whispered, "Tell me what you want."

Danica arched her body into his. "I want you," she softly moaned.

Paul bit into her shoulder as he pulled her hips to him, and Danica eagerly raised her hips higher in anticipation. Paul grunted into her neck as he drove slowly into her flesh. Danica gasped and rammed her hips into his, forcing him to go deeper. Paul responded by thrusting hard all the way into her.

"Yes, that's it," Danica cried out.

He began driving harder and deeper into her, and with every penetration Danica could feel that wonderful tingle begin rising from her groin. It climbed through the recesses of her body, tensing her muscles along the way. She gripped the bedspread as the tingle catapulted into an unbearable longing. Overcome by the intensity of her need, Danica threw her head back and cried out just as the first waves of her orgasm overtook her.

As her body trembled in his arms, Paul groaned and slammed his hips into her.

"Danica," he called out as he came inside her.

After, they lay still, soaked in a light film of sweat and breathing hard. Danica could feel his head nestled into the curve of her back.

"I never figured you to be the kind of woman who liked it that way, but I'm not complaining," he whispered.

Danica sat up on her elbows. "What way?"

He rolled off her back and on to his side. "Most of the women I've been with like being in control, not being controlled in bed. Why are you so different?"

Danica rested her head against the bed as she kept her eyes on him. "What's wrong with wanting a man to be a man?"

"Nothing," Paul admitted as he brushed a few strands of chestnut hair from her face. "It's just that in this day and age, being a man has to be tempered by a whole lot of other societal pressures. You have to juggle women's rights, sexual harassment, a whole array of politically correct terminology, while maintaining a respectful attitude and catering to her demands and not yours. By the time I get into bed with a woman, I usually let them dictate how it will go, so forgive me if I seem a little stunned to find a woman who wants me to be a man."

"I never realized how tough it was for you guys."

Paul nodded and then his deep green eyes studied her face for a moment. "Who was the one who turned you on to our little secret?"

She sighed and rolled over to her back. "Someone who wasn't encumbered by the pressures of our society. He was…well, I thought he was the one I wanted, and then you came along."

Paul pulled her into his arms. "Who is he?"

Danica stiffened with apprehension.

"What is it?" Paul asked, feeling the change in her.

Danica made her body relax against him. "I don't know how to describe my feelings for him. I mean, I care for him, but he will never be able to be there for me. I can't be with him the way I can be with you."

"Is this the guy you mentioned to my aunt?"

Danica sat up and faced him. "She told you?"

Paul grinned. "She said something to me about it at the reception. She advised me to pounce. She claimed it was the one way I could guarantee you would forget about the other guy."

"You're kidding? She actually told you to pounce?"

Paul chuckled. "Aunt Louise is nothing like my mother. Where Momma was prim and always concerned about what everyone else thought, Aunt Louise was telling everyone to go to hell." Paul tucked his arm behind his head. "So what happened with you and this guy?"

Danica cuddled against him. "We tried to find a way to make it work between us, but after spending time with you I realized it would never work. We are just too…different."

"Then my aunt was right. I needed to pounce."

Danica giggled. "Yeah, the pouncing worked."

"And you're positive it's over between you and this guy?"

She nodded against his chest. "Pretty sure."

His eyes narrowed with concern. "But not positive?"

"No, not absolutely positive."

"What would it take for you to be absolutely positive?"

Danica ran her fingers along his muscular chest. "I guess I might need a bit more convincing from you."

"How much more convincing?"

Danica clasped her arms about his neck. "Until I beg you to stop."

"I'll see what I can do," he replied, and then his mouth came down hard on hers.

CHAPTER 17

Danica awoke to a bright ray of sunshine glaring into her eyes. When she rolled over, she saw Paul's face scrunched against the pillow next to her. Her eyes lingered over his sharp cheekbones, wide forehead, and suntanned skin. As she traced her fingertips over his thin, pale lips, her body sparked with desire. He had spent the entire night trying to please her. She had lost count of how many times he had made her climax. As her body ached with pleasure, she yearned to wake him and encourage him to make love to her once more. No man had ever made her feel that way, not even Gaston. But then again, she had never awakened in the morning to find Gaston next to her. There was a profound comfort in knowing Paul was there for her. He could hold her in his arms when life got bad, and hug away all of her sadness. Despite her feelings for Gaston, she would never have such completeness with him, and she was beginning to realize she needed a physical relationship just as much as she needed an emotional one. But as she watched Paul sleeping beside her, Danica began to comprehend what Gaston had truly given her. Without him, she might not have tried again with a man, and she could have missed her opportunity to find the kind of happiness she had always dreamed of.

"You're up," Paul murmured as he stirred beside her.

"I've been watching you sleep."

Paul cringed and ran his hands over his face. "Please tell me I didn't drool or anything equally lame."

"No drooling."

He wrapped her in his arms. "Last night with you…I just want you to know it has never been like that with anyone before."

"What? You've never done it five times in a row before?"

"No ma'am. Three tops. Five is a new personal best."

Danica sighed into his chest. "For me, too."

"Glad to hear it. I'd hate to think all my mother's matchmaking efforts were in vain. She had high hopes for us."

"How high?"

Paul shrugged. "The usual…kids, the white picket fence, and a lifetime together."

Danica briefly entertained the prospect of such a life with Paul. After her marriage, she had given up on the idea of a happily ever after with any man; any living man, that is.

"You want kids?" Danica softly questioned.

Paul nodded. "That's the reason I bought this big house for Madison. The plan was to fill it with kids, but after we settled in, she began making excuses for postponing our starting a family. In the end, I realized she never wanted children…at least not with me." He traced his fingers down her back. "What about you? You ever want kids?"

Danica remembered her dreams for a big family when she was growing up. "I did before Tom. Since my divorce, I haven't really thought about kids, but yeah…I do want children some day."

He sighed into her hair. "What do you say to a breakfast of leftovers and coffee, and then we can come back up here and go for a new personal best?"

"What about your housekeeper? You said she was coming this morning to clean up?"

"I'll call her and tell her not to come."

Danica thought of Gaston and shook her head. "No, we can go for the record another time. Right now we need to get up, and you need to take me home."

Paul sat up in bed and leered at her body hidden beneath the sheets. "I have a better idea. Let's get out of here for the day. Go to the zoo or the park. It's Sunday."

She was tempted, very tempted. "Well, I can't go to the park wearing my black dress. I need to change and take a shower."

"All right," Paul agreed. "After breakfast, I'll take you home and you can change, then we can head out for an afternoon of fun."

Danica's stomach clenched as she thought of how Gaston would react. "That sounds wonderful, Paul," she heard herself saying.

He threw off the covers. "Good. Now let's get downstairs and dig into those shrimp stuffed egg rolls before Melba shows up and begins rolling her eyes at me."

"Rolling her eyes?"

"Melba is old-fashioned. When she arrives and finds you here, she will roll her eyes and insist that I make an honest woman out of you."

Danica rose from the bed. "A little late for that."

Paul chuckled. "Not according to Melba. For her, marriage is the happily ever after part of life."

Danica stood from the bed. "Happily ever after is something I would never equate with marriage."

Paul reached for his pajama bottoms on the floor next to the bed. "One day I promise, Danica, you will have a happily ever after…even if I have to slay a few hundred dragons to give it to you."

Her heart did a joyful summersault. "You would do that for me?"

He stepped into his pajamas. "Of course. Isn't that what Prince Charming is supposed to do?"

"Prince Charming?" Danica shook her head. "I've never had one of those."

Paul winked at her. "You do now, darlin'."

***

When Paul's dark green Land Rover stopped in front of Danica's cottage, her insides turned to jelly. What was she going to tell Gaston? He may not have been made of flesh and bone, but his feelings for her were just as palpable as the heavy car beneath her. She was not ready to give up on everything she had with him just yet, or at least she hoped so. But the more time she spent with Paul, the more she began to reconsider her relationship with her ghost. All Gaston's misty promises were beginning to lose their appeal when compared to the strong arms of a man who kept his feet firmly planted on the ground.

"Are you all right?" Paul asked beside her. "You've gone pale."

Danica glimpsed her shaking hands in her lap. "I guess I suddenly remembered everything that happened here and I…."

He reached for her hands and held them together in his. "Go inside and change while I drive around and try to find a place to park."

Danica's jumbled nerves eased and Paul let go of her hands. She removed her seatbelt and opened her door. "One of the setbacks of living in the Quarter, I'm afraid…no parking."

"Just call my cell when you're ready for me to come and get you. I might still be driving around by the time you're done."

Danica climbed out of the car, and as soon as she placed her foot on the curb, the porch light above her front door flickered on. She turned back to Paul, but he, thankfully, had not noticed.

"I won't be long."

"Take your time, Danica." He gave her one last crooked smile and then she closed the car door.

He waited as Danica put the key in the lock on the gated entrance and turned the handle. After she stepped into the narrow alleyway, she waved to Paul before she closed the gate. When she reached the rear entrance to her home, she took in a deep breath before she put her key in the lock.

"Did you sleep with him?" Gaston's voice reverberated in the small kitchen when she walked through the doors.

Danica slowly turned to face him. "Is that really any of your business?"

He was scowling at her from the arched entrance to her office. The light in his eyes appeared dark and somber.

"That answers that question," he growled.

She slammed her black clutch down on the kitchen counter. "Gaston, you have no right to question me about my relationship with Paul."

He came toward her. "I have every right. Do you know what I gave up to be with you?"

"I didn't ask you to give up anything. You were the one who went ahead and sold your soul to Claire for our night together. Now Claire is dead and we will never be together again…or do you plan on talking the next woman who moves into your old home into lending you her husband's body for the night?" She shuddered as she glared at him. "Do you have any idea how it feels knowing that it was Burt's body doing those things to me and not you?"

"It was me! His body was just the vessel, as is every body the soul inhabits. You felt my arms about you, not his. You felt me inside you, not him."

Danica started for her office doorway. "Thanks for that detailed description, Gaston, but you're not helping."

"So what? You're going to take up with that pretty boy until I can return to you again?"

She spun around to him. "Return to me? Christ, Gaston. How many people do you plan on killing to be with me? I can't have that on my conscience. I won't let you kill another person so we can sleep together. I can't stop thinking about poor Burt, and I don't want to be an accessory to another murder."

"It wasn't murder! Burt was weak, Danica, you know that. He had a bad heart, and it gave out with all the stress of having me occupy his body. Who's to say it will happen again?"

"Claire knew Burt would never survive a whole night of being your vessel." She pointed at Gaston. "You knew she wanted him out of her life, and still you went along with that woman's crazy scheme."

He gaped at her, floored by her comment. "I went along with it because I wanted to be with you! I didn't care how many people I had to go through to have one night with you. I don't regret what I did, Danica. I love you…I have always loved you. Doesn't that mean anything to you? Can you just cast me aside for that…foolish boy?"

"Who's more foolish, Gaston…the man who wants to seduce a woman, or the ghost who sells his soul to be with her? Am I really worth this?" She turned away.

"Don't do this," he pleaded coming up to her. "I spent a lifetime searching for the one woman who could fill my heart, and when I finally find her, I can never put my arms around her. I can only imagine what you feel like, the smell of your hair, or the touch of your lips." He stopped behind her. "I can't lose you to him."

Danica sighed as her will caved in to him. "You haven't lost me, Gaston." She slowly faced him. "Before you came to me that Halloween night, you were a dream that would never be real. Now I want more. I want you so much that last night with Paul…I guess I was hoping he could fill the void you created in me."

"Did he?" A gentle waft of air danced about in her long chestnut hair.

She gazed into his enchanting face as a sense of grief slithered through her. Paul had given her something Gaston never could…contentment. When the needs of the body and soul are met, there is physical and emotional harmony. She had wanted to share such fulfillment with Gaston, but Danica knew that theirs was a love destined to remain undone.

"Paul is not you, Gaston. You're the only man who has made me feel loved and…secure."

His shimmering eyes clouded over with pain. "But it isn't enough, is it, Danica?"

"I want to feel, Gaston. I need to feel a man's arms about me. I want children. I want a family, and all the things a woman needs in her life."

He walked past her into the office. "He can give you what I cannot. I understand."

"I don't think you do," Danica objected, following him.

He looked to his portrait above the mantle. "You are a woman with a full life ahead of you. To ask you to give up that life for me would be more than selfish…it would be cruel. I had forgotten how strong the pull of life can be." He motioned to the painting. "I'm not that man anymore. Despite what I may wish for us, I can never be that man for you."

"Look, Gaston, Paul and I are just beginning. It may not last."

"If not Paul, there will be another, Danica. The question is, can I stand by and watch you fall in love with another man?"

Danica rushed to his side. "What are you saying?"

"I think it would be best for both of us if I no longer haunted this place." He paused as his eyes explored her face. "I will never regret you, ever. You are everything to me now and for the rest of eternity."

"Gaston, wait. You can't just go away. I don't want you to go away," Danica begged, the desperation teeming in her voice.

"It may not be what you want, Danica, but it is what you need." And then Gaston Deslonde disappeared.

"Gaston!" Danica shouted. "Gaston, come back. Don't leave me like this!"

But as Danica stood in the center of her office, listening to every sound for some hint of Gaston, her heart began to break. Before she knew it, she was crumpled on her office floor and longing to see those striking sky-blue eyes gazing into hers once more.

***

Danica was not sure how long she had been crying on her floor when she heard a knock at her front shutters. Wiping her tears away, she remembered Paul and their plans for an afternoon together. When she pushed the shutters open, Paul was waiting for her with a heartwarming smile on his handsome face.

"I found a parking spot just a block away." He nodded to her black dress. "You didn't change. I thought…." His words slipped away when he saw her red eyes. "What is it?" he asked, bounding in the door.

Danica lowered her eyes. "I, ah, just got some bad news on my voicemail. A friend, a very good friend, passed away."

Paul pulled her to him and wrapped her in his arms. "That's all you need on top of everything going on. I'm sorry. We don't have to go anywhere this afternoon. I can stay here with you, if you like. How 'bout I go to the corner store and get us a bottle of Scotch whiskey?"

Danica was heartened by his presence, but confused by it as well. Her emotions, like twirling teacups on a children's amusement park ride, were spinning out of control.

She stepped back from him. "Perhaps you should go home and check on Melba and I'll—"

"I'm not leaving you like this, Danica. I'll hang out on the sofa while you make phone calls or whatever you need to do. You won't even know I'm here…just let me be here for you."

She could feel his strength pouring into her. Just the physical presence of him made her feel better. Gaston had done the same thing for her during the dark days after her mother's death, but his support had never felt unwavering like Paul's. It was not that what she shared with Paul was better than what she had known with Gaston, just different.

"You know what would make me feel better right now?" She smiled for Paul.

"What is that?"

"A cup of coffee and a beignet."

Paul nodded. "Café Du Monde it is."

"I'll just get my purse," Danica said as she went back to the kitchen.

Paul followed her through the cottage. "Do you still want to change?"

After Danica retrieved her purse from the kitchen counter, she turned and gasped when she saw Paul standing at the entrance to her office in almost the exact position Gaston had been only a short time before.

"I, ah…yes," Danica uttered, trying to collect her thoughts. "I'll just change into some jeans." She took off across the kitchen and passed Paul, heading for her bedroom.

Once she had slipped on her favorite blue jeans and a blue turtleneck sweater, Danica grabbed her casual leather purse from the bed and hurried out her bedroom door.

When she stepped into the family room, she found Paul scanning the books on her shelves.

"You have quite an impressive collection of antique books," he remarked.

Danica waved at the bookshelves. "My divorce settlement. It killed Tom to part with his prized collection, but after everything he put me through, I figured he owed me."

Paul walked up to her and took her hand. "Remind me never to get on your bad side."

"Don't worry; I've learned to speak my mind since my marriage."

He kissed her cheek. "Yeah, I've noticed."

She let him lead her out of the living room and through her front doors. Just before she was about to close the doors, Danica peered inside one more time, hoping for a trace of the ghost who had stolen her heart. But the rooms were empty, and no lingering aroma of cigars and brandy hovered in the air.

"Is something wrong?" Paul inquired.

Danica slowly closed the doors and turned to him. "No, just making sure I turned off the lights."

Paul slid his arm about her waist. "Come on, let's get you some beignets. Everything will feel better after a few hot beignets."

As they slowly strolled along the broken sidewalk, Paul's presence brought Danica an unexpected sense of comfort. With every step forward, she felt the pain around her heart begin to ease a little, but her thoughts were still consumed by the ghost she had left behind.

***

Later that afternoon, as the sun was setting over the rooftops of the French Quarter, Paul held Danica's hand as he walked her back to her cottage on Dumaine Street.

"Tomorrow night I'm having a dinner meeting with several of my engineers to go over some protocol changes, but Tuesday night I can pick you up at work and we can grab some dinner in town, if you like?"

Danica raised her eyebrows. "Just dinner?"

Paul draped his arm over her shoulders. "Just dinner, unless you're interested in a little record breaking."

Danica leaned into his chest. "Perhaps we should save the record breaking for a night when neither one of us have to get up and go to work the next day."

"Good decision."

Danica caught sight of her cottage up ahead, and suddenly the thought of Gaston not being there left her feeling cold and empty inside.

"I was thinking next weekend we could check out this Greek restaurant that opened by my house on Magazine Street," Paul went on. "What do you think?"

Danica gave him a playful grin. "Are you sure? You might want to make some time for all of your other women."

Paul tossed his head back and laughed. "I'm not good at juggling a lot of things at once, women included. And for what it's worth, when I find something I like I stick to it." He paused and worriedly furrowed his brow. "Unless you think I'm moving too fast."

"After last night?" Danica shook her head, chuckling.

"Yeah, I guess we kind of blew all the rules for dating out of the water last night."

"That's good. I don't like following rules," Danica told him.

"No rules for us then. We'll just wing it from here on out."

When they passed in front of Claire's home, Paul stopped to admire the green and white Creole cottage. "I guess I'll have to put this place up for sale once Burt and Mom's estate is settled."

"I didn't think. I shouldn't have had you come down here and see the house knowing everything that—"

He pulled her toward her doorstep. "Forget about it. I'm all right, and perhaps one day when another family has moved in, it won't be so bad seeing the old place. But I'm sure by the time that happens, you'll have moved out of your house."

Danica reached for the keys in her purse. "What makes you think I'll have moved away by then?"

He placed his hands in the pocket of his jeans and shrugged. "Maybe by then you'll have gotten a better offer to live someplace else."

Danica laughed as she opened her doors. "A better offer?" She stepped into her home. "Who would make me a better offer?"

Paul hurried inside, kicked the french doors closed, and clasped his arms about her. "Me," he whispered to her. "Maybe I don't like the idea of you living here alone. It's dangerous, and from now on I'll worry about you day and night when you're not with me."

Danica anxiously surveyed the living room. She expected Gaston to appear, or to hear his voice in her ear making some snide comment. But as she waited for calamity to strike, an eerie quiet permeated the house, and nothing happened.

"So what do you say?" Paul asked, pulling her away from her thoughts.

She looked up at him. "Say about what?"

Paul appeared taken aback. "About what I just said…packing a bag and spending next weekend at my place, so I can make sure you're safe."

"The entire weekend?" she questioned.

He frowned. "Too much to ask?"

She reassuringly patted her hand against his chest. "No, I…I just didn't expect to hear you say that at this stage in the game."

"Danica, I want to spend as much time as possible with you. I'm not looking for a fling. I am looking for a relationship, and I think you are, too."

Danica was about to agree with him when a cold breeze blew past her body, and she reflexively stiffened in Paul's arms.

"What's the matter?" Paul inquired. "You suddenly seem nervous."

Danica tried to think of something to appease him. "I guess I'm just a little tired from last night," she finally told him.

"Yeah, we didn't get much sleep," he admitted as his arms fell from her sides. "All right, I know when to cut my losses and head home." He stood back from her. "I'll call you tomorrow and we can set a time for dinner Tuesday." He went to her front doors and then mumbled, "My mind must be playing tricks on me."

Danica opened the doors for him. "What tricks?"

"I could have sworn for a moment I smelled…." He shook his head. "You're right. We're both pretty beat."

"What did you smell, Paul?"

Paul kissed her cheek and stepped outside to the sidewalk. "My mother's perfume," he answered when he turned back to her. "*First*, by Van Cleef and Arpels. I would buy her a bottle every Christmas. Could have sworn I just caught a whiff of it in your living room."

Danica spun around and stared into the room behind her as her heart rose in her throat.

"Probably my imagination," Paul added.

When Danica faced Paul again, she tried to smile, hiding her fear. "I'll talk to you later."

"Goodnight, Danica. Pleasant dreams."

But when Danica closed the doors to her home, she had an unsettling feeling that her dreams were going to be far from pleasant. She sensed something had changed within her little cottage, and that change was definitely not for the better.

CHAPTER 18

Danica awoke covered in a cold sweat with the sheets wound tightly about her body. She sat up gasping for breath as her heart pounded in her chest. Her eyes frantically searched her bedroom, but there were no shadows moving along the walls, no mysterious noises, and no faint whisperings floating in the air.

"Gaston?"

The room instantly grew colder and a slight breeze moved up from the foot of her bed, rustling her sheets as it went. She smelled the hint of a woman's sweet perfume, and then she remembered what Paul had said about detecting his mother's favorite scent in her living room.

"Claire?" Danica timidly called.

She waited, but there was no reply, and the icy feeling in the room soon lifted. Danica settled back down in her bed and rearranged her sheets, but a nagging sense of unease crept through her bones. Something was wrong…she could feel it, and when she tried to close her eyes again, a flash of a memory from the dream that had interrupted her sleep came back to her. A woman's hands had been wrapped about her neck, slowly cutting off her air, and there had been words that went with those hands. Danica's body rippled with goose bumps as the cruel voice taunting her in the dream echoed in her mind. She instantly knew it had been Claire.

Sitting up in bed once more, Danica struggled to recall the exact words Claire had shouted at her, but her memories were murky. Giving up on sleep, she climbed out of bed and headed for her bedroom door. Once in the hall, the edgy feeling within her began to ease. Danica stepped into her bathroom and flipped on the lights. After feeling reassured that there were no ghosts in her bathroom, she went to the sink and turned on the tap, eager to splash some cool water against her skin. But as she stood at her sink and stared down at her toiletries cluttering the small countertop, Danica could have sworn that everything on the countertop had been rearranged. Her brush and deodorant had been moved from their usual spots on the left side of the sink, and the soap dispenser been moved from the right side of the sink to the left. Standing back from the sink, she noticed that the drawers of her vanity had been left slightly open. When Danica checked her makeup drawer, she discovered that all of her makeup had been rearranged.

Fleeing from her bathroom, Danica ran down the short hallway to her family room. When she turned on the lights, her body relaxed with relief that everything appeared to be as she had left it before going to bed. But when she took a closer look at the books lining the shelves of the bookcase along the wall, she discovered that the books had been placed in alphabetical order. Danica remembered hastily putting the books on the shelves when she had unpacked, without any regard as to how they had been arranged.

Danica began systematically checking every room in her house. She soon discovered small things that had been moved around or put out of place. Drawings she had left in a neat pile on her desk were scattered about, and her coffeemaker had been placed on top of the refrigerator.

"This isn't good," Danica muttered as she put the coffeemaker back on the kitchen counter. "Someone is playing games with me." She turned about in her kitchen. "I never thought you this childish, Gaston," she shouted.

Danica waited for a reply, but instead of words she felt an uncomfortably cold breeze pass on her right side, then the familiar hint of perfume saturated the air.

"Is that you, Claire?"

Danica anxiously waited for a response, but there was none. Directing her attention back to her coffeemaker, she reset the timer for seven in the morning, but as she was turning from her kitchen counter, Danica could have sworn she felt a tug on her hair. She stopped in mid-stride and waited to see what would happen next, but nothing did. Reassured that it was just her imagination, she walked back into her office and turned off the lights.

Making her way through her cottage, Danica knew she would never be able to get back to sleep. When she entered her family room, she spied the television placed amidst the books on the shelf, and picked up the remote control sitting on one of the built-in bookshelves. As the television came to life, the room filled with the comforting sounds of a car chase through the streets of New York. Danica curled up on her floor and directed her attention to the images on the screen, feeling comforted by the screeching tires and occasional f-bombs emitted from her television speakers. Watching a movie about criminals being chased by the police gave Danica a strange sense of normalcy. Men with guns she could see and understand. It was the things she could not see that were beginning to scare the hell out of her.

***

The following Tuesday evening, Paul's dark green Land Rover was waiting on the street in front of the dull gray office building of Morrison and Rau. When Danica climbed into the car, Paul stared at her, appearing profoundly concerned.

"Are you all right?" he asked, taking in the dark circles under her eyes and her sallow complexion. "You look exhausted," he added.

"I haven't been sleeping well."

Paul pulled her seat belt over her shoulder. "Why haven't you been sleeping?"

She weighed the prospect of telling him about the horrible nightmares that had been plaguing her, but was not sure how much Paul would believe and how much he would chalk up to her imagination. "I just keep having these bad dreams," she eventually told him, wanting to be casual about the situation.

Paul waited and then motioned for her to continue. "Go on. What kind of dreams?"

Danica shook her head. "Just dreams."

Paul took her hand in his. "Danica, talk to me. You look like you haven't been sleeping at all. Now what are these dreams about?"

Danica looked to the street ahead, evading his worried gaze. "I keep dreaming someone is trying to kill me, or at least choke the living crap out of me."

"Kill you?" Paul sat back in his seat with an astonished look on his face. "Who do you see wanting to kill you?"

Danica swerved her blue eyes to him. "Your mother."

Paul began laughing and reached across the car for her. He wrapped his arms about her. "Aw, honey, it's just nerves, that's all. With everything that happened and her funeral last weekend, of course you're having nightmares about my mother. Hell, I'm having nightmares about her."

"Really," Danica said, feeling a little relieved. "What are your nightmares about?"

Paul released his arms about her and sat back in his seat. "Momma complaining to me about a load of stuff. Telling me the memorial service was in bad taste, and that she wanted a big funeral. Then she keeps asking me why I had her remains cremated and laid to rest next to Burt. She also tells me things about her estate, like where she placed insurance papers for Burt…you know, things like that." He put the car into gear. "The funny thing is, when I wake up from those dreams, I usually find the things she keeps pointing out to me, like the insurance papers. Found them right where she said they would be." He pulled the car into traffic. "I think we've both had a lot on our plates lately, and these dreams are just a response to all the stress we've been under."

"But what about finding those papers? You don't think she came to you in a dream and told you where to look for them?"

Paul shrugged, nonchalantly. "Not really. I was probably remembering her telling me about that before. I think that's the thing about dreams. They're just your subconscious reminding you about things your conscious mind is too preoccupied to remember. There's nothing extrasensory about all of this. There's a logical explanation for everything, Danica."

She lifted one eyebrow to him. "Is there?"

"You think there's more to this?"

She debated the need to tell him her true thoughts. "I don't know, Paul, but my dreams sure seem real. And then there is the perfume lingering in my bedroom at night. Happens every time I wake up from a nightmare. The room is cold and smells of perfume, and this morning I could have sworn I heard…."

"Heard what?" he asked, keeping his eyes ahead to the traffic on the street.

"I swear I heard a woman laughing. Not a woman's usual light tinkling laugh. This sound was cruel, almost maniacal, like whoever it was enjoyed tormenting me."

"Maniacal laughter from my mother? Now I know you were dreaming." He chuckled. "Come on, Danica, you knew her. She would never hurt a fly."

Danica decided not to pursue the subject further. She knew she would never be able to discuss what was happening in her home with Paul.

"You're right," Danica said, giving him a forced smile. "It's probably just a reaction to everything that has happened."

Paul patted her leg reassuringly. "Just wait, in a few days all of this will have gone away and we can have a good laugh about it."

As Paul headed away from the skyscrapers that shaped the city's business district, Danica pondered the reasons for her nightmares. Either it was her imagination as Paul proposed, or something else was going on at her house on Dumaine Street. The more Danica reviewed her nightmares in her head, the more uncomfortable she felt about the situation. What she needed was some good ghostly advice, but without Gaston, Danica could think of nowhere else to turn for help. As her mind began to flood with snapshots of Gaston, a warm feeling descended over her. Something had been missing from her life since the day he had vanished. There was a sense of wholeness absent from her day-to-day existence. She thought it funny how a ghost could make her feel so alive.

"Why don't we order take out?" Paul spoke up beside her. "We can take it back to my place and relax there."

Danica turned to him. "Your place? You do know what will happen if you and I end up at your place?"

He turned to her, looking completely innocent. "No, what?"

Danica laughed at his attempt at naivete.

"What if I promise to never lay a finger on you. We'll just eat and talk."

"Talk?" Danica smirked. "I don't think I'm in the mood for talking, Paul."

"Then I suggest we get something from a drive-thru," he proclaimed, pressing his foot down on the accelerator. "Because I'm not in the mood for talking, either."

***

After retrieving a chicken sandwich, burger, and some french fries from a fast-food restaurant, Paul rushed Danica up the red-bricked steps of his home. As soon as they walked inside his white-tiled foyer and placed the bags of food on a nearby table, Paul threw his arms about Danica. His lips hungrily tempted hers as he began to fumble with the buttons on her blouse.

"You don't know how much I want you right now," he murmured as he bit down on her earlobe.

Danica ran her hands down the crotch of his pants and felt his erection. "I'm beginning to get the idea."

He took her hand and pulled her toward the white oak staircase. "Come on."

Danica pointed back to the food. "What about dinner?"

"We'll eat later." Paul started up the steps, dragging her with him.

By the time they reached the top of the stairs, Paul had tossed his suit jacket and tie aside and was finishing up with the buttons on the front of Danica's blouse.

Once in his bedroom, Danica shimmied out of her skirt as Paul wrestled free of his trousers. Danica eased back on his antique bed, giggling as Paul came toward her with pure lust burning in his eyes. She sighed with happiness as he deftly removed her bra and slid her underwear down her slender hips.

"I haven't been able to stop thinking about you for two days," he softly said.

"Glad to hear I'm not the only one who was completely distracted at work," Danica replied as she slipped her hands inside his boxers, feeling the firmness of his round butt. "I had to type the same memo three times this morning because I kept thinking of your ass."

Paul reached down between her legs. "I keep daydreaming about your body in the middle of meetings, only to end up having to ask everyone to repeat themselves." He traced his fingers along the delicate folds of her flesh.

Danica's body shuddered. "I can't stop wanting you."

Paul drove his fingers into her. "You've been driving me crazy, too."

Danica's body arched as his fingers teased her. "Now, Paul," she moaned.

Paul began to rhythmically dart his fingers in and out of her, causing her body to spasm with pleasure. "I want to make this last, baby," he whispered.

Paul removed his fingers and then let his mouth meander through the valley between her breasts. He kissed her stomach, and then his lips made their way down to her firm, white thighs. He spread her legs apart and began to gently explore her sensitive folds with his tongue.

Danica groaned as she closed her eyes against the wash of white heat surging through her. She grabbed at the bedspread around her and gasped with excitement.

"Stop corrupting my boy!" a woman's voice barked next to her ear.

Danica bolted upright and Paul gaped up at her in surprise.

"What?" he asked, searching her face.

"Did you hear that?"

"Hear what?"

Danica was instantly embarrassed. Here she was having a very intimate moment with a man she cared about, and now she was hearing things.

"I know some women have heavenly visions when I'm working my magic, but I've never had a woman hearing things before."

Danica knew she wasn't hearing things. It had been Claire scolding her. She was positive of it. She rubbed her hand along her forehead. "I must just be tired, that's all."

"Too tired for this?" Paul asked as he traced his fingertips lightly between her legs.

Danica tossed her head back as her body instantly responded to him.

"Do you want me to stop?" he questioned as his fingers slowly dipped into her.

"No," Danica sighed as she fell back on the bed. "Don't stop."

Paul climbed in between her legs. "Then I won't stop," he whispered as his fingers spread her flesh apart. "I will keep going until you tell me you've had enough."

Danica curled her arms behind his neck. "I might never have enough of you."

He slowly entered her. "I like hearing you say that." He began to move in and out of her.

Danica bit into his neck as her body reveled in the feel of him. "Harder," Danica begged in his ear.

Paul grunted into her hair as he thrust forcefully into her. She clutched his round backside in her hands and wrapped her legs about his waist, allowing him to go deeper.

When her orgasm overtook her, it was riveting. For a brief second her mind cleared of her worries, and the tantalizing physical sensations numbed all the apprehension that had been knotting her muscles for days.

"Danica," Paul cried out as he arched his back above her.

Moments later, they lay nestled in each other's arms.

Paul kissed Danica's cheek and mumbled, "I swear, it gets better every time."

She nuzzled her head against his chest. "I was going to say the exact same thing."

He rolled to his side, and the sudden gurgling of Danica's stomach made Paul frown. "That sounded like an alien in there."

Danica pressed her hand over her stomach. "I skipped lunch."

"Well, I can't make love to you again with all of that going on." He laughed as he scooted to the edge of the king-sized bed. "I'll go and get the food and we can eat it in here."

Danica watched his muscular body climb from the bed and walk toward the bedroom door.

"I've got some wine in the fridge to go with our sandwiches. I'll bring that up, too," he added as he headed out the door.

Danica listened as he treaded down the stairs to the foyer. She lay back on the bed and smiled when she remembered the way he made her body tingle during their lovemaking.

"You're no good," an enraged voice called across the large bedroom.

Danica sat up in the bed and grabbed at the comforter, covering her nakedness.

"Go away," Danica whispered.

"I will never go away, Danica," the voice replied. "Not until you leave my Paul alone."

***

Later that night, Danica awoke with a start to find her body cradled in Paul's arms. They had munched on their food and drank the bottle of Zinfandel Paul had brought from the kitchen. After the food wrappers had been cleared away, and her noisy stomach had settled down, Paul had made love to her again. But instead of taking her home like Danica had asked, Paul had insisted she stay the night, claiming he wanted her by his side in the morning. Danica had not argued with him and had been somewhat relieved to stay at Paul's that night. The growing sense of discomfort she had whenever she stepped into her home made her embrace an opportunity for a night away from the cottage. But as she inspected Paul's bedroom, with its various antiques and portraits of sailboats cramming the walls, that same disturbing feeling enveloped her.

Images from the nightmare that had roused her from a sound sleep began to invade her thoughts. She saw a woman's hands wrapping around her body and attempting to squeeze the life out of her. But this time, Danica remembered what was said in the dream. The raspy voice had been Claire's, and her tone had been drenched with hatred. She had told Danica to stay away from her son.

"You're not good enough for my boy. You're Gaston's whore."

Danica's body trembled as Claire's vicious words repeated in her head.

"You're shivering," Paul whispered beside her. "You want me to get another blanket?" He pulled her closer to his warm body.

Danica snuggled against him. "No, I'm all right. Just another bad dream."

"About my mother?"

Danica nodded against his chest.

"You do know she wanted us to be together. She set us up for dinner that night. I'm sure wherever she is, she's happy to see that we are together."

"I hope so."

He kissed her forehead. "I know I'm right, so no more bad dreams, baby. I'm here. You're safe with me."

As Danica listened to the rise and fall of his chest, her eyelids became heavy with sleep. She believed she was safe with Paul. But Paul could not be with her every waking minute of the day. Whatever was going on, she was going to have to face it alone. Danica had battled enough monsters to know what she had to do. Life with Tom had taught her to conquer her fears and not run from them. The only problem was figuring out how to fight something she could not see. Danica knew that the living were capable of inflicting a hell of a lot more misery than the dead, but she debated if hatred simmering within a vengeful spirit could eventually burn its intended human victim. Did death quell anger, or could revenge always find a way to crawl back from the deepest depths of the grave? Danica prayed she never discovered the answer to that question. Some mysteries, she reasoned, were better left unsolved.

***

The following morning, Danica and Paul overslept. As they rushed around his house trying to find the clothes that had been haphazardly discarded the night before, Danica cursed their foolishness.

"Here, I found these under the bed," Paul told her as he came up to her, carrying a pair of lacey beige panties in his hand.

Danica stared at the panties. "Those aren't mine."

"Very funny." He pushed the panties toward her.

"They're not mine, Paul," she said with a straight face.

Danica watched as Paul eyed the panties. He examined Danica's features, and then detected the cocky grin rising on the edges of her mouth.

"You little...." He shook his head, smiling.

"Had you worried for a moment there, didn't I?"

"The last woman in this bedroom was my housekeeper. I assure you she cleans under the bed and has never been known to leave me...gifts before." He handed the panties to Danica.

"You can't blame a girl for checking."

"I don't lie or play games, Danica. Next time just ask instead of giving me a heart attack." He motioned to the adjoining bathroom. "Why don't you take a shower and I'll make us some breakfast."

"No time. I need to get home and change so I can get to work."

Paul slipped his arm about her naked shoulders. "There's plenty of time. I'll just get dressed and then I can take you home."

Danica stared at him. "But then you'll be late. No, I can take a streetcar to the Quarter. That way neither one of us will be late."

He pointed her in the direction of his adjoining bathroom. "Go take a shower and relax. I'll make us some coffee." He patted her firmly on the behind as he gently prodded her toward the bathroom door.

When she stepped underneath the warm cascade of water in the shower, her worries washed away. As her tired body relished the rush of warm water, she flashed back to her night with Paul. He had been gentle with her, but strong and commanding when she needed him to be. Then she remembered how Gaston had been during their night together. Paul's ardor paled against Gaston's take-charge attitude in bed. She questioned if Gaston's sexual prowess had been the result of living in a time when women were not equals, but objects. Gaston's ardor had not been tempered by modern civilities, and sex to him was primal, instinctual, and raw. Sex with Paul had been considerate, passionate, but somewhat reserved. As the comparisons between the ghost and the man continued, Danica yearned to feel Gaston's long, nimble hands on her breasts. She had hoped Paul's attentions would dissuade her from thinking of Gaston, but when left alone with her thoughts, images of Gaston would inevitably haunt her. For an instant, she wished she had been alive during his lifetime, had seen him as he was, smelled his skin, and stroked the real Gaston Deslonde in bed beside her.

"Stop it, Danica," she muttered. "He's gone. Out of your life for good."

But no matter how many times she repeated those words, Danica could never truly believe them. Part of her still longed for the mystery, fantasy, and clarity Gaston had brought to her life. Angry at her weakness for him, Danica desperately tried to scrub away all traces of Gaston from her memory, but the harder she rubbed her body with the sponge, the more her eyes filled with tears. Standing beneath the shower in Paul's bathroom, it finally hit her; Gaston was gone. Slowly, the words began to sink in, and when Danica inevitably faced the reality that she would never see her ghost again, she placed her head in her hands and cried.

CHAPTER 19

After Paul dropped Danica off at her doorstep, she was comforted by the fact that the shutters covering her front doors and window were still as she had left them the day before. She went to the gate leading to the courtyard and caught sight of Claire's closed up home next to her. The woman's voice from the previous night came back to her, and she was convinced more than ever that Claire had not crossed over like Gaston had warned.

"Hey, neighbor," Carl greeted as he headed down the small alleyway toward her.

"Hey, Carl," Danica replied, opening the gate.

"You all right?" Carl lingered over Danica's face as he stopped before her. "You don't look so good."

"I haven't been sleeping very well."

He scowled at her. "The ghosts have been keeping you up, too?"

Danica was about to deny the allegation, but then a thought gripped her. "Do your ghosts keep you from sleeping?"

He shrugged his thick shoulders. "In the beginning, but then I got earplugs and now I sleep like a rock. Being home during the day helps. The few times I am home at night, they tend to get real active."

"Have you seen…heard anything different around here lately?" she anxiously asked.

"Different? What do you mean?"

Danica vacillated over how much to tell Carl. After a few moments of uncertainty, she admitted, "I started hearing a woman's voice the other night in my bedroom. One I've never heard before, and I was wondering—"

"Was it friendly?" Carl questioned, cutting her off.

"Friendly?" Danica shook her head. "No, far from it. It almost sounded like…Claire Mouton." She watched Carl's face for his reaction.

But Carl's small brown eyes stayed on her and gave not the slightest hint as to what he was thinking. He said nothing for a few nerve-racking seconds, making Danica wonder if she should have said anything at all.

"I've seen her," Carl calmly stated. "Floating around her patio for the past three nights. She paces back and forth muttering words I can't make out. Started Sunday night."

Danica nodded her head, feeling a bit relieved. "Her memorial service was Sunday afternoon."

"Where was she buried?"

"She wasn't buried; she was cremated, along with Burt. Her son had their ashes placed in the family crypt in Metairie Cemetery last Sunday."

"That's it then. A ghost cannot haunt until the final rights have been said over their remains, or until they have been buried. The time between death and burial is called the shadow realm. A ghost hangs out in a kind of limbo until their remains have been put to rest. Then they can either haunt or cross over, but in Claire's case there will be no choice offered to leave. Suicides get to serve something akin to a jail sentence on earth."

"You think she has been forced to haunt her old home?"

Carl shook his head. "She can haunt wherever she felt at home, or haunt people with whom she had the closest ties. But why would she be bothering you? I know you were friendly with her, but I never thought you two—"

"I've been seeing her son, Paul Gaudette."

Carl gave a low whistle and then rubbed his baldhead. "That would do it. Momma may not be too happy about you and her boy. Claire was always going on about how perfect that son of hers was."

"Was she?"

"The few times I talked to her, her son always managed to creep into the conversation. I got the impression she was real possessive of him."

"Yeah, that's the impression I'm getting, too," Danica muttered.

"Watch your back," Carl warned. "I knew Claire well enough to know the woman was not playing with a full deck, and if any of that carries over from life, she may focus all of her energy on you."

"How can I get her to stop?"

Carl moved past her, shaking his head. "You can't just get her to stop, Danica. Takes a lot more magic than you or I possess to get a ghost to back off. You need a witch or a priest or someone equally skilled in dealing with the dead to help you." He stopped at the gate. "I'm just a research guy. I know there are rituals and such for removing unwanted ghosts, but I could not even begin to tell you where to start. This is out of my league."

A disheartened sigh escaped her lips. "Thanks, Carl."

Carl stepped onto the sidewalk and pulled the gate closed behind him. "Don't ignore this for too long, Danica. Claire was into all kinds of crazy crap when she was alive, and all that magic will help to make her stronger after death. Soon she may become too strong for you to stop."

Danica's stomach curled into knots. "What if I can't stop her?"

Carl frowned and scratched his baldhead. "Ever thought about relocating to Cleveland? Because if you can't stop her, you may have to." He turned and walked away.

Danica stood staring at the black gate as images of any number of worst-case scenarios tormented her. She swiveled her eyes to the cottage next to her and scowled. "Goddamn you, Gaston Deslonde. The one time I really need your help, and you stay away."

When she opened her back doors, the strong odor of a woman's perfume hit her. After she turned on the kitchen lights, her eyes grew wide with disbelief. All the contents of her refrigerator had been dumped on the kitchen floor, along with some broken dishes and shattered glasses from the cabinet above the sink.

Danica gingerly stepped over the mess and placed her purse and briefcase on the white-tiled kitchen counter. When she flipped on the lights to her office, the same disarray greeted her. All the papers and items that had been left on top of her desk were strewn about the floor, and her desk chair had been toppled over on its side. Framed pictures of her parents she had placed on the fireplace mantle were tossed to the floor, leaving broken glass scattered about the room. The only picture untouched was Gaston's imposing portrait above the fireplace.

She soon discovered every room in her home had been vandalized. Tom's books had been thrown from the bookshelves, furniture had been upended, and her clothes had been removed from her closet and flung about her bedroom. Even her toothpaste had been emptied into the bathroom sink, and her shampoo poured all over the bottom of the shower stall.

"Son of a bitch," Danica shouted as she picked up her robe from the bathroom floor. "Who in the hell did this?"

From the kitchen, Danica heard her cell phone ring tone. When she ran to get the phone out of her purse, she felt her anger abate and an inkling of panic take over. As Danica reached for her phone, she began to wonder if this wanton destruction was not caused by human hands, but by ghostly ones.

"Hello?" she said, answering her cell phone.

"I don't think I can wait until Friday to see you again," Paul's smooth voice purred into her ear. "Maybe I could come over to your place tonight. In the morning you—"

"Paul, that's not a good idea," she asserted, looking down at the pile of broken dishes on the floor.

"What's wrong? Your voice sounds funny."

Danica threw her hand up, suppressing the urge to cry. "My house has been ransacked and—"

"What? Are you still inside?"

"Yeah, but I doubt it was—"

"Get out right now, Danica. Whoever did this could still be hiding in there. I'm turning around and heading back. Go outside and call 911 right now. I'm on my way." He hung up.

Danica looked down at her cell phone. "How in the hell am I going explain this to the police?"

Just when she was about to grab her purse from the counter, a noise from her office made her stop in her tracks. At first, it sounded like a mild groaning, but then the noise grew louder and resembled something akin to a dog's growl. Part of Danica wanted to flee and never look back, but another part of her wanted to confront whatever or whoever had done this to her home. Slowly, she inched her way around the kitchen doorway to get a better look in her office. When she finally had an unhindered view of the entire room, she noticed a dark shadow forming in the far corner of her office. It was petite and built more like a woman than a man. As the shadow grew darker and more detailed in appearance, the growling became more distinct.

"You don't scare me, Claire. I know you don't want me to see your son, but perhaps you should take this up with him instead of destroying my home," Danica shouted as she stood in the arched doorway to the kitchen.

Danica's skin prickled with fear as the shape slowly morphed into a human form, but the features on the face were too dark to make out.

"Whore," the shadow shrieked.

Danica clenched her fists and defiantly squared her shoulders. "You introduced me to your son. You were the one who arranged for Gaston to come to me because you wanted to get rid of your husband. If I'm a whore, Claire, what does that make you?"

The growl turned into a thunderous roar and the room began to vibrate. Danica could feel the temperature suddenly drop and her breath became like mist before her eyes. Then, the dark shadow started moving toward her.

Danica backed away from the arched doorway and tried to make her way across the kitchen to her back doors. She kept her eyes riveted on the black mass floating across the office, but when she hopped over the pile of food on the kitchen floor she lost her footing. Danica grabbed for the counter as her feet slipped out from under her. Just before she hit the floor, she saw the dark shadow gaining speed as it entered the kitchen.

The acrid taste of terror rose in the back of Danica's throat. She kicked against the debris, trying desperately to stay upright, but just when she thought she had caught her balance the dark shadow overtook her. Danica screamed as she saw Claire's distorted face closing in on her, and then the world went black.

***

"Danica," a voice called through a thick fog to her. "Danica!"

When Danica opened her eyes, her head felt as if there were a thousand tiny hammers banging against it.

"Oh, God," she murmured as she was lifted up by unseen hands.

When her eyes came into focus, Danica realized she was being carried out of her kitchen and to the courtyard beyond her back doors. She looked over to her rescuer and saw Paul's concerned green eyes investigating every inch of her face. He set her down gently on the ground as he continued to hover over her. His fingers lightly touched the right side of her forehead.

"Are you all right?" he all but shouted in a shaky voice.

"Yeah, just have a splitting headache." She raised her hand to her right temple. "What happened?"

"You tell me." He sat back on his heels. "Your front doors and window were all shuttered up and the gate was locked. Luckily, your neighbor in the carriage house arrived and opened the gate for me."

"Carl let you in?" Danica gazed woozily about the courtyard.

"He went to his place to call 911. When we walked in and saw you passed out on the floor, I told him to go and call for help."

"They're on their way," Carl shouted as he came through the front door of his carriage house.

Danica tried to careen her head around to Carl, but the pain was too much. "Damn," she cursed, grabbing her head.

Paul placed his fingers against the right side of her face. "Looks like you slipped on all that crap on your kitchen floor and banged your head against the counter. You were out cold when we found you."

Carl kneeled down on the cement and smiled at Danica. "You okay?"

Danica remembered what happened right before everything went dark. She saw Claire's ghostly face looming over her and heard her angry growl.

"Did you see anything when you guys were in my kitchen?"

Paul gave Carl a worried glance. "Like what?"

Carl shrugged. "We were both so concerned about you, I don't think we noticed anything else. Except maybe that your house had been trashed."

Danica stared at Carl. "You didn't see anything else? Anything…different?"

Carl's eyes quickly registered with understanding. "Ah, no. I didn't see anything."

"What happened Danica?" Paul demanded.

When Danica turned and saw the trepidation in Paul's face, she could not find the strength to tell him what she had seen. Instead, she gave him a slight smile and put her hand against her right temple. "Nothing happened, I slipped on the mess on the kitchen floor when I was heading to the doors."

In the distance, Danica heard sirens approaching and her heart sank. It was one thing to explain to Carl and Paul about the mess in her house, but the police were going to ask a whole lot of questions she did not know if she would be able to answer.

Carl stood from Danica's side. "I'll go and open the gate for them."

Danica watched Carl's thick body walk across the courtyard and toward the narrow alleyway.

Paul pulled her into his arms. "You scared the hell out of me when I saw you passed out on that floor. Maybe we should take you to the ER to have your head looked at."

Danica closed her eyes and relaxed in his arms, feeling a small respite from the pounding in her head. "I'm fine, Paul."

He pulled away from her. "You're sure?"

She nodded. "I'm sure."

"All right. When the police get through here, we're packing up some of your things and you're going to stay with me for a while. I'm going to call your landlord and see what we have to do to get an alarm system installed."

"I can't afford one, and I don't think Mr. Caruso is going to want to have to pay for an alarm system."

Paul scowled. "If that's the case, you're moving the hell out of here, Danica," he declared, raising his voice.

She winced against the pain his loud voice was creating in her head. "I can't think about that right now, Paul. Let's just deal with the police first, and then we can talk about it." She looked around the courtyard. "Where's my purse? I need to call work and tell them I'm not coming in."

Paul nodded to the cottage. "You left it on the kitchen counter."

Danica tried to stand, but Paul placed his hand on her shoulder, keeping her on the ground. "I'll get it. Just stay here."

Danica heard the sirens on the street in front as Paul stepped inside her kitchen. She waited, watching the back doors for Paul to return. Seconds ticked by, but he never appeared. Danica heard voices approaching the gate to the street.

"Paul?" she called out.

Moments later Paul appeared in the back door to her home, holding her purse in his hand. Danica immediately sensed something was wrong. His countenance was pale and his eyes were glazed over.

She struggled to her feet. "What is it, Paul?"

Snapping out of his trance, Paul saw her and came up to her side, just as Danica rose from the ground.

"You shouldn't be standing up," he scolded as he handed her the purse.

She took in his ashen face and white lips. "What's wrong?"

Danica heard voices heading up the alleyway.

Paul looked down at his shaking hands. "I think I just saw a ghost," he whispered. Paul turned to see two police officers coming toward them. "Ah, here they are, just in time."

***

After questioning Danica, searching her cottage, recommending she change her locks, and giving her a report number to file with her insurance company, the policeman climbed into their blue and white sedan parked outside her home.

"No wonder none of us feel safe in this city," Paul extolled, watching the police car drive down Dumaine Street. "If the police don't consider a break-in serious, then who will?"

Danica took his hand and pulled him toward the gate. "You heard what Officer Lawrence said. They get ten to twelve of these types of calls a day in this district. If they called out the crime division for every break-in, they would have no one left to cover all the murders going on in the city."

Paul frowned as he followed her in the gate. "Another reason you can't stay here alone anymore. The crime down here is too dangerous for a woman living alone. You need to move, Danica."

She shut the gate behind him with a loud bang. "I'll change the locks like Officer Lawrence suggested, and talk to Mr. Caruso about an alarm. I'll be fine."

"We should also get you a dog, if you insist on staying here. A big one with sharp teeth."

"A dog? I'm never home enough to care for a dog."

Paul turned and headed down the alleyway. "You don't have to be home all the time to care for a dog. When you come and stay with me on the weekends, you can bring the dog with you."

Danica followed closely behind him. "You make it sound like we're going to be spending a lot of time together."

Paul turned to her and winked. "That's what I'm hoping."

"You sure I won't cramp your style?"

He came up to her and placed his hands about her face. "Maybe a little," he joked.

Danica pulled away and playfully slapped his chest. Paul slipped his arm about her shoulders and urged her toward the courtyard.

"How's the head?" he inquired as they turned from the alleyway.

"Better," she told him. "The pounding has turned into a slight throbbing."

"Let's get your things packed and we'll head over to my place."

When they reached the back door of her home, Paul froze. Danica carefully observed as his green eyes fearfully dashed about the kitchen. "Before you said you saw a ghost. Do you want to tell me what you saw?"

He released his arm from about her and turned away. "You'll think I'm crazy."

Danica laughed out loud, unable to hide her amusement. "Paul, you have no idea how not-crazy you will sound to me."

He faced her, furrowing his wide brow. "What do you mean?"

"First, tell me what you saw, and then I will tell you about all the crazy things I have seen since I have moved in here."

He looked down and placed his hands in the pockets of his casual black pants, avoiding her eyes. "I think I saw my mother," he finally admitted.

Danica patted his arm, reassuringly. "I saw her, too, before I hit my head. She was floating in this black mist, and she was pissed as hell."

His eyes became round and his jaw fell slightly. "That's what I saw. She was coming at me from the doorway, yelling at me to find a nice girl."

Danica sighed. "She thinks I'm not good enough for you."

He shook his head, appearing confused. "But she set us up. She encouraged me to see you again after dinner that night at her place. She even made a comment about what attractive children we would have together. Why on earth would she think you're not good enough for me now?"

Danica desperately wanted to tell him the truth, but the truth would have been too much for him. "Perhaps she is having second thoughts," Danica offered.

"This is crazy. My mother is dead."

"Dead, but perhaps not yet moved on," Danica explained.

"Moved on? To where?"

"Wherever we go when we die. Maybe she is hanging around trying to keep an eye on you. Make sure you find the right girl and not end up with someone like me."

Paul placed his hands on his hips. "Are you saying she's a ghost?"

"Ghosts exist, Paul. I've seen them here in this house." She nodded to her cottage. "When I was a little girl, I saw them quite frequently." She motioned to Carl's cottage. "Carl has them, too," she added.

Paul rolled his eyes, smirking. "Carl is not exactly right in the head, Danica. You saw how the police reacted when he suggested your home was ransacked by an angry ghost."

Danica stepped to the doorway of her home. "Carl has a lot of experience with this stuff. I know we have to be careful what we say, especially to the police, but just because you can't see it, does not mean it isn't real, Paul."

"Do you think an angry ghost destroyed your house?"

Danica studied his eyes, feeling as if she were at a precipice in their relationship. "I'm not sure what or who did that."

"I'm glad to hear it. I know you may believe in ghosts and such, Danica, but to attribute all of that destruction to something paranormal is a bit much."

"Do you believe what you saw was real?"

He ran his hand through his hair. "Really weird, that's for sure. What it actually was, I don't know. Maybe we have both been a little too stressed. You can see things when you're stressed."

Danica nodded her head in agreement. "I know." She paused and directed her gaze from the house to Paul. "Do you want to wait out here while I pack?"

He shook his head. "No, I'm fine. Let's get some of this mess picked up and then I'll take you home."

Danica headed inside.

"Perhaps we should pick up some scotch on the way," Paul suggested as they entered into the kitchen.

Danica reached for a broom next to her refrigerator. "Good idea."

"Yeah," Paul agreed, reaching for a broken plate from the floor. "I don't know about you, but after everything this morning, I could really use a drink."

As Danica began sweeping some of the mess on the kitchen floor aside, the memory of her father tugged at her heart. He had always believed a good belt of scotch whiskey could cure all ills. But somehow Danica wasn't convinced that the alcohol was going to help her or Paul in this situation. She had a strange feeling that what they had faced in her kitchen was only the beginning. *This is how it always begins in all of those horror movies*, she mused. *First, you reach for alcohol, and soon after you find you are running for your life.*

CHAPTER 20

The last embers of daylight were sneaking through Paul's bedroom window when Danica ran her hand through the rays of light dancing on the sheets around her. Reassured to see Paul sleeping soundly in the bed next to her, she raised her eyes to the half-empty bottle of scotch on the bedside table next to him. She remembered their feverish lovemaking after they had each consumed a good portion of the bottle. His eyes fluttered slightly beneath his closed lids and his mouth twitched. Danica considered what he could be dreaming about, and then she thought back to the events of that morning, and decided his dreams were probably not happy ones.

As she stretched out beside him, her mind filled with questions. Should she tell Paul of her relationship with Gaston? What would he think of her? Would Paul want to spend his life with a crazy woman who believed in ghosts?

Danica ran her hands over her face as the possible outcomes with Paul muddied her thoughts. She wanted to share her anxieties with him, but knew that could only end up harming their relationship, and Danica was beginning to value having Paul in her life. Tom had never been one for protecting his wife. He had always felt Danica should be able to take care of herself; it was when she wasn't willing to take care of him, as well, that Tom became violent. But to have someone who cared, who worried, and who would come when she called, made Danica's regard for Paul grow even deeper.

"No, Momma," Paul whimpered.

Danica turned to see Paul's face twisted in pain. His hands were curled into fists and his nostrils were flaring.

She gently shook him. "Paul?"

Paul startled awake and jumped back when he saw Danica. After a few seconds, he calmed and wiped his hand over his sweaty brow.

"Christ, I was having a horrible nightmare," he mumbled.

Danica brushed aside a comma of brown hair that had fallen into his eyes. "About what?"

He gave her a quizzical gaze. "Must have been the scotch." He reclined back on the bed. "It was just a nightmare. Don't worry about it."

"You sure you don't want to talk about it?"

"No," he grumbled, and rolled over on his side.

The gesture sent a bitter shockwave through Danica's heart. In that instant, she knew Claire's influence was coming between them. The Paul she had come to know would have shared his anxieties with her, but to cut her off was not at all like the man she cared for. If they stood any chance at a future together, Danica would have to do whatever she could to rid herself of Claire Mouton's malevolent presence. But what would she tell Paul? She decided perhaps it would be best not to involve him in any of her plans. The effect of seeing his mother's ghost had taken its toll on him, and Danica knew any further exposure to such experiences might be more than he could bear. She needed to spare him any more sorrow, and would have to get rid of Claire without Paul's assistance…but how? As her mind buzzed with options, Carl's words from earlier that morning came back to her. She would have to find someone who was an expert at dealing with spirits, someone who knew how to get rid of them for good.

Danica tossed the covers off her naked body and climbed from the bed.

"Where are you going?" Paul asked, rolling over to her.

She went to the dresser by the door where Paul had placed her suitcase. "I need to go out for a little while."

Paul sat up. "Out? Out where?"

Danica picked up her suitcase and brought it to the bed. "There's someone I need to talk to," she told him as she unzipped the black suitcase.

"Who do you have to talk to?"

She retrieved a pair of underwear, jeans, and a T-shirt from the bag. "Paul, I need to go back to the Quarter."

He threw the covers aside and jumped from the bed. "You're not going back there without me." He came around the bed and stood next to her. "It's not safe at night."

She waved off his concern with her hand. "I'll be fine."

He went to his dresser. “I’ll drive you.”

She put her clothes down on the bed. “I need to know what your nightmare was about.”

“What has that got to do with this?”

She sat down on the bed. “Was it about Claire? I heard you call out for her.”

He reached into the dresser and pulled out a pair of boxer shorts. “She was screaming at me, and ranting about how I needed to get rid of you. She wanted me to…send you away.”

Danica’s face remained calm. “Did it feel like your mother in the dream?”

He pulled on the boxers, keeping his eyes to the floor. “It was nothing. I’ve just been having some crazy nightmares lately. That’s all it was.”

She stood from the bed, shaking her head. “You’ve had more than one nightmare?”

He ran his hand through his hair. “I’ve had a few bad dreams about my mother, but so what?”

“When did these dreams begin?”

“Sunday night. Why? Does it matter?” He casually shook his head. “After everything I’ve been through with Burt and my mother, I would expect to have at least a few nightmares.”

Danica came up to him. “Paul, what if I said I could find a way to stop the nightmares for both of us, and in the process set your mother’s soul free?”

He crinkled his brow. “Set her free? What are you talking about?”

“I’m asking you right now to let go of everything you once believed in. When we let go of all the things we once held sacred, we find our minds are more likely to embrace a whole new philosophy. That’s the irony of belief; you have to let go of it in order to make it stronger.”

He stood calmly before her and folded his arms over his muscular chest. “What is it you want me to believe in?”

Danica walked back to the bed, picked up her clothes, and clutched them to her chest. “That ghosts are real.”

He took a few seconds to decide and then he slowly nodded. Tossing his hand in the air he said, “All right, I can accept that. If you believe they’re real, then I can, too.”

"You need to believe that your mother is a ghost, as well. You saw her today in my kitchen. I think she has been haunting my house for the past few days."

"Why is she haunting your house?"

"Because of Gaston Deslonde. You know your mother was into all kinds of spells and rituals that would open up communication with ghosts. Your aunt told me she had been fascinated with ghosts ever since she was a young girl."

Paul shrugged his wide shoulders. "All my life I grew up listening to her talk about haunted houses, or telling me scary ghost stories. I always thought her interest in spells and such nonsense was part of her fascination with the paranormal."

"It was more than mere fascination. Your mother took it a step further and tried to control the ghost haunting her home. She tried to exert her will on Gaston, but in the end she realized she couldn't compete with the only person who has ever had any influence over him."

He ran his hand over his chin. "I know I'm going to regret asking this, but who is that?"

Danica turned to the bathroom door. "Love creates its own powerful magic, with ghosts and people."

Paul bounded across the room and grabbed her arm. "Are you telling me you're in love with a ghost?"

Danica stared in horror at his hand squeezing into her arm. Images of Tom, reaching for her in the very same way, shot across her mind.

Paul saw the panic in her eyes and instantly let her go. He stood back from her as his shoulders sank with regret. "I'm sorry, Danica, but the thought of you being in love with—"

"I'm not in love with Gaston," she professed. "I thought for a while I was in love with him, but then you came along and made me realize I wasn't."

"A ghost? You're kidding."

"I know it doesn't make any sense, but it's the truth, Paul. I wanted to say something before, but I didn't know how."

His wary green eyes searched her features for the slightest glimmer of deception. "Is he the other man you were telling me about?" he eventually questioned.

"Yes, but I couldn't reveal that he was a ghost. I didn't want you thinking I was completely deranged."

Paul's stern eyes softened. "Do I have to worry about some dead guy wanting to kick my ass because you're in love with me?"

Danica intently studied his face. "I never said I was in love with you," she carefully pronounced.

He came forward and wrapped her in his arms. "You didn't have to." He hungrily kissed her.

Danica's body melted as his lips pressed against hers. She dropped the clothes from her arms and grabbed hold of his semi-naked body.

"Let's go back to bed," he whispered in her ear.

She tried to push him away. "But what about everything I just told you?"

He held her closer. "My mother and your Gaston are dead, Danica. Whatever they want, it can't harm us. We're alive, and right now I want to do the one thing with you that only the living can enjoy. After that, I'll drive you to the French Quarter so you can do what you have to do to get this out of your system."

She tensed in his arms. "You don't believe me."

"No, I believe in you, Danica; there's a difference." He picked her up and carried her back to the bed. After he placed her gently down on the blue sheets, he mumbled, "I will always believe in you, no matter how far-fetched your ideas might seem. It doesn't matter to me if you chase ghosts or UFO's or the Loch Ness Monster."

She held his face in her hands, examining his eyes. "You're not freaked out by all of this?"

"No. That's what the powerful magic of love does Danica; it opens the door to your heart so another person's weird beliefs can become yours."

Danica's heart trembled. "Are you saying you're in love with me?"

He lowered his head to hers. "Yeah, I believe I am." Then Paul kissed her, silencing all of her doubts.

As his lips began to travel the lengths of her body, Danica felt a renewed sense of strength building within her. She wasn't alone anymore, and no matter what happened, she had someone real to support and love her. The only problem was, her heart still yearned for the man who wasn't there.

***

"You're sure I can't come with you?" Paul questioned as he stopped his Land Rover in front of Jackson Square. "I'm not comfortable with leaving you alone."

"No." Danica unfastened her seatbelt. "I have to do this alone."

He kissed her cheek. "You know, I'm not afraid of ghosts. If you need a second Ghostbuster, you know who to call."

"I'll keep that in mind."

He leaned back from her. "I'll make sure my proton backpack is fully charged."

She laughed and shook her head. "I was so afraid to say anything, in case you started heading toward the exit. I want to thank you for believing in me."

"Never be afraid to tell me what you're thinking, Danica. No matter how crazy it may seem to you. I want to be included in every crazy idea, weird adventure, or paranormal event going on in your life from now on, got it?"

"Got it." She opened her car door.

"I'll be standing by, if you need me," Paul added over her shoulder. "Call my cell phone when you want me to come and get you, and be careful."

Danica turned back to him and smiled. "I will."

As she walked away from his car, Danica's eyes surveyed the darkness around Jackson Square. Despite the late hour, a great deal of street entertainers were still working the thinning crowds. Danica sighted the large oak trees on the side of the square where she had encountered Madame LeJeune. But when Danica approached the spot beneath the oaks, there was no simple wooden table or chairs sitting there. Madame LeJeune's usual place beside the thick black wrought iron fence was empty. She took in the artists on either side of her and observed a woman with large eyes and short red hair sketching something on an easel.

"Excuse me, have you seen Madame LeJeune?" Danica asked the artist.

The woman raised her misty blue eyes to her. "She hasn't been around for the past few days."

"Is there any other part of the French Quarter she frequents?" Danica probed.

The woman shook her head. "Sorry. Madame is always the real quiet type. She never says much to anyone."

Danica thanked the artist and eagerly began to circumvent the black wrought iron fence surrounding the square. She checked every artist and every fortuneteller set up in the area, but nowhere did she see the elusive Madame LeJeune.

After having gone around Jackson Square twice, Danica leaned against the corner fence post across from Jax Brewery. She noted the dark evening sky and pondered what to do next.

"I knew you would be back," a rough voice said beside her.

When Danica turned, she saw Madame LeJeune standing next to her. She was wearing a pale blue poncho and her long gray hair was piled atop her head. Her odd hazel eyes were glued to Danica's face.

"I guess the time has come for you to make that choice, Danica."

Danica's stomach knotted up. "The choice has already been made. Gaston is gone, but there is another ghost, and she's doing things to me and—"

"The woman?" Madame LeJeune asked. "She's angry with you, yeah?"

"Very angry," Danica confirmed. "You know about spirits and how to deal with them. How do I get rid of her?"

The old fortuneteller tipped her head to the side. "What you're asking takes a lot of skill and stupidity. You sure you're up for that?"

"I can't move ahead in my life if this spirit stays. She wants to hurt me and destroy my relationship with—"

"The man you were first here with. The son of the ghost you want to get rid of. You will be happy with him, but you already know that, don't you, child?"

Danica slowly nodded. "Can you help me?"

Madame LeJeune waved to a bar next to them by the corner of Jackson Square. "Buy me a drink and we'll talk."

Danica followed Madame LeJeune as she crossed the gray slate paving stones and had a seat at a round, wooden table situated on the sidewalk, overlooking Decatur Street.

"What you ask is very difficult even for an experienced medium to accomplish," Madame LeJeune began as she removed her poncho from about her shoulders. She plopped the thick material on the chair next to her. "Sending ghosts over to the other side takes a strong stomach, 'specially when they don't want to go. You think this ghost of yours is willing to leave?"

Danica made herself comfortable in her chair. "I doubt Claire wants to go. She committed suicide, and I know that ties her to the place where she died, but she is also haunting her son's home, as well." She shook her head. "We both have nightmares about her, and the other day she attacked me at my house."

Madame LeJeune's hazel eyes rounded with surprise. "Sounds like you've got a problem. But how someone dies don't make them a ghost, Danica. It's why they died that determines whether or not they will haunt one place or every place they knew in their former life."

"Why they died? I don't understand."

"What can I get you ladies?" a buxom young waitress with a long braid of golden hair asked as she stood next to their table.

"Heineken," Madame LeJeune stated.

"Just water for me," Danica informed her.

"I'll be right back with that." The young girl turned away.

Madame LeJeune waited for the server to leave before her eyes returned to Danica. "Why someone dies has a lot to do with how they lived. Death is not separate from life, but part of it. How someone lives—good, bad or indifferent—has a great deal to do with why they leave it. People who are content with the life they have lived will let go of that life at the end. They're ready to move on; whether or not they were happy or sad, they're ready for a change. But individuals who have never reconciled with their past, those are the ones who haunt. They have a harder time dealing with change."

"What about people who are murdered or who suffer sudden, tragic deaths and haunt a house?"

"Haunting is one thing. What you're talking about are impressions. Every emotion we feel is made of energy, and that energy can be imprinted on a place or thing, even a person. Sometimes what you feel in a room where a death has occurred is not a haunting, but an impression. Hauntings are very different. A haunting involves an actual spirit or soul of an individual taking up residence in their former house, or someplace where they felt safe when they were alive. When a ghost haunts, they're holding on to the past, refusing to let go of the life they once had. You can always spot the ones who will become ghosts or have a difficult time with the transition to death. How a person handles change is the key."

Danica traced her fingers over the gouges and nicks in the smooth surface of the table before her. "I don't think Claire handled change very well. Her son told me she had problems letting go when she was alive."

"Your dark man had the same problem. I'll bet he was a man who never liked change and always balked at progress. He was comfortable with how things were, and when confronted by changes that he didn't want to accept, he probably got angry or withdrew. In the end, he could not accept his physical changes, and decided to end his life, instead of enjoying the time he had left. For some people, Danica, life is less about the miracles and more about the suffering. They never see the wonder around them and can only focus on their misery. Until you can embrace the wonder of life, you will never be able to accept the inevitability of change. Change is the energy that allows us to grow. And when we don't grow…well, we become ghosts. Our energy gets trapped between two worlds, and until ghosts realize this, they can never move on."

"So how do I get Claire to realize this?"

"Some people never do. They stay trapped for a very long time until their energy fades away. In other instances, they need someone to show them the way, either living or dead. Sometimes they listen, sometimes they don't."

"But isn't there some kind of magic I can use to banish her from my house and my life?"

Madame LeJeune let out a loud cackle that made a few patrons in the bar turn their way. "Magic is nothing but a person's will personified. It's the will that makes magic happen. If you want it bad enough, you can make anything happen. The same is true for your ghost problem. You want her out, you have to will her out."

Danica leaned forward in her chair. "Will her out? What do I do, order her to go?"

"In a way, yes," Madame LeJeune responded with a shrug. "Use your words, not some incantation from a book. They must be words that have meaning to you. Tell her why you want her gone, how your life will be better without her, and believe in what you say. Words don't hold weight without belief behind them."

"That's it? Tell her why I want her gone and believe it? It sounds too simple."

Madame LeJeune slapped her hand on the tabletop. "Ain't so simple, girl. When you've got a ghost pulling all of their tricks, trying to distract you from your purpose, it can be difficult as hell, trust me."

Danica nodded her head, accepting the challenge. "All right. Is there anything else I need to do?"

Madame LeJeune waved her hand over their small table. "Four white candles need to be lit outside a circle made of salt after the stroke of midnight, when the time of the dead begins. Each candle must be lined up with the four directions of the compass. The salt is to protect you from the spirit. They can't cross a line of salt, and the white candles are to keep them from turning to the four corners of the earth to escape. The only spot open for them to go will be up. Up leads to the other side. It's sort of like herding cattle; you're driving them upward with words and light."

"And after I light four white candles, stand in a circle of salt, and tell her to go, then she'll cross over?"

Madame LeJeune sat back in her chair. "You hope she crosses over. Some ghosts just disappear for a while and make you think they're gone, but they come back."

"How will I know if she's gone?"

"There's a smell when a spirit passes the threshold to the other side. Whenever a ghost departs, there's a spark of energy as their form goes from this world to the next. If you're successful, you'll smell it or feel the energy in the air."

"Here you go, ladies," the waitress said as she returned to their table, carrying their drinks on a black tray.

She placed a tall glass and a green longneck of beer on the table in front of Madame LeJeune.

The older woman picked up the glass and handed it back to the waitress. "I won't be needing this."

The young woman nodded, took the glass, and then placed a glass of soda water in front of Danica. "That'll be thirteen even."

Danica reached for her purse and pulled out a twenty-dollar bill.

Madame LeJeune picked up her beer. "I'll be needing another one of these in a few minutes."

Danica handed the girl the money. "Keep the beers coming."

The waitress took her money, gave her a toothy smile, and walked away.

Madame LeJeune gulped back half the bottle of beer in one swallow. Danica reached for her soda water and took a quick sip.

"Make sure you ask for protection before you begin the cleansing," Madame LeJeune added as she put her beer down on the table with a thud.

Danica placed her glass on the table. "Who do I ask for protection?"

"The universe, of course. Just call to the air for protection in what you're about to do. The universe will hear you and send you protection. It always does."

Danica traced her fingers along the edge of her sweaty glass. "Can anything go wrong with this?"

Madame LeJeune's face grew grim. "More than can go right with it. You can anger the spirit or spirits in a home, and instead of calming things down, you can stir them up."

Danica grabbed her glass. "I don't think I needed to hear that."

"Be prepared for any and all things to happen when dealing with the spirit world, Danica. They're just as unpredictable as people. The only difference is you can usually see people coming."

Danica took a long sip from her drink, suddenly yearning for something stronger than water. She spotted their waitress at a table close by and nodded to the glass in her hand when the waitress looked over at her.

Danica waited until the young woman with the long golden ponytail returned to their table.

"Scotch, neat," Danica said to the server. "And keep them coming."

"Now you're getting the idea," Madame LeJeune cracked with a cheeky grin.

Danica watched the waitress as she walked away. "Yes, I believe I'm beginning to fully comprehend what I'm up against."

Madame LeJeune reached for her beer. "Child, you haven't got any idea what you're up against, but that's a good thing. You'd never be able to go through with it if you knew what was coming."

"How many times have you done this?"

Madame LeJeune peered down at the beer in her hands. "Me, never. But I've never pissed off a ghost before."

Danica gaped at the woman. "Then how do you know if it will work?"

Madame LeJeune smiled at Danica, flashing her perfectly white teeth. "I don't, but I'm sure you'll make it happen. All you have to do is believe, Danica. Believe in yourself, and that old ghost won't stand a chance."

***

Fortified with scotch and clutching the bag containing four white candles to her chest, Danica slowly turned the key in the gate next to her cottage. She could still hear Paul's protests reverberating in her head when she had called him after her meeting with Madame LeJeune to tell him of her plans.

"Are you insane?" he had yelled into her cell phone. "I don't want you going back there, let alone performing some kind of half-assed voodoo ritual to get rid of my mother."

"I need to end this tonight while I have the courage to go through with it."

"You mean the stupidity to go through with it."

"That, too," she had agreed.

"At least let me come and help you."

"No," Danica had insisted. "I need to do this on my own. I'll call you when I'm done."

"If I don't hear from you by twelve-fifteen, I'm coming over there."

"Paul, I don't know how long this will take and—"

"Twelve-fifteen, Danica. You can stop in the middle of your hocus-pocus and call me. If you won't let me come with you, then you have to stay in touch."

"All right, I'll try and call," Danica had assured him. "But I've never done this before and I don't know what to expect, so I might not be able to just step away and make a phone call."

"You'd better, or I'll have half the NOPD breaking down your door," Paul had threatened.

What scared Danica more than the prospect of dealing with Paul and the police was wondering what other pissed off entities she might awaken during the ritual. Most of her life she had known a ghost, had talked to a ghost, but never once had she been afraid of a ghost. Now she was terrified by what she could not see, and for the first time in her life, she wished she could be that naive little girl she once was; someone who had seen every uncertainty as an adventure, and who had embraced the fears only adults seemed to shun.

As she slinked down the alleyway to the courtyard, Danica's ears were tuned into every sound around her. When she reached her rear french doors, she silently prayed to the forces above to help her find the courage to see this thing through.

Inside, the cottage looked the same as when she and Paul had left it the day before. They had cleaned up most of the mess and returned the overturned furniture to its rightful place. There was not a hint of anything in the air, only the smell of the household cleaner she had used in the kitchen to wipe the floor.

She put the bag of candles down on the kitchen counter and hunted through her cabinets for salt. After grabbing the blue carton of salt and a pack of matches from her drawer, she gingerly made her way to the living room.

Once she had flipped on the lights, she rapidly went to work moving away furniture from the center of the living room and drawing out a circle on the floor with the salt. She had to guess at the four compass directions. Aligning the candles with the four plaster depictions of Aeolus in the corners of the ceiling, she hoped that was close enough to appease whatever insane god ruled over this sort of thing.

After lighting the candles, Danica entered the circle. She sat down on the floor and tried to clear her mind.

"Universe, if you're listening, I really could use your help about now, so if you're up there, I call on you for protection."

Danica let out a deep breath, shook her hands, and closed her eyes. She pictured Claire as she had appeared in life, and then Danica began slowly telling the image in her head why she had to leave.

"That won't work," a man's deep voice said beside her.

Danica's eyes snapped open and saw Gaston standing at the edge of the circle, staring down at her.

Her heart thudded with happiness as she jumped to her feet. "Where in the hell have you been?"

"It's good to see you, too, my treasure." He stepped over to the brown sofa Danica had pushed against the far wall and had a seat.

"Where did you go?"

"Did you miss me?"

"Of course, I missed you," Danica shouted. "You went away and I have missed talking to you and—"

"But you found someone else to listen to you." He leaned back on the sofa. "I know, Danica. I know your feelings for Paul, and I'm happy for you both."

She cautiously stared into his disconcerting eyes. "You're happy for us?"

"I was wrong to pressure you into committing to me. How can you love someone who isn't real?"

"You're real to me, Gaston, and how I feel about Paul doesn't change what we have. It's not better or more fulfilling, it's just...different."

"It's human," he told her with a sad smile. "I guess that's what I realized when I was away. You're human, and you need another human being to make you feel complete. It's what every human needs while they are bound to this earth."

"Is that why you came back? To tell me this."

He shook his head. "You called for protection." He pointed his finger at his chest. "That would be me. I've always been your protector, Danica. I took up that mantle the first day I saw you sitting in your bedroom and playing with your dolls. I swore then I would always protect you from harm."

"If you're my protector, where were you the other day when Claire was attacking me in the kitchen?"

"You didn't ask for protection then. I can only come when I am summoned."

She was about to leave the circle when he held up his hand to her. "Stay inside that. If you step outside the circle, she will attack you."

Danica's blue eyes nervously searched the room. "She's here."

He nodded. "And listening to every word we say."

She cocked her head to the side. "What did you mean when you said this won't work?"

He leaned forward on the sofa and folded his hands before him. "Claire doesn't want to go to the other side, Danica. She must be forced to go."

Danica threw her hands up. "How in the hell am I supposed to force her to the other side?"

Gaston stood from the sofa. "I can help you, but you must promise to do something for me."

"Of course, Gaston."

He came to the edge of the circle and gazed into Danica's eyes. "Be happy, Danica. Grab hold of that man and build the kind of life you always dreamed of since you were a little girl. I will be happy, if you are happy."

Danica's eyes anxiously searched his. "What are you saying, Gaston?"

"You know what I'm saying. It's time for us both to move on."

"Gaston, no; please tell me you're not going to do anything stupid. I need you, here with me. I came back to this house to be with you."

He raised his head and listened. "Claire knows something is going to happen." Gaston turned away. "Time to begin." He waved his hand about the room. "Call to her. Tell her to leave. Be forceful…be strong." He glanced back at her and grinned. "Be you," he added.

"What is going to happen?"

"Not to worry, my treasure, all will be well."

He smiled and Danica felt as if she were a little girl again with her best friend standing by her side, encouraging her to conquer all those mountains life shoved in her way.

Remembering what Madame LeJeune had said about using words that had meaning to her, Danica summoned every ounce of courage she possessed and called out, "Claire, Claire Mouton, I demand that you come to me. I want to talk to you. We need to settle this. I will not have you interfering with Paul and me. This is my life, and you're not going to ruin it. Do you hear me? You want to fight, well, here's your chance."

"She hears you," Gaston advised. "But she is hesitant." He lowered his head and whispered, "You know what you have to do. Don't be nice."

Danica nodded and balled up her fists. "Get your ass over here, Claire," she shouted into the air. "I want to talk to you, you manipulative, selfish, stupid, old hag!"

Gaston chuckled. "That should do it."

A deep, malicious laugh resounded about the room.

Danica's fear welled up inside her.

"Keep at it," Gaston entreated.

"I want you out of here, Claire." Danica locked eyes with Gaston. "Stop haunting me and your son. He doesn't want you around anymore. He wants me. He doesn't need his mommy protecting him. You can't give him what I can, and you need to go."

"Whore!" an evil-sounding voice bellowed as a strange mist began to swirl around the circle.

"Don't listen to anything she says," Gaston directed. "You can do this, Danica. I know you can. Remember, she can't touch you in the circle. No matter what you see, no matter what you hear, stay in that circle." He pointed to the circle of salt around her.

The mist grew thicker, but Danica ignored it and held her head high. "Get out of my house, you old, worthless cow! I order you out of this house and out of my life. You can't touch me, Claire. You can't hurt me. You're dead, and you don't belong here anymore."

The mist gathered into an unrecognizable form right in front of Danica. She swallowed back the abject terror rising from her depths. Her eyes turned to Gaston. He nodded to her, giving her encouragement to go on.

"You filthy, little slut!" a craggy voice called from within the mist. "You can't order me. You don't have the power to make me do anything, girl."

The mist intensified in shape until Claire appeared. She looked as she did in life, but her skin was translucent, her eyes almost black, and her lips were as red as blood. She was hunched over and wearing a pair of taupe jeans and a casual long-sleeved, cream-colored shirt. It was then Danica noted the small reddish brown bullet hole to her right temple.

"You're dead, Claire. You took your own life and have no power over anyone anymore. You gave up, but I haven't. I have power over you because I'm alive. I treasure life, I live every day, and that gives me more power than you'll ever know."

Claire let out an ear-piercing shriek that made Danica want to cover her ears, but she did not flinch.

"I was made strong by black magic. I have more power than you will ever know."

Claire grinned at Danica as the room began to quake. Danica stared wide-eyed around the living room as furniture shook and pictures fell from the walls. A brass lamp on the table next to the front door suddenly flew across the room at Danica. She tried to duck out of the way, but the lamp just grazed her head, knocking her to the floor.

"Danica!" Gaston shouted as he made a move toward her.

Danica shook her head slightly, and then her heart froze when she saw where she had landed. Her body was outside the circle of salt.

"Now you're mine, you stupid girl," Claire snarled, leaning over Danica's figure. "I'll show you power, the power of pain."

Danica tried to drag her body back into the circle, but something was pinning her to the floor. She could not move, and the air was growing thin around her. She was rapidly growing weak, as if her energy were being siphoned away. Her mind began to drift and thoughts of giving up slowly seeped into her consciousness. Danica questioned if her life was really worth fighting for. She was tired of it all, tired of the constant battle of living. She wanted to close her eyes and sleep, forever.

"No!" Gaston yelled as he slammed his shoulder into Claire.

But instead of shoving her aside, he simply bounced off her ethereal body and fell to the floor.

Danica anxiously looked to Gaston, sprawled out across from her. She connected with his shining eyes, and then a funny thing happened. In that instant, Danica's desire to live returned.

Danica mustered her voice and shouted. “Get the hell out of my house, you bitch!”

She fought back against the force holding her down, and inch-by-inch she gained control over her body. Ever so slowly, she pushed up from the floor and back toward the circle. With every movement she made, Danica could feel her body growing stronger. She recalled Gaston’s words about love helping spirits to cross over, and she realized that was her weapon to use against Claire.

“You can’t hurt me, Claire. I’m stronger than you ever were or ever will be, because I have something you never had…the love of a good man. You hated your husband. You put up with his abuse, and instead of walking away, you killed him. That’s the coward’s way out, Claire. That’s what you are, a coward.”

“You know nothing of my life,” Claire screamed as her pale white face drew back in an ugly grin.

“I know everything about your life,” Danica returned, getting her body back inside the circle. “I had your life, but I chose to rise above it. I walked away and found happiness with your son. You were too afraid to walk away. That’s your weakness, Claire; you were afraid while you were alive, and you’re still afraid.” Danica pulled her body from the floor and stood before Claire. “You’re pathetic,” she growled.

For the first time, Danica saw fear in Claire’s black eyes. The woman’s glowing body took a small step back from the edge of the circle, and Danica could not help but smile. She was winning.

“Get out of here, Claire. Leave me alone and never haunt me again. You’re nothing. You will always be nothing.”

Without warning, a beam of light appeared above Danica’s head. The area within her circle became filled with the warm, comforting white light. A feeling of peace floated through her, reinforcing her determination to end Claire’s stranglehold.

“Keep at it,” Gaston told her as he stood from the floor. “It’s working.”

Danica tried to squint up into the light shining down from her ceiling, but she had to raise her hand over her face and block the painful rays from her eyes. “What is that?”

“The gateway to the other side,” Gaston replied.

Danica shifted her gaze to Gaston’s sky-blue eyes and noticed the same odd light from above beginning to shine within them. His body became immersed in the light and started to shimmer like diamonds in the sun.

"Gaston? What is happening?"

"Finish this, Danica," he urged, never taking his eyes from her.

Danica mustered all of her remaining strength, squared her shoulders, and faced Claire. "Claire, you have to go. This is my world, my house, my life, and you will not be a part of it. You had your chance at happiness, and you blew it. You're finished here. Get out!"

The light from above became brighter and began pulsating.

As Claire fearfully raised her face to the bright light, Gaston grabbed her hand.

"Time to go, Claire," he told her. "We must go together."

Claire snarled at Gaston, fighting against his grip.

"Wait! What are you doing?" Danica shouted.

"Someone has to take her to the other side. I am bound to her. I'm the one who started this, and now I must end it."

"Gaston, no!" Danica cried out. "You can't leave me."

Claire was struggling furiously against Gaston's hand, but he never let her go.

The living room began to hum with energy. Danica could feel her body tingling as the humming grew louder.

"You don't need me anymore, Danica," Gaston called over the noise. "You're going to be just fine. You're going to be happy."

"Let me go," Claire hissed, thrashing against him. "I won't go there."

Gaston began rising from the floor as he held on to Claire.

"Gaston, I can't lose you," Danica hollered as the noise grew even louder.

"You won't lose me, Danica. You can never lose me. I'll always be here for you, but I want you to promise me something."

"Gaston, please, don't do this," she begged.

"Live your life, Danica." He smiled fondly into her eyes. "Cherish every minute, and when it's done, we will be together again, my treasure. I want you to remember that I will love you forever, and I will always be waiting for you on the other side." Gaston turned away and his face became awash in the splendor of the white light. Slowly, he began to ascend into the shower of light from above.

"Nooo!" Claire screeched as her feet lifted off the floor.

Claire's protests filled the room, and then a rush of warm air knocked Danica off her feet, sending her tumbling to the ground and outside the circle of salt. As she cowered on the floor, the frenzied vortex of air spun in the center of the circle, roaring like a freight train barreling ahead at high speed. She covered her ears against the painful sound, and just when she thought her head would explode from the pressure filling the room, Danica heard a loud popping noise. When she opened her eyes, everything was still. There was no bright light, no vortex of warm air, no Claire, and no Gaston. The white candles were still burning and the circle of salt appeared undisturbed. Then, Danica detected a faint odor, like an electrical charge, lingering in the air.

"It must have worked," she whispered, recalling Madame LeJeune's instructions.

As she stared up at the ceiling where the bright light had once been, a tear cascaded down her cheek. "I promise to be happy, Gaston. I promise to live a full life. I'll never forget you. Good-bye."

"Danica!" a man's voice shouted from outside her home. "Danica, are you in there?"

She heard banging coming from the rear entrance to the kitchen.

"Danica, it's Paul? Are you all right?" Paul's voice clamored from the other side of the door.

Danica stood from the floor and ran to the back doors. When she flung the french doors open, she saw Carl and Paul standing there. Carl had a crowbar in his hands and Paul looked panic-stricken.

"Thank God!" Paul embraced her. "I've been banging on this door for ten minutes, screaming your name."

Carl held up the crowbar. "Yeah, we were about to break in."

Danica stood back from Paul. "What are you doing here? I told you I would call you at—"

"Danica, it's after one in the morning," Paul interrupted. "I've been calling your cell phone since midnight."

"One? I just walked in here a few minutes ago. It can't be after midnight."

"Time flies when you're messing with the other side," Carl commented.

Danica's round eyes gawked at Carl.

"I heard him banging on the gate. When I went to open it for him, he told me you were performing a cleansing ritual." Carl snickered.

"Gotta hand it to you, Danica. I'd never have the balls to pull off somethin' like that. Did it work?"

Danica nodded her head. "I think so."

Carl rested the crowbar against his shoulder. "Maybe I should let you have a go at my house. It could use a good cleansing."

"No thanks, Carl. I've had enough of ghosts."

Paul hugged her close once more. "Does this mean you're finally finished with all of this ghost stuff?"

Danica relished the feel of his strong arms about her. "I'm done, Paul." Her eyes traveled back to her beloved cottage. "All my ghosts are gone."

EPILOGUE

The crisp early December air tickled Danica's nose as she carried a large box from her doorway to the U-Haul truck parked on the street in front. She placed the box on the bed of the truck and looked back at her French Quarter home. Her eyes meandered to Claire's house next door and the bright red For Sale sign secured against the dark green shutters over the front door.

"This is the last of it," she told the tall and tanned man with the handsome face as he tied down the large portrait of Gaston Deslonde in the back of the truck.

"I don't know why you want to keep this thing." Paul Gaudette motioned to the portrait. "Maybe we should leave the picture of your boyfriend behind. My house is already packed with Mom's old stuff and mine. I don't know where we will hang it."

"We could have a garage sale?" Danica suggested.

Paul scowled at her as he approached the end of the truck bed. "You're making me nervous."

"Why? Because I'm suggesting a garage sale?"

He shook his head and jumped down from the back of the truck. "No, because you will probably want to get rid of my stuff and not yours."

"How 'bout a fifty-fifty split? Half mine and half yours?"

Paul wiped his hands on his blue jeans. "Only if you promise to sell that painting."

Danica shook her head. "Not a chance."

"Are you always going to be this difficult?"

"Most definitely."

Paul rolled his eyes. "I think I'm in trouble."

Carl emerged from the black side gate. "Hey, you guys heading out already?"

Danica turned to him. "Just about."

Carl came toward the truck. "I'll bet old man Caruso is sorry to see you go."

Danica tucked her hands in the back pockets of her jeans. "He understands."

"He'd better," Paul asserted with a snicker.

"I guess I won't see you two again until the wedding next month," Carl commented as he stood beside Danica.

Paul slipped his arm about Danica's waist. "Yeah, just look for the happy couple standing by the altar at St. Charles Presbyterian Church on the twenty-third."

"Looking forward to it. I'm glad everything worked out between you, considering…." Carl nodded to Claire's old home.

Paul looked over at his mother's house. "Sometimes things happen for a reason. If Mother had not married Burt and moved down here, I might never have met Danica."

"It was fated. The universe has a plan. It always has a plan," Carl assured him. "Just be happy, you two. Happiness is the glue that holds the universe together."

Danica scrunched up her brow. "I thought that was love."

Carl shook his head, chuckling. "No, it's happiness. You have to create happiness before you can find love, Danica."

"Before? I thought happiness came after love," Paul returned.

"You have to be happy with who you are and what you are in order to find love. Love isn't something that is wasted on the heavy-hearted." Carl motioned to Danica's cottage next to them. "All the souls trapped here never figured that out. When you're happy, you are content, and contentment is the key to letting go at the end of life. Only then can you cross over and begin again."

Danica stared at Carl with a hint of wonder in her blue eyes. "Where did you read about that?"

"Something I figured out from my years of paranormal research. That's why I live here and do what I do. Before I moved to New Orleans, I worked for the FBI as an operative. Gave it up after I almost died in a shoot-out several years back. Now I just enjoy life and people. I'm creating my happiness, so I figure love is right around the corner."

Paul reached for the handle on the back door of the truck. "Carl, you never cease to amaze me."

"Me, either," Danica added.

Paul pulled the roll down door on the truck closed, and then turned to Danica. "Why don't you lock everything up and do one more walk through to make sure you didn't leave anything behind."

Danica headed inside the front doors of her cottage and secured the shutters behind her. She strolled through each of the rooms, checking the bare floors and carpets for any last items that might be left behind. When she stepped into her office, she folded her arms about her body and sighed as she eyed the spot where Gaston's painting had hung above the mantle. Her mind drifted back to her time with Gaston and their one night of passion.

A beam of the afternoon light from the skylights made the oval-shaped diamond and emerald engagement ring on her left hand twinkle. Danica smiled, knowing she had more memories to create, and though her happiness with Gaston would always be in her heart, it was time to move on.

As she walked out to the shady courtyard, Danica felt a renewed sense of purpose in her life. The possibilities for the future were limitless, and not since she had graduated from college had Danica been so energized with hope. When she turned to close the french doors behind her, a whiff of brandy and cigars floated by.

"Gaston?" she whispered into the kitchen.

As Danica peered into the darkness, her heart raced and her palms became sweaty. Then as quickly as the scent had manifested, it disappeared. An unfamiliar emptiness settled over her as she remembered Gaston's smile and his thrilling eyes. But Danica could no longer feel his presence around her. He was gone. For years his spirit had filled the home like a warm fire on a cold winter's night. Now, it was just a building with a long history and perhaps a few secrets, but it was no longer the emotional haven it had always been for her. As the cracks in her heart created by Gaston's departure once more tugged at her, Danica shut the back doors and locked them.

When she emerged from the side gate, Paul and Carl were chatting at the back of the truck.

"Are you all done, darling?" Paul called to her.

The fading afternoon light haloed her fiancé's tall, muscular figure. "All done," she proclaimed.

"Well, I'm off to work. Take care, you two." With one last wave, Carl sauntered down the sidewalk toward Royal Street.

Danica went to the truck and climbed into the front cab. As she waited for Paul to take the driver's seat beside her, she turned to her window and beheld her childhood home.

Once inside the cab, Paul patted her thigh. "You okay?"

"I'm good."

He placed the key in the ignition. "No last minute regrets?"

"I'm never going to regret anything ever again." She smiled at him. "I'm going to enjoy every second of my life and always be happy."

Paul turned the key in the ignition. "That sounds like a good plan."

Danica shook her head. "It's a promise, actually. A promise I once made to an old friend."

"Will you be inviting this old friend to our wedding?"

"No, but I'm sure he'll be there in spirit. He'll always be there in spirit."

Paul nervously gazed over at her. "This isn't another ghost, is it?"

"No, just someone who always believed in me."

He let out a relieved sigh and put the truck into gear. "I'm glad to hear that. I don't think I can handle any more ghosts. I'm still creeped out by my last encounter."

Danica eased her body back in her seat. "Ghosts are just people, Paul. There's nothing scary or creepy about them. If anything, we should think of them as comforting."

Paul eased the truck slowly into the street. "How can a ghost be comforting?"

Danica watched from the passenger window as they moved further away from her cherished cottage. "They're a confirmation that everything we are in life continues on to the other side."

Paul gave her a skeptical side-glance. "The other side?"

Danica turned to him. "Where all souls go when they depart the earth. It's a place where all the love we created in life gets to live on."

"You're talking about Heaven, right?" Paul inquired.

"Yeah, I guess I am." Danica smiled as she remembered Gaston's warm laugh and magical eyes. "Heaven will always be waiting for me on the other side."

THE END

ABOUT THE AUTHOR

Alexandrea Weis is an advanced practice registered nurse who was born and raised in New Orleans. Her first novel, *To My Senses,* introduced readers to the world of Nicci Beauvoir and garnered numerous awards and rave reviews. Her popular second Nicci Beauvoir novel, *Recovery,* won the Gold Medal for best romantic suspense from The Reader's Favorite Book Awards 2011, was named best Romantic Suspense novel by the Spring 2011 NABE Pinnacle Book Awards, and was a Finalist in the ForeWord Magazine Book of the Year Awards in 2011. Her fourth novel, *Broken Wings*, won best Contemporary Romance by the NABE Pinnacle Book Awards in 2012, was a finalist in the USA Book Awards for Romance in 2012, and was a finalist in the Reader's Favorite Book Awards for Contemporary Romance for 2012. Her sixth novel, *Diary of a One-Night Stand,* was released in August 2012 and was named a Paranormal Romance Guild's Best Reviewed of 2012. A permitted wildlife rehabber with the Louisiana Wildlife and Fisheries, Weis rescues orphaned and injured wildlife. She lives with her husband and pets in New Orleans.

Made in the USA
San Bernardino, CA
28 August 2013